Bethia did not trust him!

Simon could not remember anyone in his long life doubting him. He was a de Burgh, and his honor was not suspect. Ever. He felt a surge of frustration. How would he gain her faith? He had only his word, and none had ever questioned it.

Nor did anyone refuse him. At Campion, his word was law, and so he lashed out at her, angry at both her denial and her disloyalty. "You *will* come with me, for as your liege lord, I command it!" he snapped.

"You are not my liege lord," she said dryly. "'Tis my father who owes your brother allegiance."

Her calm manner set off his temper, and Simon slammed a fist against his hand. "By faith, you will obey me, or I will toss you over my shoulder and carry you there, mile by mile!"

Bethia hooted in disbelief....

Dear Reader,

Entertainment. Escape. Fantasy. These three words describe the heart of Harlequin Historicals. If you want compelling, emotional stories by some of the best writers in the field, look no further.

Deborah Simmons is one of those writers. Since her debut with Harlequin Historicals in 1992, Deborah has written twelve novels, alternating sassy Regency tales with spine-tingling medieval stories. *Robber Bride* marks the third book in her wildly popular medieval DE BURGH series, based on the powerful de Burgh men, all knights. In this novel, the strong, arrogant de Burgh brother, Simon, finds his match in a runaway bride who is hiding from her despicable would-be husband. It's great!

The Tender Stranger by Carolyn Davidson is the heartwarming tale of a pregnant widow who flees from her conniving in-laws and later falls in love with the bounty hunter they've hired to find her. Award-winning author Ruth Langan is back with *Rory,* the first book in her brand-new miniseries, THE O'NEIL SAGA. In this suspenseful tale, an English noblewoman succumbs to the charm of a legendary—and very handsome!—Irish rebel who is wounded in battle and falls under her care.

Rounding out the month is *Father for Keeps* by Ana Seymour. In this stirring reunion romance, a handsome heir returns to Nevada to win back the woman who secretly had his child.

Whatever your tastes in reading, you'll be sure to find a romantic journey back to the past between the covers of a Harlequin Historical.®

Sincerely,

Tracy Farrell
Senior Editor

Please address questions and book requests to:
Harlequin Reader Service
U.S.: 3010 Walden Ave., P.O. Box 1325, Buffalo, NY 14269
Canadian: P.O. Box 609, Fort Erie, Ont. L2A 5X3

ROBBER BRIDE
DEBORAH SIMMONS

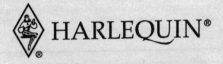

TORONTO • NEW YORK • LONDON
AMSTERDAM • PARIS • SYDNEY • HAMBURG
STOCKHOLM • ATHENS • TOKYO • MILAN • MADRID
PRAGUE • WARSAW • BUDAPEST • AUCKLAND

ISBN 0-373-29055-1

ROBBER BRIDE

Books by Deborah Simmons

Harlequin Historicals

DEBORAH SIMMONS

A voracious reader and writer, Deborah Simmons began her professional career as a newspaper reporter. She turned to fiction after the birth of her first child when a longtime love of historical romances prompted her to pen her first book, published in 1989. She lives with her husband, two children and two cats on seven acres in rural Ohio, where she divides her time between her family, reading, researching and writing.

For Arlita Jean Smith

Chapter One

Simon de Burgh was looking for a fight.

Although he would have denied it, Simon deliberately took the forest road, as if daring brigands to attack his train. He was bored, and routing a band of ruffians—should they be foolish enough to attempt a raid—would well remedy that complaint.

When he had taken on this errand from his brother Dunstan, it had promised an escape from the peace of his father's hall, but after endless uneventful days on the road, Simon was restless. Although his destination, Baddersly Castle, lay not far ahead, the prospect of overseeing his brother's lands like some glorified steward held little appeal.

All his life Simon had felt in competition with his six siblings, especially the elder Dunstan, who had served King Edward in Wales and received his own demesne. Although the driving need to prove himself had eased in the past two years as he took on more responsibilities, Simon still felt impatient for challenges, for some kind of glory that was lacking in his life thus far.

And it would not be satisfied by a foray into the

woods, he knew, even as his destrier moved forward under the huge elms. The men behind him fell into silence, and for a while the only sound was the creaking of leather and mail and the tramp of hooves over packed ground. Simon realized that his brothers would not have chosen the forest road. In fact, he could almost hear sensible Geoffrey reminding him that they did not have a large train, just a small group of horsed guards. Did he intend to be so reckless with their lives? The warning, like a prick from his conscience, soured his mood, and he spurred his mount onward.

But it was too late to regret his course, for in the shadowy darkness in front of him, Simon could see the shape of a huge tree lying across the roadway. Knowing that its placement was no accident, he suspected that his hoped-for fight was at hand. Silently he raised a hand in the air as warning to those who followed. Then he reached for his sword.

"Hold and state your purpose here." The voice rose in challenge from behind the wide trunk, and Simon wished he could trade one of his knights for a good archer. He watched through narrowed eyes as the speaker rose to stand on the fallen wood.

A rogue, indeed, the fellow sported a dark brown tunic and braies so as to blend in with his surroundings. He brandished no weapon, but stood with his legs spread apart and his hands on his hips in a cocky manner that made Simon grit his teeth. He wore a small sword and some sort of shortened mail, no doubt stolen from a fallen knight, Simon thought, and the knowledge infuriated him.

"Move, knave, for I answer not to you," Simon called out.

"State your name, your allegiance and your business

in these woods,'' the ruffian responded. He appeared to be no more than a lad, and a foolish one at that, Simon thought, for unless the forest hid scores of men better equipped than this shabby fellow, he could hardly hope to prevail against hardened warriors.

"I am Simon de Burgh, loyal to my father, Earl of Campion, and my brother, Baron of Wessex, and my purpose is none of your concern. Do not make the mistake of challenging me. Now begone or be killed.''

"Nay! It is you who has made a mistake in coming here, Lord de Burgh, if that is truly your name. Lay down your weapons, for you are surrounded!''

Simon rasped out a laugh at the absurd order, couched in fair speech for a brigand. "And by what are we surrounded, beyond yon leaves?'' he asked. Even if the youth had a host of his fellows behind him, they could do little against armed and mounted men. Surely even this brash boy must see the folly of his challenge and be on his way.

"Greenery, indeed, my lord, and archers as well,'' the youth said. His claim was followed by a rustling and low murmurs among the men in the train. With a scowl, Simon glanced upward and saw several rogues poised high in the branches like birds, arrows at the ready. *Archers?* How had ordinary outlaws become so well trained and well organized? Simon gritted his teeth, for he could almost hear Geoffrey's rebuke for endangering his men needlessly.

"Lay down your arms,'' the youth repeated with a boldness that infuriated Simon. He was not accustomed to taking orders from anyone, let alone some brash bit of brigand. Arrows be damned! He was not going to surrender without a fight. Lifting his sword, he let out a mighty roar and sent his horse forward, intent upon separating the braggart's head from his body. Here, at last, was the battle he had been seeking and, along with his rage, Simon felt the familiar surge of excitement, like no other, that came with the clash of weapons.

Dimly he heard the echoing war cries of those behind him as he leaned forward, eager for blood, but his sword arced in the empty air as the boy leaped out of the way. Before he could charge again, Simon felt a blow to his back. It was so sudden and forceful as to knock him from his mount, and he hit the ground hard, his sword struck from his hand and his breath buffeted from his body. Dizzy and dazed, he nevertheless rolled to a crouch, shaking off the man who had landed upon him with a heave and a grunt.

Arrows were flying, but he could see the youth shouting orders to his fellows from behind the relative safety of the fallen oak, and the boy's cowardice enraged Simon further. Uncoiling from his low stance, he launched himself at the slim form, sending it sprawling into the dirt behind the tree.

"Get off me!" The braggart's voice rose to a high pitch with his panic, and Simon knew a moment's satisfaction before he felt the prick of a blade at his throat. It might have given another man pause, but Simon had never been known for his cool head. With a roar of outrage, he dashed the dagger aside, ignoring the pain as it sliced through his skin on its way to the earth. When it landed out of reach, he grabbed his opponent's neck, eager to choke the life from him. The boy wiggled like a fish out of water, thrashing wildly, and Simon grunted as a knee connected with his groin.

Doubled over in pain, Simon nevertheless managed to keep hold of the youth, and, vowing to give one better than he got, he reached for the fellow's bullocks.

A quick squeeze would have the lad singing in an even higher voice. But it was Simon who gasped when his fingers found nothing but empty braies. Baffled, he tightened his grip only to feel the smooth contours of woman's body against his palm.

"Bastard!" his opponent whispered heatedly. Startled, Simon lifted his head, but before he could get a good look at the strange creature in his grasp, he felt the sharp impact of a stone above his ear. He blinked once in astonishment as the boy's features faded into those of a woman, and then the world went black even as he ground out a protest.

Simon returned to awareness with a sudden jolt when he felt the sting of something wet against his flesh. With a growl of displeasure, he jerked away only to find his hands held fast behind him. Struggling violently, he snarled in fury.

"Hold still, you fool!" The words, uttered in a husky female voice heavily laced with exasperation, brought him up short, and Simon blinked as a face came into focus in front of him. It was a youthful visage, with skin gilded golden by the sun, sculpted cheekbones, a regal nose and thick-lashed hazel eyes. For a moment, Simon stared as he tried to place it.

"You!" he sputtered, finally recognizing the boy turned girl with whom he had struggled. This was the brigand, and a female at that!

"Who else?" she said, slapping more of that wetness against the side of his head. "I didn't want to hurt you, sir *knight*," she said in a scornful tone, "but I take exception to your manner of fighting."

Simon was so furious he could not speak. How dare this...this impudent chit talk to him in such a manner?

"If you don't want to be taken as a man, you shouldn't dress as one," he finally muttered, raking her up and down with a contemptuous look.

"Pardon me, but I didn't realize that the knight's code of honor included grabbing each other's privates," she answered in a disgusted tone.

"You tried to unman me first!" Simon shouted, forgetting, for a moment, that this was not one of his brothers, but a female. When he remembered, he was stunned by her insult. No woman had ever spoken to him of such things and in so bold a manner. He wondered if she was a doxy, but even the most hardened of whores wore skirts. Indeed, he had never heard of a female taking on male garb. Who was this creature?

"I was only protecting myself," she said. "And if you had laid down your weapons, as I told you to do, you would be unhurt. Now you have injured men, and I'm forced to treat their wounds." With decidedly ungentle fingers, she swiped some noxious mixture across his neck. "I must admit that I've often hoped to see a man slit his own throat, but have never witnessed it before today."

Simon felt an unreasoning flush climb in his cheeks. Though he had done nothing more than fight valiantly, the wench again made it sound as if he were an inept clod. He jerked viciously at his bonds, but they held tight, enraging him further. He bellowed an oath.

"Have you a death wish?" she hissed at him. "If your wounds are to heal, you must remain still, and if you don't stop making such a noise, I'll have to gag you."

Gag him? Speechless with fury, Simon sought her gaze and held it with a glare known to reduce grown men to terrified quakes. She didn't even blink.

''I have little enough respect for you, mercenary,''
she said, returning his fierce look with a cool one that
roused him further, ''and given any excuse, would
gladly kill you.''

She kill *him?* Simon choked back a laugh. Although
he had not served the King as Dunstan had, he had
seen his share of fighting and had even regained his
brother's castle when it was taken by a warring neighbor. ''No *man* has ever bested me and certainly no
wench in boy's garb! You are more the fool, if you
think you can!''

She smiled, a mocking grin that drew his attention
to her wide mouth. It lingered there as she drew a slow
breath. ''Ah, but I already have,'' she said. Pausing to
glance pointedly at his bound feet, she turned on her
heel and walked away from him.

The arrogant claim set his blood boiling; that it was
true was all the more maddening. ''Come back here!''
Simon roared.

''Perhaps when you're in a mood to talk, not shout,''
she said over her shoulder. As he sat up, trussed and
bound like a goose, and watched her walk away, Simon
realized there was no mistaking her sex now. A long
braid the color of fine wheat fell down her back, and
her hips, clad only in a male's braies and tunic, swayed
slightly despite her long stride.

''*Wench!*'' Simon screamed at her, but her steps
never faltered, and he felt a kick from behind.

''Quiet, you!'' a gravelly voiced man muttered.

And for the first time in his life Simon felt utterly
helpless. When Dunstan had been tossed into his dungeon, Simon had been eager to rescue his elder brother,
but he had never thought such a fate could be his own.
No one would ever capture *him.* Least of all a woman!

Now he could just imagine how his brothers would jeer if they could see him caught and held by a mere female. He gritted his teeth at the thought until he realized that before laughing their heads off, they would aid him.

With that knowledge came a surge of strength that swept away his momentary chagrin, for he did not need anyone to deliver him from his predicament. He would free himself, and then…then he would have his revenge, he thought savagely. With steely determination, he banked his temper and surveyed his surroundings, intent solely upon escape.

They were in a small hollow surrounded by ancient trees that provided natural concealment. Several men dressed in the same brown garb as the female served sentry on the fringes of the encampment, while others stood guard over Simon and the wounded. At least he assumed they were men, Simon mused, narrowing his eyes in study, and a quick assessment of thick calves and burly shoulders assured him of their sex. But why they took their orders from a slip of a female was a mystery to him.

The whole business was odd, he realized now. Noting the fat quiver of arrows that nearly all of them carried on their backs, Simon wondered again why simple outlaws were so well trained and equipped. And surely most brigands would have slain them all, taken their horses and weapons and fled into the forest.

Not these. They had killed no one. Would they ransom him and his men? It was common enough to pay for knights won in battle, but not everyone in a train, travelers all! Simon scowled, furious at the possibility of his father being forced to give good coin to these ruffians because of him. Because of his misjudgment.

The thought brought on more rage, and Simon struggled uselessly with his bonds for long, futile minutes before regaining control of his temper. Breathing deeply, he tried to concentrate, as Geoffrey would do. He had scoffed at his brother's scholarly ways and cautious plans often enough, but now even he realized the necessity of clear thinking.

He glanced around the area, looking for some clue as to these rogues and their purpose. Not only had they spared all of his men, but they were treating the wounded. It made no sense to Simon, who was not used to solving puzzles, guessing at motives or studying his enemies too closely.

At the thought, his gaze flicked to the girl, bending to tend Aldhelm, who had taken an arrow in the shoulder. The wheat-colored braid slid across her shoulder only to be tossed over her back once more, and Simon's attention followed. Her lower legs in their braies and soft boots were clearly visible, and although he decried the sight, he could not help eyeing each slender curve.

Finally he forced himself to glance upward. But that view was no improvement, for she leaned forward, her face intent as she pulled back Aldhelm's sleeve. While Simon watched, she applied that noxious mixture with her fingers, and the sight of her stroking the soldier's skin made him feel as if something had kicked him between the ribs.

Scowling, Simon twisted to look behind him, but no one stood near. Perhaps he had some wound of which he was unaware, he thought, taking a deep breath, but the pain was gone as swiftly as it had come. Having never been prone to aches, he blamed the wench and glared at the woman who was defying every law of God and man by strutting around in her short mail as if she were a knight. Bah! He had little enough use for females when dressed in their own garb. His mother had died while he was young, and though he had known a child's fondness for his father's second wife, she, too, had passed on, leaving him with the perception that women were weak creatures.

It was well-known that they were smaller, less intelligent and less able than men, and their interests of home and hearth were not his own. Although their bodies could provide a certain pleasure, Simon rarely indulged himself, and when he did, he purchased the use of their flesh as he would any other commodity. Indeed, no matter what his father might say on the subject, Simon had always thought women inherently inferior. Dressing in men's clothes could not change that fact.

Smiling slowly, he recovered his innate arrogance. After all, he was a de Burgh and a knight, his father's second son, and no one could hold him for long. Then he would punish this slip of a female for her impudence. He would tie her up himself and see how she liked it—or make her his slave! The idea of the haughty chit bowing to him gave Simon a small measure of satisfaction, but he could not afford to indulge in his coming victory as yet. Glancing away from the distracting sight of her, Simon schooled his thoughts to strategy and began assessing the condition of his men—and hers.

He carried a knife in his boot that even his brothers did not know about, and it had served him well on more than one occasion. If he could get off this accursed log, he ought to be able to reach it with his bound hands and free himself. He need only wait until the cover of darkness to make his escape. From the looks of the men he could see, none were severely injured or closely guarded. He would take as many as he could with him, but without more weapons, their exit might be hampered.

Eyes narrowed, he searched the glade, but he could not mark where the wench had put his sword and mail. He felt naked without them—another reason to despise her—but forced his thoughts once more to his plan. It had been his experience that all but the most highly trained of men took their ease at night, and these brigands were even more likely to drink too much ale and seek their rest. And then, with or without his men and his weapons, he would slip into the trees and make his way toward Baddersly.

Assuming, of course, that they were still near the place where they had been attacked. Swearing softly, Simon glanced up at the sky, as if seeking a sign, and cursed the clouds. If they cleared away tonight, he could find his general direction by the stars. Fie, he would *sniff* his way, he thought angrily. And although Dunstan did not keep a large fighting force at the castle, he would lead them right back here to seize this wench and her pitiful band of followers.

The thought brought a slight curve to his lips, and so, when the absurdly clad female approached him once more, Simon was able to affect a more stoic demeanor. He was a good warrior, with an eye for the most advantageous position. In fact, Dunstan had compared his skills to those of the King! And since he had laid his plans, no brash girl would stop him. With narrowed eyes, he watched her step forward.

"Now what?" he asked.

"That depends upon you, mercenary," she said, sitting gingerly on the edge of a tree stump. To Simon's astonishment, she drew one leg up to her chest and wrapped her arms around it. He wondered if she always deliberately flaunted her limbs in this manner or if she only taunted him. If so, for what purpose? He scowled, his gaze lingering on the dark recess where her tunic dipped low.

"How much is he paying you?"

"Who?" Simon asked, jerking his attention back to her face.

The female laughed in a low, husky tone. "Do not jest with me, de Burgh, if you are who you say."

If he was not, how did they expect to ransom him? Simon wondered, but he could not let the insult go unremarked. "No one impugns my good name or my honor, wench. You have only to travel with me back to Campion or Baddersly, if you would know the truth."

That startled her. Simon saw a flicker of it in her hazel eyes before she lowered her thick lashes. Her jaw tightened, and he suddenly wondered at the muscle there that held it taut. "And just what do you at Baddersly?"

"I come upon an errand for my brother, who is lord there," Simon answered. *And who would crush outlaws who prey upon his lands,* he did not add. Dunstan had no patience for brigands, but the thought of this one's death made Simon grow uneasy, and he snapped impatiently at her. "If you release us now, he might be persuaded to show you mercy."

She laughed. She actually laughed at his offer, insincere though it might have been, and Simon had to restrain himself from diving at her, bound or not. Only the presence of the other guards and his own wounded men kept him from recklessly throwing himself forward. Instead he remained seated and silent, cursing the flush that mounted his cheeks and this female's ability to call it forth as none had before her. Abruptly he was aware that he was the one blushing like a girl, while she questioned him as would a knight, and the reversal of their positions pleased him not. He grunted angrily, though the girl seemed unaware of his discomfort.

"And what is this important errand, de Burgh?" she asked, leaning forward slightly as if intent upon his answer.

"I am to oversee his demesne," Simon replied through gritted teeth. As one who was accustomed to giving orders, he could barely sit still for her impudence, let alone answer. "Those duties will be varied, though they might well include eliminating any outlaws that plague his lands," he added spitefully.

"So you are here to destroy us?" she accused.

While he had not been sent there for that purpose, the notion held a certain appeal that Simon did not plan to admit. "Wench, I have no idea who you are or what you are doing here, but I advise you to move on, for Dunstan will allow no raids upon his lands," he said, growing impatient.

She cocked her head to one side, as if to study him, and her braid slipped over her shoulder. It slid down her chest, and Simon's attention caught and held for a moment. The soft curves of her breasts were discernible beneath her tunic, and he had a sudden urge to cover her from prying eyes other than his own.

"And what of Brice Scirvayne? Can you claim you are not his hired mercenaries?"

Annoyed at his wayward stare, Simon jerked his gaze back to her face. "I grow weary of your questions, wench. I know not of this Scirvayne, nor has a de Burgh ever been a mercenary. We serve only Campion and Edward!"

"If not mercenaries, then soldiers, come to Baddersly to aid his cause," she said bitterly.

"What cause? Who is Scirvayne? Where does he rule?" Simon asked, curious now. The girl's jaw was tight, her hazel gaze fierce and probing as that of his brothers.

"He rules not!" she cried. "He is nothing more than a thief, a conniver!" She rose to her feet, her eyes blazing with such magnificent fury that Simon felt a surge of something akin to the thrill of battle rush through him.

"Bethia." As she turned her head toward the soft voice behind him, Simon drew in a sharp breath, startled by the hot thundering of his blood. For a moment, this odd female had seemed like a warrior, strong and willful and full of blood lust. Simon frowned, shaking off the impression, for her short mail and burst of temper did not make her a knight. Far from it. She was nothing more than a girl, dressed up as her betters.

When Simon glanced back at her in disgust, she appeared calmer, though her eyes had not lost their dangerous glow. "If your mission is peaceful, as you say, it should be easy enough to check," she said, her mobile mouth curling with contempt. "Bring his pouch!"

Outraged, Simon could only fume as she easily caught the heavy leather bag someone tossed to her and opened it to rifle through his brother's correspondence. There was not much of interest, he knew, a letter to the steward, a proclamation to be read at the next manorial court and an order giving him the right to speak in Dunstan's name.

Simon remained stiff and silent while she looked through the documents, surprised that she could even read them. What kind of outlaw was she that she possessed such a rare skill? And what cared she of mercenaries? He knew that there were parts of the country where lawlessness went little checked, but was this band so powerful that they feared destruction only from soldiers? Nay, he decided, for surely no such group would answer to this slip of a female.

She looked up then, her expression softening slightly, and Simon wondered how he could have ever thought her a boy. She was a striking woman, with those high cheekbones and the firm jaw that had unclenched as she read.

"Perhaps you speak the truth, de Burgh," she said, returning the correspondence to its place. "Or perhaps, like Brice, you prefer to hide your true doings behind clever words and smoke screens."

"Him again! Who is this unknown that he should have power over me?" Simon ground out the words, as revolted by his momentary admiration of the wench as with her continued suspicions. "And who are you to hold a de Burgh hostage to a whim? Explain yourself!"

Overcome by his mounting frustrating, Simon nearly surged to his feet without waiting for nightfall. But even he was not that reckless. Behind him and all around the clearing the archers were scattered, ready to take aim at him should he make an untoward move. Sinking back against the bark beneath him, Simon silently seethed as one of the brigands pulled the girl aside for a heated discussion.

Eyes narrowing, he watched them, and he wondered if the short, squat fellow was trying to talk this Bethia out of enlightening him. Was he her lover? With a snort, Simon rejected the notion. She held herself like a warrior, tall and straight, without the slightest hint of subservience, though she gave the fellow her full attention. A woman with that kind of bearing did not share herself with all and sundry—or did she? Simon knew nothing of the wench and it looked as though he would learn even less, for she and the squat man walked off into the woods, disappearing behind the heavy growth.

Pulling futilely at his bonds, Simon's disappointment mounted. He prided himself on his skills, holding himself above all of his brothers. He might not be as learned as Geoffrey, but he had a better understanding of warfare, and he made everything to do with it his business. He knew Baddersly and its environs well enough, having secured the castle for Dunstan two years past, yet he had never heard of any Brice Scirvayne. Obviously this wench and her band had appeared sometime since his last visit, as had the infamous Scirvayne, whoever he may be.

Simon scowled. He was not accustomed to being uninformed and unprepared, and it gnawed at him. Fie on the female, with her taunts and her mysteries! He would know his fate and have done with it rather than sit here in humiliation. With a low curse, Simon struggled once more, earning him a swift kick in the back from some bastard behind him. The reminder of his unseen guards made him rein in his temper.

Nostrils flaring, Simon drew in a deep breath and schooled himself to patience. Nothing could come of drawing his enemy's attention. Instead, he must remain still and silent, pretending defeat, no matter how painful the posture, if he would seize the final victory in this battle. It had been midafternoon when they were attacked, and soon it would be full evening.

In the meantime, Simon would play at Geoffrey's game and watch and wait—until he could unman this girl in male clothing as surely as she had him.

Chapter Two

Bethia felt the knight's frustration even across the long stretch of grass and the curtain of leaves that separated them. He was a fine specimen of a man, the fittest she had ever seen, with dark hair and eyes the color of brightly polished mail. Tall, strong and as fierce as a cornered animal, he would make a powerful enemy, and Bethia felt a prick of dread crawl up her spine.

Ruthlessly she tamped it down. She could not afford to be cowed by this man—or swayed by his demands, even though he reminded her of an untamed beast chained and caged against his will. Against nature. *Stop it, Bethia.* The last thing she needed was to feel anything for Simon de Burgh, for like a wild thing he would surely turn on her should she loose him.

But it was difficult not to harbor some grudging respect, at least, for her captive. Simon de Burgh had neither offered to bribe her, in the way of Brice and his kind, nor had he brought his family into it. Although she knew little of Campion, Bethia had heard of the powerful earl, and she knew well that this knight could have threatened her with his mighty ties. But he had not.

Instinct told Bethia to trust him, and perhaps she would have, if she were the only one whose future depended upon her decision, but she had others to think of, others who looked to her for protection and leadership. And right now, that mantle weighed heavily upon her. Firmin, one of her more hotheaded archers, had already clamored for the blood of the prisoners, but Bethia could not condone outright murder, especially since these men might well be innocent. Neither did she wish to rouse the Earl of Campion, bringing a vast army down around their heads.

Bethia had listened to Firmin's arguments, and she had to admit that he had raised one interesting point. If she did not want the captives killed and could not release them without certain retribution, just what was she going to do with them? Thanks to a recent raid, she was well provisioned, but she had not the supplies or the manpower to watch a dozen men, especially once the injured regained their strength.

Although Bethia had a vague idea of carting them away to abandon them at some distant site, she had a feeling that Simon de Burgh would not easily forget— or forgive—his imprisonment. No doubt, he would return with additional forces to crush her small band.

Bethia swore softly as she considered such retribution, and her gaze immediately traveled to the man who sat on the old stump in the clearing. Although he was motionless now, Simon de Burgh exuded power and strength in a manner she had never seen before. It was there in his fierce expression, in the rigid pose of his warrior's body, and in the cold glint of his eyes. He wore a grimace for which she could hardly blame him, and yet Bethia suspected that he rarely smiled even in the best of circumstances. At first glance, she had thought him cold, but she had witnessed a fierceness that did not come from lack of passion. The thought made Bethia shiver, and she took a step backward.

Of course, there was one other possibility that Firmin had not mentioned—that Simon de Burgh and his men could be persuaded to join her. In her heart, hardened though it might be, Bethia held out that small hope, but she knew better than to suggest it to the archer. Firmin had a dislike of all those in authority, and he would surely scoff at the idea of this knight coming to their aid. And yet, as lord of Baddersly, Simon de Burgh ought to be concerned with injustice against his people. *Ought. Should.* Bethia choked on a laugh, for she had learned that the truth did not often prevail. And being in the right counted for nothing.

Still, unlike Firmin, Bethia saw no reason not to discuss the situation with Simon de Burgh. If he knew nothing of her forces, as he claimed, then he deserved an explanation. And if Firmin was right, and he was being paid by Brice to hunt them down, he might as well hear her side of things. And if he had an ounce of knightly honor in him, then he would join them!

Unfortunately, judging from her earlier experience with him, Simon de Burgh was not the most chivalrous of men, warrior or no. Bethia remembered the feel of his hands on her, restraining and then touching her where no man ever had before. She shivered, suddenly hot, as she glanced toward him only to stiffen in dismay when she saw him rise to his feet. Calling a warning to one of the guards, Bethia drew her sword and stepped out from under the canopy of trees.

"Stay where you are," she commanded, as he stood

tall and arrogant despite his bonds. He was an imposing sight, more than six feet of warrior and every inch proclaiming his strength and pride. Bethia's growing admiration for him nearly robbed her of her purpose, but she could not ignore the danger he presented to them all—even tied hand and foot. Nor would she reveal his increasingly disturbing effect upon her. With a curt motion, Bethia bade him resume his seat, but instead of obeying, he eyed her with a stony expression.

"I have a need, wench, that cannot wait," he said roughly.

In light of her recent musings, Bethia nearly flinched. Surely he did not suggest that she satisfy his...lusts? Just as her heart began a sudden, violent clamor, he spoke again.

"I don't suppose you have a garderobe here?" he asked dryly, his gaze raking the clearing.

Bethia swiftly hid her relief. It would not do to show this man any weakness, for he would seize it to his advantage without a moment's hesitation. Keeping her sword at the ready, Bethia returned his cold stare. "I am sorry, but you will simply have to make do."

The slow, contemptuous perusal that followed was nearly her undoing, but Bethia steadily held his gaze. Finally he shrugged. "Will you do the honors?" he asked, flicking a glance down at the braies he could not manage while bound.

It was his cool control that told Bethia he was planning something. She had seen his rage and frustration before, and she suspected that relieving himself in front of an audience would normally humiliate Simon de Burgh beyond endurance. Yet now, he seemed so detached that Bethia found it difficult to believe him. *Very difficult.*

Stepping closer, Bethia lifted her sword and pointed it directly at his nether regions, just in case he thought to cause some mischief. "You are aware, I assume, that the guard behind you has an arrow at the ready, to plant in your back should you make any wayward moves?"

Only a shadow passing through those silver eyes gave notice of his annoyance, and Bethia knew another rush of admiration for this man. Although he would subdue her if he could, he was different from Brice, and Bethia felt an odd thrill, as if she were finally facing a worthy opponent.

As long as he didn't win.

With a slight smile, Bethia carefully raised her sword as if to slice through his clothes herself, and the spark in those silver depths was well worth her effort. Still she knew better than to toy with such a man for long, and without removing her gaze from him, she called to Firmin.

"Help this knight with his braies," she said.

But the archer's bray of laughter told her he had no sympathy for the captive's plight. "Let him wet himself like a babe!" Firmin taunted, stalking off into the woods.

Bethia noticed the change in Simon's expression immediately. "Such insolence should not go unpunished," he said, and for a moment, Bethia felt akin to him. Here was a man who understood the difficulties of leadership, of rising above defeat to fight again, of giving everything to a cause.

And yet Bethia could hardly use the same methods as Simon de Burgh. She could well imagine how he would deal with disobedience—or disloyalty—but her men were bound to her by nothing except their will. Although she tried to impose a code of behavior upon them, she could not enforce it as strictly as a knight, or a lord his subjects.

"Well? Will you do the honors?" Simon asked, and Bethia shifted her stance to cover her confusion. Although she would not force Firmin to return and do his duty, neither did she intend to yank down Simon de Burgh's braies herself. She might have abandoned most of her modesty when she took to the forest, but the thought of putting her hands upon the great knight made her shiver—and not out of embarrassment. No matter whether she knelt in front or behind, she would get a closer view of the man than she had ever intended.

Besides, Bethia thought, determined not to dwell on that rather disturbing image, she had no intention of placing her neck anywhere near Simon de Burgh, even if he was tied. Nor would she allow the archer behind him to abandon his post. Instead, she called curtly to the young man who stood watch, and, after a rustling of leaves, he dropped to the ground nearby.

"Jeremy, help this knight with his clothing," she said.

"Coward," Simon whispered to her, and Bethia glanced toward him in surprise, startled to see something flickering in his silver eyes. Was it anger, or could this harsh warrior be teasing her? He did not seem like the type of man to flirt with a maid. More likely, he wanted to distract her, Bethia thought, setting her mouth firmly.

"Nay, only prudent, sir knight," she answered. "Go ahead, Jeremy," she urged, and the boy knelt hastily in front of Simon.

"Prudent or prurient?" her prisoner asked, cocking a dark brow toward her. "Do you intend to watch? I have heard of those who seek their pleasure in viewing others.''

Shocked by the shaming taunt, Bethia nearly turned away. Only the certain knowledge that this man was too dangerous to leave unattended on any side kept her motionless as Jeremy gingerly unfastened his braies and lowered them. For a moment the young man hesitated and then, standing back as far as he could, he lifted the knight's tunic.

Immediately a stream hit the ground near Bethia's feet, and she stepped back swiftly. Although outraged, she kept her sword aimed at her opponent's torso and her eyes on his face to prove to him that she was no fool. Bethia prided herself on her discipline, learned from her father many years ago and recently honed, and yet, when Simon had finished, her gaze dropped, as if against her will, to glimpse muscular legs and a dark thicket of hair from which his heavy male sex protruded.

"Enough!" he bellowed. Bethia winced, horrified to be caught staring at her prisoner's bared body. But when her fleeing wits returned, she realized that Simon had spoken not to her, but to Jeremy. The young man quickly dropped the material he held and fumbled with fastening the knight's braies though hampered by the tunic. When at last his task was completed, the youth bowed and hurried away, eager to be off. Bethia could hardly blame him, for one look at the bound man was enough to frighten even the most stouthearted.

As he sat back on the stump with a furious grunt, Bethia cocked her head to study him. Was he angry because whatever plan he had attempted had failed, or was it the indignity of being attended by another that galled him? Even as Bethia hoped that it was not her swift perusal of his privates that had roused his ire, she told herself it did not matter. Still she was moved to tender an apology of sorts.

"I regret that we are not better prepared to serve you here, but we are unaccustomed to guests," she said in an attempt to placate him.

"Oh, it appears that you are well equipped to serve," Simon answered. He raked her with a contemptuous look that told her in no uncertain terms it was her presence that bothered him. But, as a hardened warrior, he must know that she could not trust a captive, Bethia mused, her own part in his distress rankling her in a way she could not have explained.

"Did you look your fill? Or would you have the boy strip me at your leisure?" he asked, his silver eyes glittering dangerously. "Or is that for later? Are you so desperate for a man that you have to capture one and force him at sword point to ride you?"

His words so stunned Bethia that she nearly lunged for his throat. Or was that what he wanted? Did he taunt her apurpose? If so, he was to be disappointed, for she would neither put herself in that vulnerable position nor would she give him the satisfaction of knowing just how much he had insulted her. Instead, she carefully composed herself to return his scorn.

"If I did, I would not choose you, my lord, but someone with a...heftier tool!" she lied coolly.

He flushed, and Bethia knew a heady sensation of victory at having bested him. She sensed that Simon de Burgh rarely found himself in that position and told herself that humility was good for the soul. It was only after she caught a glimpse of his eyes, glittering dangerously, that Bethia realized that this was not the way to win the man over.

Did it matter? Firmin would tell her she was wasting her time anyway, for no one outside of Ansquith cared of their struggle, least of all a mighty de Burgh. And no amount of explanation or persuasion could sway him to the cause. With one last glare at his stony face, Bethia turned away.

She had learned long ago to fight her own battles, for no knight, including this one, would ever ride to her rescue.

Simon watched the sun dip above the trees and bided his time. Soon he would have his chance, and then that wench would pay for her misdeeds in kind. He felt himself flush again at the memory of her eyes upon him and stifled a curse.

When he had first felt the urge, Simon had hoped that the woman would untie him, or at least give him some privacy, so that he could seize the opportunity to escape earlier than planned. After it became apparent that she would not give way so easily, he had jeered at her, thinking she would meet his challenge and come close enough for him to seize her weapon.

But when she refused to take his bait, Simon thought she would simply turn around or walk away. He had never imagined that she would stand there, cool as you please, sword drawn and pointed directly at him. Like an astute warrior. Or a base whore! Simon grimaced, unable to reach a satisfactory conclusion about this Bethia or her bizarre effect upon him.

There was simply no explaining it! He had grown up among six brothers, fought and shared encampments, lived along the road and turned a blind eye toward the kind of women who sometimes approached the battle

weary. Fie, he had bathed publicly in the closest stream
when necessary, without a moment's hesitation.

So when the wench had remained there, he had been
merely annoyed that his tactic had failed, but gradually
he had begun to feel…odd. The sensation grew until
he had never been so intensely aware of a woman, and
for once in his life, his body rebelled against both his
rigid discipline and his good sense. At first, it was the
realization that she could witness him being unclothed
in any way that began to affect him. Then her presence
but a few feet from him while he was exposed to her
made him react in a most inexplicable and embarrass-
ing manner.

Fie on the wench, but he had become aroused! And
it had infuriated him. If he hated her before, now he
despised her for the reaction she had culled from him
without obvious effort on her part—and without his
consent. Frantically he had urged that fool boy to cover
him, so she would not see his rod stiffening for no
reason. He would not have her know she affected him
in any way, least of all in that manner.

Had she seen? He thought not, but what was that
comment about a heftier tool? Simon scowled. His
brother Stephen said all the de Burghs were well
equipped, but he had never considered the claim. Perhaps this wench was so well used that only a staff the
size of… But no. Suddenly he found that train of
thought not to his liking. At all.

As if directed by something other than his own will,
Simon glanced around the glade, seeking her. Obviously accustomed to stealth, the brigands lit no fire
even to cook their meal, but ate only bread and cheese,
berries and nuts. Bah! Woodland fodder fit only for
birds, Simon thought in disgust. His stomach growled

for a slab of venison, but he would be lucky to get anything this night.

At last he found her, striding toward a tall oak where she spoke softly to her fellows. Although he had been listening for hours in the hopes of gaining information about her and her men, these ruffians were a silent group, moving among the trees with faint rustlings that were barely audible. Sly devils!

But even as he seethed with contempt at the whole lot of them, Simon's attention was drawn to their leader. He sucked in a sharp breath as she took her seat upon a thick tree root, straddling it as if it were a horse...or a man. Cursing his suddenly errant blood, Simon grunted angrily.

He glanced away, yet soon found himself drawn back to her, as if by some unseen force. Like the men near her, she broke off a hunk of a loaf of bread, but unlike them, she did not gobble it down in haste. She tore off a small piece and tossed it into her mouth in a manner he had never seen before. Careless yet efficient, graceful yet spare.

Simon found himself watching her throat as she swallowed, her hands as they worked the bread, her skill with the small dagger she used upon a hunk of yellow cheese. When she lifted a fat berry to her wide mouth, he swore and looked away, unable to bear the sight as a certain hunger grew within himself, fierce and unyielding.

Perhaps his head wound was deeper than he thought and was even now affecting his humors. But no matter what imbalance drove him, Simon could not help gazing toward her. She was rising to her feet, not with a woman's fussy daintiness, but with a nimble movement that spoke of capability, strength, leadership. As he watched, she lifted a jug and went around to the wounded, pouring the liquid into a wooden cup. Water? Ale? A sleeping potion? Simon vowed to drink nothing from the woman's hand, and when she stepped toward him, he jerked his head away only to stare in surprise. "Milk? You have a dairy here?"

Her expression hardened. "Let us say that I can rightfully lay claim to a herd, even if it isn't tethered close by."

Simon snorted, frustrated at her cryptic comments, but he leaned forward as she began to tender the drink. If she would just get a little closer. As if suddenly realizing her error, she caught herself and Simon gritted his teeth. He would gladly have butted his head into her chin and taken her hostage, but the wench was too wary.

"Jemmy, will you aid me again?" she said, and the youth who had handled his braies returned to lift the drink to his lips. Although Simon felt like spitting it upon her, his chance at escape was rapidly approaching and he would not waste it on such petty displays of temper. He would wait, for when he took a captive, it would be no useless lad, but the leader herself.

Two cups of milk assuaged the worst of his hunger pangs, and the boy fed him a hunk of bread, too, before moving silently into the shadowy canopy of trees. What kind of men were these to scurry like squirrels among the branches? For a long moment, Simon simply stared at the rustling leaves above him, feeling a strange yearning. It was so quiet here, without the constant noise of Campion, the raillery of his brothers, the ever-present need to prove himself.

When at last he dropped his gaze, the wench was leaning against a nearby oak studying him, and Simon was annoyed at his momentary lapse of attention. A warrior did not take his eyes from his opponent. Scowling, he glared at her. "Waiting for another display, wench?"

"I have no designs on your body, fine though it may be," she said with a cold expression. Then, grabbing a blanket from a passing youth, she threw it at his feet. "I'd advise you to get some sleep, but should you think to hop away," she said, glancing toward his bound legs, "be warned that the forest has eyes and ears—and bows—at the ready."

With a grunt, Simon fell to his knees on the makeshift bed and then turned onto his side, biting back a smile of triumph. This was really too easy, he thought contemptuously. Eyes and ears and bows notwithstanding, as soon as the camp settled in for the night, he would simply ease his boots up toward his bound hands and retrieve his knife.

He had to stifle a laugh at the poor wench who thought to keep him captive. Soon the tables would be turned, he vowed, as he watched her move away in the growing darkness. Apparently she was accustomed to sleeping in the open, and Simon struggled against a growing admiration for her. Not many females would make a bed beneath the trees without complaint.

Nor would they look so easy doing it, Simon thought. Something caught in his throat as he saw her remove her sword. His mouth was suddenly dry. Surely she didn't intend to take off anything else, did she? Although he had more than once thought her a whore, she did not resemble in the slightest any of those women he had known. She was too graceful, too confident, too...pure looking, like some Norse goddess of war.

Her thick braid slid over her shoulder, and she threw it back with a toss of her head just as Simon felt a kick in the chest. He glanced around furtively. Had some jeering archer tossed a stone at him? Seeing nothing, he turned his attention back to the wench, who was stretching out on a blanket, her sword at her side. She could sleep with it lodged within her fist and she would be no better for it, he thought.

Silently he concentrated on his breathing, keeping it even and low, despite a sudden, inexplicable rush of blood that he put down to his imminent escape. It had nothing at all to do with the sight of the woman lying prone not far away from him, nor the memory of her watching him.

And as a man who had never been the slightest bit vain—unlike his showy brother Stephen—Simon swore that it certainly had nothing to do with the sudden, sharp memory of her calling his body "fine."

Simon waited until the last sounds of human activity died away and then inched his feet up behind him so that his fingers could delve for his knife. It was an awkward business, but he was skilled with his hands, bound or not, and he soon had the well-honed dagger slicing through the rope that held him.

Once freed, he resisted the urge to stretch cramped muscles and lay still and silent, listening for the guards that Bethia claimed watched from the trees. But even if one or two remained still awake, they could not see much; the darkness was complete except for a twinkling of stars and a moon that was still on the rise behind the forest.

Finally, after silence reigned and naught stirred but night creatures, Simon began to move. Gradually he

rolled and inched across the stretch of grass to where
his adversary lay, having marked her position so well
that he could have found her with his eyes closed.
When at last he reached her, Simon silently unsheathed
her sword, then slid one hand over her mouth while he
held the point to her throat.

She did not disappoint him, but awoke instantly and
jerked away from him only to be halted by the pressure
of her own weapon. Simon smiled, her look of dismay
surging through his veins like a war cry. The battle had
been joined, and he was the victor.

Clasping her to him, Simon rose to his feet, stealthily
moving into the forest to the sound of snoring rising
from one of the men nearby. She was not a dainty
woman, but he had carried heavier loads with ease and
certainly none that had given him quite as much satisfaction.

It was really too easy, Simon thought, just before he
felt a set of sharp teeth clamp into his palm. Without
pausing to flinch, he kept walking, ignoring the discomfort as he would the sting of a bee. But there was something about Bethia's mouth on his flesh that made him
draw in a harsh breath unrelated to pain. Again he
wanted to give her one better, to lower his head and
nip at the golden skin of her neck or the lobe of her
ear.

Simon grunted in annoyance. Fie! He could not afford undisciplined thoughts, not when one of her snoring companions might turn over to find her gone and
send up an alarm. He spared a fleeting regret for his
men, but he could not free them without raising the
camp, and right now his hands were full. Gripping her
tighter, Simon vowed to ignore the press of her buttocks against his groin as he marched onward.

Even without the distraction her woman's body presented, it was slow going. The trees kept out all but the faintest light from the night sky, and Simon was not very familiar with these woods. He continued in the general direction of Baddersly, if not the road itself, until the stiff form in his embrace had relaxed against him.

Unless her precious archers could sprout wings and hop from branch to branch in their pursuit, Simon did not see how they could follow, and at last he stopped, pausing only to twist the rope he had brought with him around her hands. When she realized his intent, she struggled, knocking aside the sword, but once on her feet, she stumbled, and Simon sent her sprawling onto the mossy ground.

Although she fought him anew when he bent to bind her feet, to Simon's surprise she did not scream or weep. Nor did she wail or plead as he would have expected any other woman to do. As he was rapidly coming to discover, this wench was like no other, and Simon was not sure whether the knowledge pleased him.

"There, wench, how do you like playing the captive?" he asked as he straightened to tower over her. The triumph he had expected to feel at their reversed positions was short-lived, however, for as he stared down at her in contempt his gaze drifted to the front of her tunic, where her now-unmistakable breasts rose and fell rapidly. His attention lingered there, and Simon wondered if she bound her chest to disguise herself. Abruptly he felt a surge of heat in his blood, just as he recognized the uniqueness of the situation.

He could do whatever he wanted with her.

The thought shot through him like a lance. She had

attacked his train, taken his men and humiliated him. Who could blame him for exacting a fitting revenge? Had he not vowed to? Suddenly his heart pounded and his blood ran hot as he realized he could take her now on the forest floor.

Simon turned away with a rough curse, shaken by his own thoughts. One did not torture or dishonor adversaries, but held them for ransom, as was accepted practice. Though such rules might not apply to an outlaw, he could not abuse a prisoner—even a female.

Female! There was the problem, for Simon had never before been faced with an enemy like this one. Still that did not explain the odd temptation that seized him. He had never been with any woman except a paid consort, having always prided himself on a discipline of mind and body that went far beyond that of his brothers. He was not about to lose that control just because this creature in men's clothing would distract him. It was probably her intent to make good use of her woman's wiles, he thought as he eyed her sprawled at his feet.

Turning his head to catch his breath, Simon faced her again with a harsh glare. "Come along," he said, tethering the rope to himself. "It is time you walked." He did not help her to rise or wait for her to follow, but began marching, the tautness of the line his only reminder of her presence.

And so he picked his way through the King's forest, stopping only to listen and study the night sky. When at last the trees thinned out, Simon halted to gaze through leaves, where an overgrown area yielded to tended pasture beyond, faintly illuminated by the partial moon.

Although he did not want to travel in the open, neither did he care to stay in the outlaw's domain, which she knew far better than he. Pulling his captive behind him, Simon skirted the edge of the woods, looking for a shepherd's hut or somewhere in which to spend the rest of the night. This was sheep country, and he hoped for an abandoned cot to keep them hidden, but he found nothing until he came upon a broken trail and an old Roman shrine.

"Inside, wench," Simon whispered, pushing her before him. The air was musty with old leaves that had collected in the corners, and weeds grew through the cracked tile, but the abandoned site would provide shelter from prying eyes, should her men manage to get this far.

Come daylight, Simon would be better able to get his bearings, and, if not, he could ask one of the shepherds who roamed these hills. The outlaws, meanwhile, would be bound to their shadowy realm, unable to take to the open as honest men.

But just in case they ventured forth, he still held their leader, Simon thought with a grim smile. Pulling her down beside him, he stretched out upon the cold floor, fully expecting her to complain. But she said nothing, continuing the silence she had maintained since her capture.

It irked him somehow that her wide mouth should remained tightly closed against him, but with a grunt, Simon decided it was just as well. Right now, the quiet would keep them from discovery, and he just might be able to get some rest in preparation for tomorrow's travel.

Closing his eyes, Simon mused with satisfaction

upon the days ahead, when there would be time enough to gain the information he sought—and to get back some of his own from the wench who had so foolishly thought to hold a de Burgh.

Chapter Three

Simon awoke at dawn and came to attention immediately, his gaze swiftly taking in the shadowy coolness of the old Roman shrine, his fist gripping the hilt of the sword still in his clasp. It was lighter than his own, and he wondered at the female who wielded it so easily. Having fully expected her to try to take it from him even while he slept, Simon knew a brief disappointment that she had not.

He felt a hum of excitement in his blood, not unlike that which presaged a battle, at the thought of clashing with her again today. He had a deep, compelling urge to look at her, which he defied for the sake of his own discipline. Did she continue to rest, or was she glaring daggers at him even now? Smiling grimly in anticipation of the contest between them, Simon at last allowed himself a glance in her direction.

He turned his head slowly only to jerk upright, an oath upon his lips. Rising to his feet, Simon stood gaping at the empty ropes that dangled from his waist, unable to believe his eyes. He swiftly scanned the small interior of the shelter as if he would find her crouching in a dark corner. But no one shared the space.

She was gone.

Raising his fists in the air, Simon fought back a war cry that would have rivaled Dunstan's. Only the knowledge that he might be heard by enemies kept him from howling his rage to the skies. It coursed through him, bitter and fierce, a boundless anger at the wench who had somehow escaped him—and at his own negligence for letting her.

Drawing a deep, fortifying breath, Simon tried to deduce how she had flown from beneath his very nose. When he yanked impatiently at the ropes, he saw that the ends were cut, but she had not used his sword. The edges were ragged as his own had been, and he gritted his teeth at the realization that she must have had a dagger secreted on her person, just as had he.

He had underestimated her. Again. Simon cursed himself for it and for sleeping so soundly that he had not heard her efforts. He was a warrior, and, as such, he should be aware of a gnat landing upon him in the night. His very life depended upon it! Yet this woman had sliced through her bonds and fled without him taking notice!

With a distinct sense of unease, Simon lifted his hand to his neck, rubbing against the wound still encrusted with some kind of salve. He doubted whether the wench could have slit his throat before he would have overpowered her, but the notion made him chary. As did the thought that she might have left him alive for reasons of her own.

Simon slammed a fist against his hand, chastising himself for not questioning her last night when he had the chance. How would he find out the identity of this woman who led a band of men? Why didn't they act like common outlaws? And who the devil was Brice, the man she had accused him of coming to aid? The questions came fast and furious, but now he would have no answers. Slamming his fist again, Simon ground out a curse at yet another misjudgment on his part.

Worse yet, underlying all his rage and frustration and disgust ran a strange feeling of loss. It ate away at him like a canker, gnawing at his vitals in a way he did not understand. With another low oath, Simon nearly turned on his heel and headed back into the woods the way he had come, vowing to find the camp, free his train and destroy the outlaws.

But as he took a step forward, he could almost hear Geoffrey decrying his recklessness. Even if he could rescue his men, how could they fight, weaponless, against the band of archers? With a grunt, Simon realized that, rather than hare off into the forest again, he needed to get back to Baddersly and arm himself with both men and information before he returned.

He smiled grimly at that, for he *would* return to claim his own back, the wench included. He wanted her here beside him with a fierceness that he dismissed as a need for revenge. If there were other forces at work, he refused to consider them. She was a clever adversary, but not his equal, he thought with typical de Burgh arrogance. And soon she would know it.

Whoever she was, Bethia had met her match.

From her perch high in the ancient oak, Bethia watched him go with a combination of relief and regret. Foolishly she wished that things could have been different between them, that this knight would have come to her rescue, vanquished her enemies and…the denouement to her dream was vague and unsettling.

Releasing the breath she had been holding, Bethia

knew she ought not bemoan the loss of what could not be, but instead send up thanks that he had not discovered her perch. The thought of facing all that righteous de Burgh rage had her shivering, despite her stout heart.

It had served her well when she had awakened to find her own sword at her throat and herself a captive of her prisoner. It had taken all of her strength not to cry out uselessly, for her men would never have attacked while he held her hostage. And once schooling herself to silence, Bethia had remained so, for there were other dangers abroad besides Simon de Burgh, although sometimes when the moon gilded his harsh profile, it was hard to remember that. Or anything else.

Bethia shied away from the memory of him binding her in the darkness, of how she had fallen, breathless, onto her back, while he towered above her. In that moment, she had embraced her fear rather than give in to the other feelings that rushed through her, including her consciousness of her own gender—and his. She had never known anyone like Simon de Burgh, arrogant, powerful, skilled, and for an instant, she had forgotten everything else.

Bethia released a low, shaky breath, grateful that the moment had passed and that he had soon dragged her behind him like so much excess weight. She had welcomed the forced march and the respite from his intense regard. Simon de Burgh sizzled with strength and vibrancy in a world of pale, callow men, and only the reminder of her precarious position had turned her thoughts back to herself.

And she had managed to keep them there even when he pulled her down beside him and stretched out to sleep. Her startling awareness of him had worked for her then, keeping her awake even after he slumbered, keeping her painfully attuned to every breath he took and every nuance of his great body, while she used her dagger on the ropes.

But after she freed herself, Bethia had felt no triumph, only a sickening dread that he would discover her yet. Although well accustomed to moving silently through the forest, she feared that any noise might send him after her, so taking but a moment for her most pressing needs, she had climbed a nearby oak, putting herself well up and out of reach. And there she had remained until dawn.

Even now, watching him take long strides through the meadow, Bethia trembled in reaction to her narrow escape. She had been very lucky. What if he had guessed her ploy and looked for her? A dread that was both excitement and terror flooded through her although she realized that he would not think her clever enough—or brave enough—to hide in plain sight.

Fool! For all his great strength, Simon de Burgh was a dolt in some respects, especially where she was concerned, and Bethia longed to educate him. Most men saw women as nothing more than pretty ornaments, bound by birth to household tasks beneath their own exalted status. They refused to acknowledge that women had brains, and just might think as well as they.

Last night, for just a moment Bethia had been tempted to prove this arrogant knight wrong by capturing him once again. She could have done it, too, by pricking him with her small dagger while he slumbered. But something stayed her hand; a gut-level desire not to hurt either his fine body or his exaggerated pride had joined with her own good sense to stop her.

For Firmin was right. Simon de Burgh was trouble and Bethia could hardly keep him prisoner forever.

Now that he was free, perhaps he would leave them be, especially once she released his men, as well. Surely, as lord of Baddersly, he would have more important business than to concern himself with her small band.

Although Bethia knew a nagging doubt, she still thought it better to be rid of such a dangerous man than to try to hold him. Besides, she was not entirely certain that she could have bested Simon de Burgh there in the darkness of the abandoned shrine. The thought of struggling with the fierce warrior brought to mind their first encounter when he had touched her too intimately, and Bethia wondered if she could have kept her wits about her if so sorely tried again.

No matter, for now that the great knight was disappearing into the distance she no longer had to worry about such things. Her jaw tightened at the thought, for it brought Bethia no relief. In its place, she had plenty of other burdens to tax her, including the possibility that Simon de Burgh, once unleashed upon the countryside, would do far worse.

Simon jumped out of the cart with a scowl. As much as it annoyed him to use such transportation, he had reached Baddersly more quickly than on foot. Of course, the freeman who owned the smelly conveyance was reluctant at first to take up a stranger, but Simon persuaded him in a voice that brooked no disobedience.

Grunting at the memory of the woman who had not only taken his pride, but his men, his supplies and his warhorses, Simon vowed that his destrier had better be returned to him in prime condition. If the thieving wench thought to sell the mounts, she would suffer his wrath tenfold, he swore, fisting his hands angrily at the thought. His mood was not improved by the guard at Baddersly's gate, who stepped forward to question him.

"Halt, stranger! What business have you here?" the guard asked, his hand on the hilt of his sword.

Although aware that he little resembled a knight when stripped of his mail and nearly all else, Simon had no patience with the man. "Put away your weapon, fool. 'Tis I, Simon de Burgh!" he answered, and the steel in his tone must have pleaded his case more effectively than his appearance, for the fellow's manner changed at once.

"M-my lord Simon! I beg your pardon! We've been expecting you, but where is your train? Your mount?" he said, looking about in bewilderment.

"I met with trouble on the road," Simon muttered, forestalling the young man's questions with a frigid glare. "And I am in haste to reach my hall."

"Of course, by all means, my lord," the guard said, bowing as if remembering his place. With a curt nod, Simon passed swiftly by him and strode into the outer bailey. Although his keen eyes took in his surroundings, he spoke to no one as he made his way to the inner bailey and the great hall.

The fewer who knew about his irregular arrival the better, Simon decided. He certainly had no intention of telling all and sundry that the mighty de Burgh party had been set upon by brigands—or that he had been taken captive by a mere female. His reputation would be ruined if that small piece of information got out, and how his brothers would howl! Simon's blood boiled again at the thought, and he stormed through the wide doors to the hall.

Once inside, he ignored the luxury that greeted him, the tapestries, the cupboard that held expensive plate and the smattering of heavy chairs and settles. He was as comfortable on the road as in a fine castle, so such things meant little to him. But Baddersly had one thing that he would well appreciate: a decent meal.

With that in mind, Simon bellowed for food, and several servants ran to do his bidding. Everyone else in the vicinity hung back, mouths gaping, with the exception of a few knights who were clustered near the hearth. Heads lifting from the after-supper conversation, they leaped to their feet, and Simon waved them alongside him as he headed toward the solar.

Designed as a private place for the lord of the hall and his family to gather, the room was empty, and Simon took a seat in the massive chair that stood at the head of the long table, motioning for the three knights to join him. Leaning back in the place of authority, Simon felt some measure of calm return as he surveyed those who attended him.

One he knew well, for young Thorkill had come with him from Campion, eager for new challenges two years ago when he had set the holding to rights for his brother. The elder Quentin had arrived with him, also, having been at Wessex with Dunstan. Only the portly one, whom Simon recognized as Leofwin, had served at Baddersly for any length of time. Although he had once marched on Wessex, Simon did not hold that against him, for several knights had transferred their allegiance to Dunstan after the death of the tyrant who had once held Baddersly.

All three Simon deemed trustworthy, yet he hesitated, uncertain how much to tell them. Not only was he reluctant to share his recent disgrace, but something else held him back, something about Bethia and her men. How much, really, did he know about them? Were they simple outlaws? Or was there more to their thievery?

Simon suspected that his mocking brother Stephen would laugh at his ambivalence, for he was usually the most decisive of men. But he was not at home. It had been two years since his brief stay here, and he was not as familiar with the area as he would have liked. Nor could he claim to know what had transpired in his absence, beyond the steward's reports he had barely glanced over at Dunstan's request.

Caution, as much as he disliked it, just might be well-advised, he thought, with a nod to the absent Geoffrey. With it came a need to keep his own counsel. And as he gazed at the men surrounding him, all trained in the ways of war, Simon felt something else—an odd protective instinct. For he was sure of one thing: he would not let these knights slay the brigands, at least not until he had some answers. And as for their leader…he would deal with Bethia himself, Simon vowed with grim resolve.

The knights before him waited in silence, obviously wary of his harsh mood, until finally Thorkill spoke. "Is something amiss, my lord?" he asked.

Simon eyed him steadily. "We were attacked on the forest road. All of the train was taken," he admitted. "Perhaps to be held for ransom." A flurry of outraged grumbling greeted his words, but none seemed surprised that Simon alone had escaped, and he savored the small balm to his sorely injured pride.

"Who was it?" Thorkill asked, indignant. "Enemies of Campion, your father?"

"Or your brother, the Wolf of Wessex?" Quentin asked.

"Or Baddersly? It has long been envied for its wealth," Leofwin added with a gruff sigh.

Simon shook his head. Although Bethia could well have been lying, he did not believe she knew of his identity when she attacked his train. Indeed, she had accused him of being a mercenary, he thought with a grimace of disgust. The memory tempted him to ask about the mysterious Brice, but, again, Simon held his tongue. "Simple outlaws, I suspect," he said.

"Devils!" Thorkill exclaimed. "We have heard warnings about brigands plaguing the forest, especially Burnel Chase, but I knew not that these ruffians were preying on innocent travelers."

The young knight immediately snared Simon's attention, for Bethia was after more than the usual poacher, and the miners who delved for iron ore in those woods were hardened men with little to steal. "Who else would they prey upon?" Simon asked, watching intently as Thorkill exchanged a glance at Leofwin.

"Well, I know nothing for certain, but rumor has it that there have been sheep and supplies stolen from Ansquith," Leofwin said, looking uncomfortable under Simon's regard. "I have not heard of them taking captives or harming anyone," he added hastily.

"Ansquith," Simon said softly. "The demesne that claims the chase?"

"Aye, my lord," Leofwin said, nodding in agreement. "'Tis a prosperous holding with a fortified manor house and rights to what was once part of the royal forest."

"And 'tis sworn to Baddersly," Thorkill added with a pointed glance at Quentin. Simon watched the interplay between the three knights with interest. Was there a personal dispute between them or were they keeping something from him? Simon leaned back just as the servants entered with ale, bread, cheese and a bowl of dried dates, raisins and figs.

When the servants left, Simon eyed each knight in turn. "And?"

Leofwin gazed longingly at the food, and silence reigned until finally Quentin cleared his throat. "Oh, the braying ass of Ansquith has been demanding our help, but none here thought his whining worthy of attention."

"We did not know they would bother travelers!" Leofwin protested, but Thorkill, obviously the dissenter, held his tongue.

Simon's eyes narrowed as he reached for a fig. Apparently the knights feared he would call them to task for neglect of their duty, as well he might. If they had investigated the outlaws earlier, his current misfortunes might have been prevented, and yet, Simon found the notion oddly unpalatable. Despite the indignities of his adventure, it had roused his blood more than anything had in years, aye, in a lifetime, and he could not bring himself to regret the encounter. *The battle had been joined....*

"Who is the braying ass of Ansquith?" Simon asked. "I seem to recall an old man holding the demesne quite peacefully."

"Sir Burnel," Quentin said, relaxing slightly in his seat. His hair was nearly all white now, and Simon realized he must have a wealth of information with his years. "Aye, that rich piece of property has been in the Burnel family for a long time, and he had done well by it."

"Yet you refused him aid?" Simon asked.

Quentin snorted. "Not Sir Burnel! He's ill from what

I hear. It's the ass who claims to speak for him who has been complaining. What's his name, Thorkill?''

"Brice. Brice Scirvayne," the young knight answered.

Simon hid his flicker of reaction by leaning forward to reach for the food. The mysterious Brice, at last! He nearly grinned in triumph. "And exactly who is this Brice?''

Quentin shrugged. "No one knows. A relative of Burnel's perhaps—or a friend.''

"He claims to have been betrothed to Burnel's daughter," Thorkill said, his face rigid with what looked like disapproval.

"Aye," Leofwin said. "But now that she's dead, what claim has he on the place?''

"I do not recall Sir Burnel having a daughter," Simon said, tearing off a hunk of bread. He ignored Leofwin's avid attention to his actions, for the knight was well fed enough. Any more weight would sorely strain his mount.

"She was gone for a long time, fostered out since she was just a young thing and wild as a boy," Quentin explained. "I remember her then, for she traipsed after her father and his guards, just as if she were one of them. Burnel allowed it, since he had no sons, but after his wife's death, I think he came to regret his laxity, for he sent her off quickly enough.''

Simon frowned. Listening to the elderly knight reminisce was getting him nowhere. The old neighbor's dead daughter was of little interest to him beyond her connection to this Brice, who seemed to be at the very center of whatever was happening here.

"Ah, pretty thing she was, too, that Bethia, with her

light hair and—'' Leofwin stared at Simon ''—my lord?''

Simon's hand hung in the air halfway to his mouth, and he swiftly took a bite of the bread to cover his surprise. But deep inside him, he felt the thrumming of excitement that came only with an approaching clash of weapons. ''The old man's daughter, Bethia,'' he said, after he had swallowed. ''You say she is dead?''

''Aye, my lord,'' Thorkill answered, his expression grim. '''Twas not long after she returned to wed this Brice, several months ago now, that we were told of her death. And little enough mourning they did for her, too, from what we have heard.''

Quentin grunted. ''He's an ass, that Brice, a bullying braggart, who did not deserve the girl or the lands she brought to him.''

''But he's no worse than many a landholder,'' Leofwin muttered, with a swift glance at Simon. ''Few are as fair and just as the de Burghs.''

Although Simon acknowledged the praise with a curt nod, his thoughts were no longer upon Brice. Reaching for his cup, he took a drink of ale while envisioning his captor. Tall and slender, with a braid the color of fine wheat and habits that could well be described as wild and boyish, she could easily be the adult version of the girl Quentin mentioned.

For unless there were two Bethias, the outlaw wench was the daughter of Sir Burnel and decidedly not dead. It made sense, in a way, for what other female could claim such unique training? Not only could she read, but wield a sword and a rope. She had some knowledge of healing herbs, he thought as he absently rubbed his throat, and a rudimentary understanding of battle tactics, as well as a certain aura of...leadership.

An image rose before him of her standing straight and tall, her lovely face intent, her weapon poised, and Simon's blood flowed in response. *The battle was joined...* Struggling against the hot surge of excitement that rushed through him, Simon concentrated on arming himself with information. Yet, though he questioned the knights further about her, they could tell him little. Even Quentin had naught but snatches of recollections to offer him.

Finally Thorkill dropped his blond head and spoke reluctantly. "I saw her once, riding her palfrey. She was beautiful, as pale and fine as an angel," he mumbled as if dumbstruck by awe.

Simon stared at him, unable to summon up a caustic scoff at a young man's fancy. Normally he would have been the first one to dismiss such chivalrous words. Instead, he tasted a bitterness in his mouth at the notion of the youth pining after Bethia.

Bah! Thorkill was no match for the wench, Simon knew that much, and the thought made him smile grimly. Should the young knight try to bow before this angel, he might find himself skewered through the gullet. Better that he believe her dead than have his illusions of feminine sweetness shattered.

For Bethia was not sweet, but neither was she tart, in the off-putting manner of some women, though her tongue could cut like a blade. No, the wench was something entirely different, and Simon intended to find out exactly what strange breed was she. Unfortunately, his knights could add nothing more to his store of knowledge.

Relations between Ansquith and the castle had been strained ever since Harold Peasley, the uncle of the rightful heir, had held Baddersly in a cruel grasp. Al-

though Dunstan had killed Peasley, he had been busy
with his own demesne ever since and had done no traveling at all at his wife's insistence.

And Simon had done little visiting during his past
stay here. His job had been to reorganize the castle
forces and select a trustworthy steward to manage the
household in Dunstan's absence. He had no time to
cement petty alliances, and, apparently, Burnel had remained wary of his new lord.

According to Quentin, there had been little exchange
at all between Ansquith and the castle until the arrival
of this Brice. Then, rumors had filtered in about
changes at the manor, that the villeins were over-
worked, and the freemen, too, coupled with grumblings
of interference with the prosperous wool production
and alienation of the chase miners.

Still, as Quentin noted, such hearsay was no cause
for alarm and of little concern to those at Baddersly.
As long as Burnel paid his annual scutage to Dunstan,
the castle was obligated only to provide him with protection, should his lands come under attack.

They had not, and neither Quentin nor Florian, steward of Baddersly, had deemed it necessary to send
knights into the woods because of minor thievery on
lands belonging to Ansquith. And rightly so. Although
the three warriors eyed each other warily in anticipation
of Simon's reprimand, he found no fault with them.

But, now, as if to make up for their previous inaction,
they clamored for revenge against those who had dared
to attack their lord. And Simon, usually the most eager
for battle, found himself in the strange position of
dampening their enthusiasm.

"Let us lead a large force into the chase and be done
with them," Quentin said dismissively.

"Nay. 'Tis unwise to pit horsed soldiers against skilled archers," Simon muttered.

"Then let us take archers!" Thorkill said. "I would test Baddersly's against any in the land!"

"And how familiar are they with the chase?" Simon snapped. "Can they climb about the trees like squirrels, searching out their targets, both above and below?"

The three men looked at him in varying degrees of astonishment, and Simon shifted uncomfortably. He was not used to urging caution, but he was not prepared to mount an attack, either. What if he sent archers into the woods and one of them killed Bethia? Simon rubbed his hand across his chest, where a sudden, sharp sensation struck him, as if from a troubling wound.

Annoyed by the feeling, he grunted and glared at them all, daring them to question his judgment. "And what if this Brice wants us to send all of our soldiers haring off into the woods? What if he seeks to trap us or attack Baddersly in our absence?"

Although Simon did not think such a thing remotely possible, he was rewarded by three gasps of surprise. "I had not considered that, my lord," Thorkill said, hanging his head in shame.

"I doubt that—" Leofwin began, but Simon cut him off by sliding the remains of the bread in his direction. The rotund knight grinned happily and tore off a large chunk.

"Nay. I would rather take a small group of highly skilled men, leading them myself," Simon said. That way, he could be assured that Bethia would not be harmed. Aye, he would decree it! Never had he taken such a keen interest in an enemy, but neither had he been so humiliated before, and he vowed that the next victory in their little war would be his.

Although Simon would have liked to go first to Ansquith and find out more about this Brice and his dead betrothed, the better to arm himself with knowledge of his foe, he knew an urgency to find her again, to see her, to triumph over her…and the wench still held his men. Simon intended to get them back as soon as possible, as well as his prime horseflesh.

The question was how to do just that, without endangering the woman herself. Leaning back in his seat, Simon considered his options, and for once, he was not sure how best to proceed against so elusive an opponent. It was a challenge, one such as he had never faced before, and Simon found himself smiling in satisfaction as he took it up most willingly.

The battle had been joined.

Chapter Four

Simon was roused just after dawn by one of the servants, wide-eyed and wary to disturb his rest. "You are wanted out at the gate, my lord," he said, backing away to escape through the door of the great chamber. With a grunt, Simon rose and dressed quickly. He had chosen mail and a sword from the weapon stores to replace those stolen from him, but having no squire, he was forced to don them himself, and he grunted in annoyance as he hurried from the room.

A mount was ready and waiting when he strode out of the great hall, and Simon grimly wondered who could be at the gates at this hour. Had the mysterious Brice arrived? Or some enemy of whom he was not aware? Although he knew of no one who would march against Baddersly, Simon would not have been surprised by an army laying siege along the outer wall, for he had been trained to expect anything.

Except this.

Simon reined in by the gatehouse, masking his shock at the sight of an old cart full of his men, bound hand and foot, blocking the roadway. His first reaction, past surprise, was anger, swift and sure. How dared she?

Just when he was determined to get back some of his own, that wretched female had returned them all to him, as if they were a gift. He could almost picture her laughing at him, and the thought made him seethe in frustration.

As he glared at the evidence of his own incompetence, the castle guard stepped forward. "My lord! We found this cart abandoned on the road not far from the gate, and these men, they claim to have come south with you." Simon could hear the disbelief in the guard's voice, for what kind of men-at-arms were these to arrive tied and caged?

Raking them all with a contemptuous glance, Simon knew a fleeting desire to deny their identity, even their very existence, but their capture could only be blamed on his own recklessness. *And her.*

"Loose them," Simon said with a nod toward the guard. "But, heed this," he warned, giving them all a hard look. "Any man here who can't hold his tongue best be prepared to lose it."

Most needed not the threat, Simon knew, for they were loyal to the de Burghs. And what man would willingly reveal his defeat at the hands of a woman? Simon gritted his teeth at the memory, followed by this new humiliation. He watched as one by one the men were freed, most unharmed, a few with minor wounds that would soon heal, and again he wondered what game she played.

She had not held them for ransom, nor even kept all of their belongings. What kind of outlaw was she? Instead, she had left them here like so much fodder, as if to throw them in his face. Did she have such contempt for his skills that she did not think him capable of freeing them himself? Simon felt the flush rise on his neck and cursed it. Did she think that he would not pursue her now? If so, she was wrong. Dead wrong.

The war was just beginning.

"What should we do with the cart?" the guard asked, pausing to frown as he studied the old wooden piece. Simon was just about to tell the fellow to burn it when another gatesman stepped forward. "Why, I think this belongs to the smith."

Naturally, Simon thought angrily. She had stolen the blessed thing! As he glanced at one broken end, Simon grimaced suddenly. "Where are the horses?" he asked through gritted teeth.

"She said—" one of the wounded men began, only to break off hurriedly when he caught a glimpse of Simon's face. "We, uh, I think we'll find them at the smith's."

"She?" the guard whispered, but he was hushed by his companion. All eyes turned fearfully to Simon, who sent them a fierce glare. He had no intention of enlightening anyone as to the identity of the thieving wench who was responsible for his men arriving at Baddersly in a pilfered wagon.

With a harsh call to his squire, Simon turned his mount, intent upon gathering some knights and heading toward the village, where he would best not be overcharged for his own horseflesh.

With a movement of his hand, Simon bade his small group halt before the stables. Although the village situated near Burnel Chase was fairly prosperous, the smithy was small. Indeed, the low stone building and enclosed ground could barely hold the large destriers and packhorses that now crowded it. And the sight of

them there only made Simon angrier at the female who
had bested him—and continued to prove it.

Gesturing to Quentin and his outriders to wait,
Simon dismounted and headed inside to find the owner
calmly grooming a tall roan. He was a big, rough-
looking man who did not pause in his task at the in-
terruption, and Simon had half a mind to toss him in
the dungeon for dealing with thieves. But first he
wanted information about the outlaws, preferably their
leader.

"You have my horses," Simon said, making the
statement a demand. His hand drifted to the hilt of the
sword at his waist, and he stepped forward, prepared
for anything.

But the smith appeared undisturbed. "Thought as
much," he said, halting to spit on the hard-packed earth
beside him. "Might as well take them, then," he added,
continuing with his work.

Simon was nonplussed, a condition with which he
was becoming increasingly familiar. Ever since he had
stepped into the chase, the world seemed skewed. There
was no order here, no rhyme or reason, and it was
enough to task even his ironclad discipline. "And just
how much are you asking for them?" he queried.

"Me?" The fellow turned with a look of dull surprise on his harsh features. "Nothing. You said they
were yours."

Simon gritted his teeth. "They are. But how did they
come to be here?"

The man made a low sound in his throat. "I'm thinking you would know more about that than I would, my
lord," he answered.

Simon stood back to study the fellow through narrowed eyes. Heavily built and muscular, with a shock

of thick reddish hair, he looked formidable, but his wits were obviously lacking. "Are you telling me that you don't know where they came from?"

"They're yours, so I'm thinking they came from you, my lord. They were here when I got up this morning."

"And you didn't hear a thing during the night?"

The man shook his head, and Simon gritted his teeth in frustration. On the surface, he appeared to be wasting his time, for the fellow was little better than a fool, but somehow he sensed that the smith was not quite as dull as he pretended.

He knows her, Simon thought grimly. *You know her!* He wanted to shout the accusation to the skies, to grab the idiot and throttle the truth from him. But he curbed his reckless urges and continued his questions as evenly as he could. "And you weren't surprised to find them here this morning?"

The fellow shrugged. "I was thinking that someone would come by to get them."

"And you're just handing them to me, free of charge?" Simon said.

"They're yours, aren't they?"

Simon had to restrain himself from lunging for the man's throat. He was getting nowhere. If the smith was not an utter fool, he gave a very good impression of one. Simon studied him suspiciously, trying to gauge the truth. If this man knew more than he was letting on, was he frightened of retribution from the outlaws, or was he protecting Bethia and her men?

Difficult as it was, Simon tried to imagine what Geoff would do or say. Turning his head away for a moment to rein in his temper, he fixed the man with a fierce look. "How do you know that the animals are mine?'' he asked. ''Might they not belong to some local, those at Baddersly, for instance...or Brice Scirvayne?''

''Pah! That lout!'' the fellow said. Rewarding Simon with a grimace, he proceeded to spit on the ground once more. ''I do no business with him!''

''And why is that?'' Simon asked evenly.

''He's a cheat and a liar! 'Tis common knowledge that he's not well liked around here,'' the fellow answered.

''Why?''

But the man must have realized his mistake, for he shook his head, refusing to say more. '''Tis not my place to speak of my betters, my lord,'' he said, the blank expression returning to his face. ''Here, now, I'll help you round up your mounts.''

Simon nearly charged after him, for now he was certain that the fellow knew more than he was telling. Was he in league with the outlaws? And, if he was, were there others here who sided with Bethia and her band? Simon glanced around the village, where tradesmen and freemen and miners moved to their tasks, and he wondered where their allegiance lay.

Then, as if through a will of its own, his gaze drifted toward the chase. Where was she? Was she standing just inside the trees, laughing at him? Simon flushed at the thought, and his hands fisted at his sides as he fought the urge to go after her, to find her. He felt it in his very blood, like a call to battle, rousing him to action. Indeed, if Bethia thought to placate him with the return of his horses, she was sadly mistaken. He was not finished with her, by any means.

Yet, even as he was drawn to the forest, Simon knew better than to hare off into the woods without a plan.

The more he learned about her before he confronted the wench the better. And here in the village, he had discovered that loyalties were mixed, making him even more cautious. And curious.

Perhaps it was time to pay a call on the mysterious Brice.

Bethia gazed out over the hillside, admiring the gentle slopes dotted with sheep, while behind her the great oaks and beeches rose in leafy splendor. These were truly beautiful, prosperous lands, but how much longer would they remain so? It seemed that more of the forest was being destroyed every day for its wood, and already Brice was squeezing dry the people who lived and worked on the Burnel demesne and the chase.

And Simon de Burgh, what would he do? The thought of the great knight sent a shiver through Bethia, and her fingers dug deep into the bark of the tree beside her. By her reckoning, he should be at the smithy now, retrieving his mounts—and cursing her name, no doubt. She smiled a little at the thought of his rage, for he was too arrogant by half, but her amusement faded as she wondered just where he would direct his displeasure.

"He is at the smithy." The echo of her thoughts made Bethia turn abruptly, but it was only Firmin, looking grim and furious. "'Twas folly to leave his horses there! What if he imprisons the smith or punishes the whole village? He could set every cot to the torch!"

Although she, too, had worried about such a possibility, Bethia kept her voice even and couched in reason. "He has no quarrel with the village," she said.

"Neither has Brice, but that has not stopped his heavy fist from being felt."

Bethia sighed, for this was a long-standing argument with the archer. "Not everyone is like Brice."

"No! This man is worse, a powerful lord, with the army of Baddersly behind him! We should have killed him!" he raged.

Bethia ignored the sharp pain that came at the thought of Simon de Burgh dead, his noble blood on her hands. Instead, she looked out over the hills, seeking their peace. "Then we surely would have roused an army, not only from Baddersly, but Wessex and Campion. The de Burghs are mighty beyond even Brice's imagination."

Firmin swore low and harsh, but Bethia let his wrath spill over her out of long habit. Unlike the archer, she could not afford to be reckless or passionate—two words that turned her thoughts, once more, toward Simon de Burgh.

"You should have kept the horses. He is so wealthy that he has no need of them, and we could have used them, or sold them for a fine profit!" Firmin argued.

But Bethia refused to be drawn into heated debate. "He would never have rested until he had them back," she said softly, for even though she had known him but briefly, she felt as if she recognized Simon de Burgh all too well. She suspected that he valued his mounts more, perhaps, than his men, and their theft would be an outrage he could not ignore, one for which he would never have forgiven her.

Startled by that unruly thought, Bethia took a deep breath and turned to face her companion. "Besides, I will not stoop to the theft of innocents."

"Innocents?" Firmin repeated with a bitter laugh. "Simon de Burgh is not one of those, and you will rue the day that you released him."

Although she shrugged off Firmin's words as she stepped past him to return to the woods, Bethia nearly laughed aloud at his prediction. For Firmin was too late with his warning. She already regretted releasing the great knight, but not for any reason the hotheaded archer could comprehend.

Indeed, Bethia was not sure if she understood it herself.

Simon sent half of his force back to Baddersly with the horses, while he and the remaining men rode directly to Ansquith. Despite deliberately skirting the chase, they reached the fortified manor house in good time on their fresh mounts. Simon had seen the place before only in passing, but now he paused to admire the building, large and well protected by a wall and a gatehouse.

"Halt and state your business here," a soldier called out roughly as they approached.

"Is the gate always shut?" Simon asked in surprise, turning to Quentin, who rode beside him. In peaceable times, it was unusual to see a home barred during the day, especially when the owners did so much trading in sheep.

"It never used to be," Quentin answered with a frown. "Perhaps it is closed because of the outlaws."

Simon grunted in acknowledgment, but his eyes narrowed. If this Brice feared a few archers, he was a coward. Simon's contempt for the man grew, as did a certain uneasiness, for he knew that there were two reasons to bar the entrance: to keep intruders out and to hold the residents inside.

"You! I asked you a question!" the soldier at the

gate shouted, and Simon eyed him with no little astonishment.

"I am Simon de Burgh, lord of Baddersly," he snapped, unaccustomed to such treatment. "Open this gate at once so that I might speak with my vassal, Sir Burnel."

At Simon's response, the soldier's brashness left him, and when he peered through the narrow slit in the wall, he looked pale and nervous. "I have orders not to open the gate to anyone, my lord."

"Then go speak to your master," Simon advised.

The fellow shook his head. "I cannot leave my post."

Quentin let out a low, harsh laugh. "What's the point of having a guard at the gate if you're not going to open it to anyone?" he muttered.

But Simon, growing impatient, did not share the knight's amusement. "Then summon your superior, but do so at once!" he commanded.

"It will do no good, for none are to enter," the soldier admitted, glancing over his shoulder warily. "If you would tell me your message, I will see that it is passed on to Master Scirvayne."

"Scirvayne! What of Sir Burnel, owner of these lands?" Simon growled.

Again the guard appeared apprehensive, and he paused to wipe some sweat from his brow. "Sir Burnel is ill, and Master Scirvayne rules here in his stead."

Simon fought back his growing anger. If this Brice hoped to gain the support of Ansquith's liege lord, barring him from entering was not the way to do it. "Brice, then," Simon said through gritted teeth. "Send for Brice, who asked for the aid of Baddersly against a band of outlaws."

"Aye, my lord, the brigands are most plaguesome, stopping the supplies, stealing sheep, inciting the free-man and villeins to…" The soldier trailed off, again appearing uncomfortable. "I'm sure he will be most pleased with your aid."

"I did not *offer* to aid him, but I wish to speak with him concerning this matter…and others," Simon said, struggling against an urge to strike down this minion and storm the gate without further useless chatter.

"I will pass on your message," the soldier said.

"You fool! Do you not know to whom you speak?" Quentin shouted. "Open this gate at once!"

"I cannot," the guard said. Then he ducked his head back into the gatehouse, as if to end all communication with them.

Simon watched the man disappear with amazement. What was it about this trip, alone among all his travels, that allowed others to defy him at every turn? All his life he had been granted the respect due his position as a de Burgh and as a knight, but now he had been sum-marily dismissed by a mere soldier!

The slight sat poorly on him, and he shifted in the saddle, his temper sorely strained. In times of peace, it was unheard-of for a castle or manor house to refuse visitors. Even strangers—travelers and pilgrims—were allowed some food and a place to rest, at least. But to deny one's liege lord admittance bordered on treason. He ought to charge the wall and take the house in return for such insolence!

With a grim smile, Simon contemplated his attack. This was no castle, but a manor with simple fortifica-tions, and he had more than enough men at Baddersly to bring it down. His nostrils flared, as if scenting battle, and his blood thrummed with the anticipation of a fight.

But thoughts of war brought to mind another opponent, the only one who had ever bested him. In memory she rose before him, strong and lithe and taunting, and Simon grunted in annoyance. Even when she was not present, the blighted female continued to spite him, for until he was certain of her identity, how could he proceed? What if she really was Sir Burnel's daughter, and the old man lay ill inside Ansquith, unable to speak for himself? Simon could almost hear Geoffrey warning him not to attack the holding without more provocation, or more information at least.

"Shall we stay, my lord?" Quentin asked.

"Nay, we wait not upon another's leisure," Simon answered. His plans had been thwarted for now, so he would simply have to make others, and at that realization, the urge that he had been fighting all day returned in full force. A slow smile broke upon his features as he turned his mount. If he could not talk to Brice, then perhaps it was time to speak to Bethia herself.

Immediately Simon felt his blood surge in anticipation of such a conversation. He lifted his head and looked off into the distance where Burnel Chase rose behind the pastured hills, and he pictured a tall, slender woman in men's clothing. Where was she? Harrying travelers? Stealing someone's purse? Or simply hiding away among the trees, her sword at the ready? His body tensed at the promise of the clash to come and the triumph that would surely follow.

"Do we return to Baddersly, then?" Quentin asked.

"You may go, and take the rest with you." Simon said, inclining his head toward the small group of outriders. "I've other business to attend to—alone." He had already decided that any companions would hinder his search for the elusive outlaws. A group would be too easily seen, while one man riding off the main road could go unmarked by any watching eyes. And this time, Simon vowed to catch the wench unawares.

"But—but, my lord! You cannot mean to go off without an escort!" Thorkill protested.

Simon turned a harsh stare upon him. "Do you think me incapable of traveling by myself?"

"Nay, my lord," the young knight hastened to reply. "But I would serve you! If it is privacy you wish, let us fall back, nearly out of sight, but do not go by yourself!"

Privacy. Simon turned his head away as the suggestion sent a rush of excitement through him, though he told himself that he needed no such thing. He only wanted information from the wench—and a chance to get some of his own back, to prove his superior skills in a way that would leave no doubt as to the victor. He swung back to Thorkill with a fierce grimace. "Do you argue with me?"

"Nay, my lord, but after what happened... " Thorkill halted awkwardly, obviously stopped by the force of Simon's murderous glare. Did they think he needed guards, lest he be bested again by a female?

"Be off with you!" Simon snarled. "And do not look for me until tomorrow!" Ignoring the startled glances of the men, Simon urged his horse in the opposite direction from Baddersly. He told himself that he would need ample time to find Bethia and pry some semblance of the truth from her. He had no wish for his knights to be combing the countryside for him should he not return by nightfall.

That was all, he thought grimly. It was not the idea of sharing a blanket with the wench that prompted his hasty words, for he had no desire for a woman in men's clothes, no matter what fleeting urges had struck him during their last encounter. This time, he was firmly in charge of both the situation and his own state of mind. Let her flaunt her limbs, for it would affect him not, he swore grimly.

His mood had not improved by the time he reached the chase, for one look at the narrow paths told him that he could not take his horse in without announcing his arrival to the world. Instead, he headed into the adjacent valley, where he hailed a shepherd boy, promising the youth good coin to watch his horse.

"But what if you don't come back, my lord?" the boy asked. Simon drew up short, astonished that everyone in these lands from landholders to the most ragged youth questioned his power.

"I will return," he said with a harsh look.

The boy blinked but nodded toward the woods. "There's brigands abroad, my lord. Are you sure you want to go in there on foot?"

Reaching for the hilt of his sword, Simon uttered a low string of oaths, before something in the boy's tone halted him. He paused, eyeing the shepherd more closely. "What do you know of brigands?"

The boy dropped his gaze to his toes. "Nothing, my lord. I have only been told to be wary of the forest."

Simon's eyes narrowed, and he wondered if everyone for miles around was allied with Bethia. He was beginning to think that each man, woman and child knew of her, and protected her, as well.

Fie! He had no time for such fancies or for foolish boys! Tossing the child a coin, he offered another upon his return. "I will be back tomorrow, lad," he added with a warning look. "See that you are here with my mount, or you and yours will pay dearly."

"Yes, my lord," the boy answered primly, but he ducked his head as if to hide a smile.

It was enough to send Simon charging through the forest in search of the author of all his troubles. The notion drew him up short, however, as he wondered if word of his capture had spread from the brigands outward to the workers of the land, making him a butt of jokes in every cot and castle. Slamming a fist into his palm, Simon vowed to make the wench pay well for her deeds.

Although his blood urged speed, Simon's head argued caution, and he took but a few steps before turning to watch his young subject. If the boy ran to report his presence…but the shepherd stayed where he was and made no overt signals to hidden companions, and finally Simon turned, grunting at his own suspicions.

He was dealing with a small band of ruffians only, not a widespread system of spies and traitors. Even if some of the villagers disliked Brice, they were not clever enough to join together to stand against him. Even Geoffrey would be hard-pressed to develop such a scheme, Simon thought, his innate arrogance returning.

And so he struck off through the forest, careful yet confident. Though it had been dark during his last trek through the trees, Simon was certain he could find his way by the position of the sun, landmarks, and his own sense of direction. It took longer than he thought, however, and by the time he reached the clearing where he had been held, he was hot and short-tempered. Still he had enough sense not to charge forward recklessly, and he circled the area, alert for enemies both around him and above. But he noticed no one and when he stepped into the glade at last, he saw why.

All traces of habitation had been removed, making him wonder if he had the location aright. Indeed, any sane man would question his memory when eyeing the pristine area, but Simon was too sure of himself for that, and upon closer inspection, he could see the flattened grass that spoke of human steps and, hidden beneath leaves, the dark stains of blood from the wounded.

Ha! They had been here, Simon realized. But his elation was brief, for they had obviously covered their tracks well. Although he checked the edges of the former camp carefully, he could find no trail leading elsewhere, and he swore harshly. Tilting his head back, he glanced up at the trees, wondering if Bethia and her men had hopped from one leafy branch to another like squirrels.

Armed with heavy mail and weapons, Simon could hardly follow, even if he trusted his skill at climbing, which had not been tested since his youth. Fie! Now how would he find them? Simon wished he was more familiar with the chase and the royal forest beyond. His lack would make his task even more difficult, for he sought not a particular place, but men who blended in well with these surroundings.

Already the afternoon was hurrying by, making his errand even more pressing, but Simon would not turn aside from the first real challenge he had faced in many a year. Gritting his teeth, he left the clearing more determined than ever. No matter how long it took, he would find the outlaws and seize their leader.

Just as long as they did not find him first.

Chapter Five

Simon moved quickly and silently through the chase, though he hated the need for stealth. He would rather face an opponent on an open field of battle than skulk through the trees. Bethia's men could be anywhere, including above him, so he made his way carefully, remembering all too well the feel of one of the ruffians landing on his back.

The memory roused his ire, for he had always thought himself nearly invincible. From a young age, he had soundly trounced all of his brothers and anyone else who gave him challenge, excepting Dunstan, of course. Frowning, Simon considered his long-standing competition with the eldest of the de Burghs. Dunstan would always be the firstborn and older by several years, yet Simon still strove to be his equal. Or better.

His frown turned into a grimace as he considered his failing efforts since his arrival, and the thought of his brother's laughter spurred him onward. He might not fight for the King, as Dunstan had, but he served his family well and he would set aright whatever was wrong here, including disbanding one infamous group of outlaws.

A faint odor of charred wood caught his attention and he followed it, knowing disappointment when he came upon an old smelting site. Trees had been cleared and felled for use in the small bowl furnace, and piles of slag gave testimony to the process, but, like many such areas throughout the adjacent royal forest, it had been long abandoned.

Perhaps his nose had deceived him, but Simon did not dismiss the lingering scent of smoke so easily, and he knelt to examine the ground more closely. Some of the grass looked trampled, arguing for recent usage, and he followed a nearly imperceptible trail to the nearby mine that had once provided iron ore.

Simon drew himself up slowly and eyed the dark opening of the tunnel with distaste. He never had cared for being closed in. Stifling castle rooms and even caves were one thing, while a mine with its narrow passages, dripping walls and foul air was entirely different. All too easily, the earth that had been excavated could crash down upon a man, crushing the life from him.

Simon's eyes narrowed, but he was no coward, and he stepped closer, pausing to lean inside and listen. Although no sound came from below, he waited before moving forward again and blinking into the black interior. Still he heard nothing. Unless the brigands were deep under the ground or totally silent, no one was within, but they had been here, he was certain of it. And they might well return. All he had to do was find a good vantage point from which to wait and watch.

Exiting the tunnel swiftly, Simon drew a deep breath of fresh air and moved into the trees, looking for a likely hiding place. He had barely gone a few steps when something caught his eye, and he stilled. Indeed, his very heart seemed to stop as he realized just who it was before him at last.

She was seated on a chunk of wood, her head bent as she strung a yew bow, but the simple task took on an otherworldly cast as the sunshine filtering down through the tall oaks dappled her in light and shadows and gilded the pale color of her hair.

For a long moment, Simon simply stared, unable to explain the strange sensations rushing through him. Certainly there was the thrill of discovery, of a challenge met and a battle to come, but even as excitement roared through his veins, he recognized something else, an alien feeling with an edge of danger unlike any he had ever known.

He shook it off, telling himself that it was the scent of his prey, nothing more, but still he hesitated, drinking in the sight of her like a man long without water. Everything about her seemed brighter and fiercer than he remembered, from her fat braid to her thick lashes and the carved bones of her cheeks. She might have looked too starkly beautiful but for the wide mouth that curved in concentration. Those lips... Simon could just imagine what his brother Stephen would have to say about them.

And the rest of her. He had seen women's legs before, but never encased in braies that left little of her shapely calves to the imagination. The material hugged her so well that Simon's mouth went dry as his gaze traveled upward to where her tunic rode high, giving him a glimpse of her thigh.

He must have made a sound because she suddenly glanced up, her eyes bright with alertness, and stared right at the spot where he stood. Although Simon thought himself well camouflaged, she must have seen

him, for she bounded to her feet immediately. He was
out of the trees and after her in a thrice, capturing her
and dragging her to the ground as he had once before,
but this time, he was well aware that it was a female
he held, struggling in his arms.

The knowledge only hampered his efforts, for Simon
tried not to hurt her as he subdued her, all the while
remembering the dagger she might have secreted somewhere on her person. He did not intend to get his throat
sliced open a second time, so he threw his considerable
weight over hers, trapping her kicking legs with his
own and her arms with his hands. It was no easy task,
for she tried to strike him with her fists and butt him
with her head.

Finally he lay full upon her, his face resting near the
top of her head, where a few tendrils of hair brushed
against his nose. The scent was intoxicating, and he
might have lost his advantage if she, too, had not
stilled. Uncertain whether she was feigning surrender
or if he had somehow hurt her, Simon ran his hands up
her arms, stopping as he grasped her above her elbows.

Jerking his head upward, he stared down at her in
astonishment. "You have muscles," he said, his fingers
finding the hard shape of them beneath her sleeves.

Apparently she scorned his admiration, for she glared
at him with obvious contempt. "Yes! Just as many as
you, I'll warrant."

Her claim was absurd, of course, and Simon would
have laughed but for the feel of her beneath his stroking
hands. Something about her strength excited him, and
he felt himself stiffen against her stomach, eager to
match his power against hers. She noticed, her surprise
evident in the flicker of her thick lashes, and he smiled
grimly down at her.

"Perhaps," he said, in answer to her boast. "But there is one muscle I possess that you do not." He was willing to share with her, however. Indeed, in that one heated moment, Simon knew a dizzying need to give that part of him into her keeping.

But she did not want it. With a shocked look, she pushed him away, and Simon loosed her. He was both disappointed and annoyed at her rejection—and his own body's betrayal. He was not some randy youth like Stephen, and he prided himself on his control. Anger at himself was swift in coming, for this was no purchased doxy with whom he dallied, but a woman like none he had ever known, with skills beyond most females. Although he hardly thought her capable of besting him once more, he was uneasily aware of his own lapse of attention.

She rolled to her feet and Simon followed, covering his discomfort with a low growl. "'Tis not a good place to stay, wench," he said. "These mines have been known to collapse. Surface water drains into them, and air is scarce."

Ignoring his words, she turned on him, fire bright in her hazel eyes. "What are you doing here? Are you mad? Anyone could have seen you and buried an arrow in your back! Where are your men?"

"I am alone," Simon said. Despite his own ire, he felt an absurd desire to smile at her. She was magnificent in her fury, facing him with an intensity that nearly robbed him of breath.

"You *are* mad!" she cried. "Only a madman would walk knowingly into a host of his enemies. You could have been killed!"

"A host?" Simon said, lifting his brows. "I hardly think your band so large. And your concern for my welfare is misplaced, for it is your men who should be wary of me.''

Simon bit back a grin as she sputtered, her cheeks flushed with her outrage. ''I care nothing about you! 'Twould please me well to see you with a shaft through your heart, for 'twould mean one less problem for me!'' Lifting her chin, she tossed her thick braid over her shoulder and crossed her arms over her chest in an impatient gesture that drew his attention to her breasts. ''Why *are* you here? What do you want?''

Want. The word echoed in Simon's head as his gaze lingered on the top of her tunic, where her rounded mounds strained at the fabric. Did she bind them to appear more like a boy? he wondered again, and he suddenly ached to find out. Dismissing such foolishness with a low grunt, he cursed the heat that rose through his traitorous body.

''I have come for information,'' he said.

Her expression grew harder. ''What kind of information?''

''Simple answers, Bethia,'' Simon said, emphasizing her name. Only a flicker of her thick lashes gave away her reaction, and his admiration for her grew. He leaned back against a thick oak. ''Answers like why you returned my men and my horses.''

She made a soft sound of exasperation. ''What difference does that make? Can't you simply take them and be gone?''

He snorted in disgust. ''Would you?''

She turned away, giving him her reply in a whispered oath that was far too coarse for a female's usage. He scowled, pushing from the tree to follow her as she strode away from him. Fie on the wench, for he would find out what he wanted to know, if nothing else!

He reached out for her, his hands closing over her slender arms, lean and muscular. ''Tell me, Bethia. Why did you capture us only to loose us? What keeps you here in the forest, playing outlaw when you could be living in luxury? Who are you, really, *Bethia?*''

She stared at him then, her hazel eyes wide and a startled expression parting her lips before she recovered. Again Simon felt a twinge of respect for her control. ''Let go,'' she said, shaking off his hold. He dropped his hands willingly, struck by the realization that this woman in men's clothes had more dignity than any female he had ever known.

She did not weep or faint or screech her outrage. He had never heard her complain or beg for mercy. She simply collected herself and faced him, like a man. Only she wasn't a man. The knowledge was dizzying. Absently Simon lifted a hand to rub against his chest, where his mail suddenly felt heavy and hard.

''Very well. I will tell you, Lord de Burgh.''

''Simon,'' he found himself saying, wanting to be set apart from his brothers, needing her to speak to him alone. ''My name is Simon.''

She eyed him warily. ''Simon,'' she echoed. ''But don't blame me if the answers are not to your liking. Come, then.''

She turned toward the clearing, and Simon followed, though he remained alert. Was she leading him into a trap once more? Even as his instincts told him to trust her, he was not so naive as to do so.

Pausing, she looked up at him again. ''And then you must go, before you are seen,'' she insisted with renewed intensity.

Simon did not reply, for he wondered what lay behind her words. Concern for his life? He nearly scoffed aloud. Nay, Bethia had her own reasons for wishing him gone, but he would soon discover them. Aye, he would not stop until he had searched out each and every one of her secrets, he vowed, smiling in anticipation.

He had come, as she had known he would, and Bethia hid her dread in a cloak of anger. He was a fool to have returned! If Firmin had seen him, he might very well have been killed. Although she had wished to do murder more than once these past few months, Bethia shied away from the thought of this great warrior wounded, or worse.

It disturbed her, so she pushed the image aside, concentrating again on his recklessness. How he had made it to his age without getting himself killed, she did not know. He needed someone to keep an eye upon him, to restrain his rash urges! But the idea of restraining Simon de Burgh made her shudder with wild, half-formed thoughts from which she also shied away.

Would that this man leave her be! Tamping down the sharp edge of fear that came from recognizing the danger to herself, even *within* herself, Bethia hurried toward the mine where they had made their camp. If, as he claimed, he simply wanted information, perhaps when he heard her story, he would go away. No longer did she cling to the hope that he might aid them, for she suspected that the price of his help would be too steep for her to pay.

Swiftly, as if to conclude this business as soon as possible, Bethia stepped into the shelter of the entrance, but Simon did not follow. His face was a hard mask that did not reveal his thoughts, yet she sensed his anger, along with something else as he ducked his head.

''Nay, I'll stay where I can breathe, and you should

not be going in there, either,'' he muttered. Surprised, Bethia shot him a sideways glance. Was this big, brave knight afraid of going down in the mines? She gave no indication of her suspicion but motioned toward the woods instead. If they could not be hidden from prying eyes, then they had better move away from camp.

Not only would she protect him from Firmin's short temper, but it would be easier for the two of them to talk without the distracting questions and suspicions of her men. She was simply making a leader's decision, Bethia told herself. And yet, she knew that part of her yearned to be alone with him, if only to gain some of this warrior's knowledge.

How long had it been since she had spoken with an equal? Never, Bethia decided, as she led him through the trees, away from the nearest sentinel. Or at least, not since she had been a young girl following the teachings of a father who looked upon her as his prize pupil. Shrugging away those memories, Bethia realized that as the son of an earl, Simon de Burgh would hardly consider her *his* peer.

Indeed, the very thought made her lips curve in amusement, for the great knight obviously thought very little of women. But, to Bethia, who had spent years among witless relatives and now found herself directing a diverse group of former servants, freemen and miners, he was the only person she had ever met who understood the life of a warrior and a leader.

That, of course, is what drew her to him, among other things, she acknowledged ruefully. But, just as ruefully, she knew that the lure of their shared interests, their similar traits was a danger, for the flame that warmed and soothed could also burn. And she would be wise to get rid of this one before he had a chance to scorch her.

Keeping that thought in mind, Bethia found a broken log and took a seat, motioning for Simon to do the same. Although he smiled tightly as if amused by her courtesy, he remained standing, and she could see his gaze probing the leaves above and around them.

"We are well away," Bethia assured him, though she knew that in his position, she would not trust her words.

"Are you so certain that they do your bidding?" he asked, coolly, and Bethia flashed him a glance. He was referring to Firmin, of course, in some effort to unnerve her, but she would not fall for the ploy. Tossing her braid over her shoulder, she drew up one knee and leveled a serious gaze at him.

"Yes," she said.

His face grew grim and hard. "A certain code of thievery?" he mocked, his eyes narrowed.

"We are not thieves!" she said. "My people are honest freemen and villeins struggling against injustice."

"And part of that struggle is the capture of travelers along the common road?" Simon asked her.

His pride still smarted from being bested, Bethia realized. "Only when our coffers are in need of funds. Do you wish answers or an argument, my lord?"

"Simon," he said harshly. "And I would like answers, most especially to why you have stolen the identity of a dead woman."

"*Stolen?*" For a moment, she nearly gave way to her own seething outrage. She had not asked him to come here. Indeed, he ought to be grateful that she had released him with nothing but a few scrapes and bruised pride to show for his trip through the chase. "I have *stolen* nothing that did not belong to me, including my own name. I am Bethia Burnel, whether you choose to believe it or not."

He met her glare evenly, and she had the odd sensation that he already knew who she was and was only seeking confirmation. The suspicion disturbed her. She knew this knight was strong and skilled, but she had not thought him particularly clever. Perhaps she should be more wary in her speech with him.

"And your father?"

"Is Costin Burnel," she said, watching him intently.

"He who holds Ansquith?" Simon said.

"He did," she said. "But now he is a prisoner in his home. If you are who you claim to be, then as lord of Baddersly it is your responsibility to free him." Something made her say it, to poke him in his fine pride, although she no longer entertained hopes of this man's aid.

"You have a strange manner of treating those whom you would ask for help," he said, glaring at her.

"I did not ask for help," Bethia argued. "I am but reminding you of your duty." And he did not like it, she realized as his eyes narrowed once more. Did he think her impertinent, or was he disturbed for a far more insidious reason? He could still be in league with Brice, Bethia admitted to herself, his presence here naught but a ruse to scout her camp, her plans, her strengths, her weaknesses. She studied him closely, her heart pounding at the possibility of this man's betrayal.

It would be worse than Brice's, worse, perhaps, than her father's, Bethia thought, though she did not know why it should strike her so painfully. Because you admire him, she told herself. Because he is strong and handsome and a knight, which means he should be honorable. But what if he was not?

"Mayhap you should explain how this Brice is holding your father prisoner in his own home?" he suggested, and Bethia hesitated. She could refuse to answer, but that would only prolong his stay, a thought that nearly made her shudder. And what could he do with the truth that he could not without it? She decided, swiftly, to treat with him, but to watch her tongue.

Shifting slightly, she looked down at her worn boots. "I was my father's only child, and he looked upon me as the son he never had...until my mother died. Then, a visiting relative expressed horror at my boyish ways," she said dryly, startled by the pain that lingered from that long-ago betrayal.

"Why did he not stand up for you, if he had encouraged you to behave in such a fashion?" Simon asked, his tone rough.

Bethia slanted him a glance, surprised that someone who looked so thickheaded could be so perceptive, but there was no softening to his rigid features, only an impression of impatience restrained. She shrugged. "He was grief stricken. He thought that his aunt knew what was best for a young girl." The explanation was difficult for her to voice, for she too had wanted her father to speak up for her and for the dead wife who had approved and joined in the rearing of her.

But Gunilda could be persuasive, even reasonable when she chose, and her father had let his aunt separate her from everything she held dear. "So he fostered me out to her, in the hope that I might be brought up in the ways of a proper maiden." Bethia choked back a laugh, for instead, she had labored as little more than Gunilda's servant, dressed in female clothing, but of rough wool, not her great-aunt's fine fabrics. Oh, yes, she had learned soon enough of her woman's place in the world, but they had not broken her fierce spirit.

And she had never stopped writing to her father, hoping that he would rescue her from her enslavement, the prison that was the direct opposite of how she had spent her childhood, strong and free. Bethia swallowed hard, tossing the braid that had slipped forward over her shoulder. But no word at all had she received, no one had come to rescue her or claim her until recently.

"A few months ago I was summoned home—to marry," she said, refusing to look at the man who still stood beside her as she recalled how her elation had turned to anger. She was certain God would forgive her for uncharitable feelings when she realized she had been brought home not because of any sentiment, but to be bartered away. Having learned the truth of a woman's role in Gunilda's household, she had no desire to be under any man's rule, but she had come, yearning for her father's welcome.

What greeted her instead was Brice Scirvayne. "I returned home to discover my father had aged," she said, swallowing hard. "Not only was he older, but frail and sickly, when he had once been the most robust of men. I—I can only think that his judgment must have been impaired by his…illness," she said. "For I soon discovered that my suitor, Brice Scirvayne, was most unworthy."

"Was he not young and handsome enough for your liking?" Simon accused her in a harsh voice. Surprised, Bethia looked up to see a scowl on his face, which she could only blame on his own unfortunate gender. As a man, he would defend his sex to the death, no doubt.

Disgusted, Bethia held his glare with her own determined gaze. "Oh, he was young and handsome enough, with smiles and fine words aplenty, but he was also a liar, a fortune hunter and a conniver."

Something flickered in Simon's eyes. She knew better than to hope it was understanding, and so she went on. "Appalled, I began to investigate. I found that Brice had only been at Ansquith for a month or so, after having appeared at the gates, claiming that his train was attacked by brigands."

"A common enough happening in these parts, it seems," Simon said, with a mocking look that made her want to kick him in his taunting white teeth.

"It was not common then, from what I have heard," she answered stiffly.

"So you set out to change all that?"

Bethia made to rise to her feet, but Simon stopped her with a grunt. "Sit," he said, and she stayed, poised over the stump, for she would take orders from no man. "Go on," he muttered, and she sank down once more, this time straddling the bark.

"Although he talked of his many holdings and great wealth, none at Ansquith saw any evidence of it. Nor could I, through discreet inquiries, find any who knew of him. I came to the conclusion that all that he said was a lie, certainly his great doings and such, perhaps even his name."

Bethia could not keep the contempt from her tone, but when she looked up to judge Simon's reaction, she found his eyes held a glazed, hot look, and were focused on her private parts. For a moment she was too startled to move or speak, but then his gaze rose to hers with a fierceness that made her think she had been imagining things.

"And what did your father do?"

Bethia frowned, uncertain of this man. But dismissing her recent observations, she took a deep breath and concentrated on finishing her tale. "From my arrival, I was leery of Brice's influence, and as I discovered more inconsistencies in his stories, I tried to broach the subject with my father. It was impossible," Bethia said with a low sound of frustration.

"He came between us at every turn, and soon my father took to his bed where Brice's guards stood watch to prevent my entering the chamber!" She pressed her palms over her knees as the old rage enveloped her, and drew another long, slow breath.

"Obviously Brice ingratiated himself well into my father's confidence. He is an old man who married late in life, and after my mother died, he kept to himself, even more so when I too was gone, or so I have heard. Apparently, Brice's unscheduled arrival caused much excitement. His many...tales of his travels and heroics are amusing to some and must have appealed to a man who had not been entertained in years."

She paused to slant Simon a glance. "Make no mistake, Brice can smile and speak so smoothly that only the wary and vigilant would look twice."

"And you were both?"

She met Simon's probing stare. "I had no particular wish to be married, so I was more cautious than most," she admitted. "But after a time, when none of his great wealth or innumerable attendants arrived for him, it became apparent to even the most easily swayed that something was wrong with his story. Unfortunately, by that time, his hold upon my father, the household and the guards, was firm and unyielding."

"Even to you?"

Bethia let out a small croak of a laugh. "Especially

to me, for only some of the older servants remembered me well, and even fewer retained their loyalty.'' It was those few who saved her, but she was not about to offer that information to Simon, who might or might not be in league with her enemies.

The thought made her swallow hard again, this time in dismay. Her tongue had run away with her, she realized, and she wondered how this taciturn man had encouraged her to speak so easily that she had nearly forgotten herself.

''And the marriage?'' Simon asked roughly.

''It did not go forward,'' Bethia admitted, wincing at how close she had come to that calamity. ''When I refused to wed him, he tossed me in the dungeon, and…I managed to escape,'' she explained, leaving unmentioned the aid of two of her most trusted servants.

''I disappeared into the woods,'' she added, refusing to indict those who had taken her in. She had been told later that Brice, being too full of himself to consider that a mere female might be able to fend for herself, had screamed like a babe when his search party returned empty-handed. She smiled slightly at the thought of thwarting him, for it was all that gave her pleasure.

''And this business of your death?''

Bethia lifted her head and shrugged. ''I assume that Brice thought it better to be rid of me permanently, whether in truth or fiction, but the celebration of it was a bit…premature.''

''He would have you dead?'' Simon's harsh query sliced through the air, startling in its sudden ferocity. Though he did not move, the knight seemed to radiate a threat that was so intense Bethia would have stepped back if she were standing. Thankfully, she was not and could hide her discomposure with a bitter laugh.

"Naturally," she answered. "Why do you think he is hiring mercenaries? My father's money is being used to kill his only heir." The words hung in the air, hard and cold and bleak, but Bethia stood by them.

"But why would you allow him to do this? Why not return to where you were fostered or to the King or even a neighboring demesne, Baddersly, by faith!" he said, as if her actions aggrieved him.

"Those who fostered me would not aid me," Bethia answered. They might well have taken her in, but she preferred the freedom of the forest to the prison of that household. "All they ever wanted was an unpaid servant, and the King doesn't care about this small part of the world."

No one does. Deliberately Bethia cast aside her bitterness, for it did her no good. "As for our neighbors, how could anyone take me in when I am officially dead? Few enough have seen me since my arrival, fewer still remember me from my youth. How would I convince anyone of my identity? It would be my word against Brice's, and he is well entrenched."

The resentment crept back into her tone, but she could not stay it. "After he claimed I was dead, he took complete charge of the household. He tells all that my father is ill, but keeps him cloistered away, so that none I trust have seen for themselves. I fear the worst, that he is dead or dying."

Simon's agitation was fueling her own, and she rose to her feet. "As for Baddersly, what know I of it, except that we all kept well away from Harold Peasley?"

"Peasley is dead," Simon said with a rough grunt that conveyed impatience. "Baddersly is my brother's now."

"And what know I of the de Burghs?" Bethia challenged, facing him squarely. She was aware that she should not bait such a man, but she could not help herself. How could she trust him when she had nothing but a blind instinct to guide her?

"The de Burghs do not hire themselves out as mercenaries, nor do we side with petty usurpers. In fact, my brother wrested Baddersly back for his wife, who was the true heir to the castle. If you had come to your liege lord, my brother, as you should have, you would not be living like an outlaw in the woods!" he growled, sweeping a hand toward their surroundings.

His accusation stung, as did his tone. "And I am to take *your* word on the honor of the de Burghs? I think not!" Like two spitting cats, they faced off, Bethia tilting her head back to view him better. His hands fisted at his sides, and for a moment she thought he might strike her. Let him do so, and he would regret it, she thought, for she had bested this great knight more than once.

"Our honor is well-known across the entire land, you foolish wench, and I will not have you impugn it!" he said.

"Then prove it! Prove yourself," she dared. "Rout Brice!"

Her words hung in the air, a challenge that a true warrior would not refuse, a cause an honorable knight could not forsake, and Bethia realized she was holding her breath, hoping once more.

But again, she was only to be disappointed, for he snarled an oath that was clearly a denial. "And just how am I to do that when I cannot get past the gate? Is it war you want, Bethia?" he asked her, his features setting into a harsh grimace. "Because if it is a battle you wish, then I can raise an army the likes of which this countryside has never seen.''

His promise sent a thrill of excitement through her, as Bethia envisioned crushing her enemy with the combined might of the de Burghs. She could see it now: knights, archers, foot soldiers, spread over the hills, all converging on Ansquith. With battering rams and bores, ladders, axes, longbows, fire…Bethia's elation left her, replaced by the frustration that so obviously seethed through the man who faced her.

''And if this Brice does not surrender, are you prepared to have us lay waste to your father's demesne, perhaps to his manor itself?'' he asked.

Bethia choked back a sound, half sob, half rage, and he stepped closer, lifting his hand as if to touch her, only to let it fall in a fist to his side. ''Perhaps you do not realize the consequences of a long siege, but I do. Are you prepared to starve the inhabitants of your old home, to seize all that can be taken from the surrounding area, from villeins and freemen alike, to feed your army?''

Bethia shook her head, ashamed that she had not considered the attendant realities of such a course, while this man, whom she had dismissed as reckless and thickheaded, knew better. ''And what of your father?'' he asked, his voice a low rasp.

Bethia took a deep breath, casting aside the last lingering dream of taking her home back from the interloper, for she could well guess at the answer. ''Brice would surely kill my father, and then all of it would be for naught,'' she whispered.

''Aye,'' he said gruffly. ''You have it aright. Damn! There must be some way to—'' He broke off, turning away from her, and Bethia's heart lurched. She could almost believe that he wanted to help her, and her wariness to let him join her faded away in the heat of the moment. Without volition, she reached for his arm.

"We need not a siege army to strike at him. We have been harrying him with but a small band, although more join us each day—freemen thrown from their homes, others discontented with his heavy hand. He is charging the miners more to work the ore in the chase. He is taxing the freemen and calling the villeins back to new fields."

Simon looked down at her hand on his massive arm, and Bethia dropped it, as if it suddenly burned her. "And what do you do? Buzz at him like a pesky fly! That is not a fight!" he said, stomping away to stare off into the woods.

Painfully aware that this man might not be what she wanted so much to believe, Bethia marked her words. "We waylay sheep, payments, supplies." And they waited for Brice to come out, but so far he had remained, like a spider in his web, too cowardly to emerge from his fine new home. "We make a difference," she said softly.

"Let him bring on the mercenaries, and I will crush them!" Simon said with a growl. "But I have no stomach for this outlawry." His voice was naturally harsh, growing more so in anger, but there was something about it that appealed to Bethia. It was like the man himself—strong and fierce and arrogant—and if she did not keep her wits about her, she would let him sway her.

But she could not. He might be lying still, toying with her, waiting to ferret out her secrets and destroy them all. He could do it, too. Even without an army, he was a threat. Bethia could feel it, pulsing in the air between them, for danger came in more than one guise.

Slowly she flexed her hand, as if she could still feel the steely hardness of his arm beneath her fingers. She had never thought to touch a man, but she had reached out to this one without even thinking. His back was to her, and Bethia's gaze leaped to his wide shoulders, dropping down his long torso to his muscular legs. Any woman would admire his form, his strength, his will, but she was not any woman. She had no desire for a man, least of all one who would not fight for her rights.

"There must be some way to get to him without endangering your father." So great had the silence been that Simon's muttered words startled her, and Bethia stepped around to face him. "He is a coward who hides behind the manor walls," Simon said with open contempt. "He would not let me in, but would he answer an invitation from his liege lord?"

Bethia held her breath, afraid to hope once more, but something flared in Simon's eyes that sparked an answering excitement in her, a heady rush of something indefinable. He looked down at her with a tight grin of triumph on his harsh features, his voice low and rich with promise as he spoke, and Bethia held her breath.

"Perhaps we can draw him out."

Chapter Six

For a moment Simon thought she might throw her arms around him, such was her joy at his suggestion. Oddly, even when she didn't, he still felt...good. Better than good. Like the greatest knight who had ever lived. Greater even than Dunstan. With a grunt, Simon pushed aside that thought, for he knew that inviting Brice to Baddersly did not guarantee his cooperation, but surely even Brice would not ignore his liege lord. It was a start—and had to be more effective than stealing sheep and risky outlawry. Perhaps, now that they had a plan, he could convince her to give up this foolhardy existence and return with him.

"Are you hungry?" she said suddenly, startling Simon from his thoughts. When he glanced toward her, she was smiling, her wide mouth curving upward in a way that did something to his insides. Absently he rubbed his chest as she spoke. "It's getting late. I thought to take down a rabbit or other small game," she said.

Now it was Simon's turn to smile. Had she wearied of her diet of woodland nuts and milk stolen from the Ansquith dairy? If she longed for meat, she had only to ask him, and he would gladly oblige her. She needed not this pretense of doing for herself. ''I'll see what I can find,'' he said with a smug grin. Instead of nodding gratefully, Bethia crossed her arms over her chest and looked up at him with a stony expression.

''And what do you intend to do with only a sword?'' she asked.

Simon felt himself flush, and once more, he cursed this woman's ability to make him feel the fool. She spoke the truth, of course, for instead of his usual entourage, he was accompanied by no one. He had no dogs, no falcons and no arrows, for he had not come prepared to seek game. ''Lend me your bow,'' he said tersely, reaching for the weapon she had but recently restrung.

''No,'' she answered, stepping away from him. ''I will do my own hunting, thank you, as I have been doing these months past, with no help from you, my lord.''

Simon didn't know what irritated him more, her sharp tongue or the way she used his name only when it suited her. Did she think he would stand by idly while she did a man's job? His eyes narrowed as he took in her rebellious stance. Wretched wench, who did she think she was to gainsay him? Someone ought to put her to rights. The thought led to another, and Simon smiled grimly.

'' 'Tis illegal to poach from the King's forest, unless you have warren rights, or are you still claiming that you are no thief?'' he asked.

Instead of paling and protesting, she turned and flashed him a superior grin that made Simon grit his teeth. ''We are not in the royal forest, but Burnel

Chase, which means that the game here belongs to my
father...and me!''

With that she stalked away, and Simon angrily sank
down onto the stump she had recently vacated. He
watched as she positioned her bow in her slender hands,
and gradually his rage was replaced by diversion. Although she seemed to handle the weapon with ease, her
familiarity did not assure competence. His natural confidence returning, Simon leaned back against the crag
of a nearby beech. This he had to see.

''By all means, fetch us supper,'' he taunted.

She slanted him a fierce glance for disturbing the
silence but gave him no argument, simply lifting the
bow higher. It was smaller than usual to accommodate
her shortened reach, and she carried her arrows in a
bundle tucked through a loop in her belt, as did many
unmounted archers.

Simon was not prepared for the way her shoulder
slipped back, her muscles straining as she notched one
of them. Faith, she was strong, and the knowledge
spread heat throughout him as he watched her. She
moved silently, and he grudgingly had to admit his respect for her stealth. As she slipped away, though, he
stood, determined that she not simply disappear into the
trees.

He thought he had won her trust, at last, but nothing
about this lady-turned-outlaw was predictable, and so
he peered through the greenery as she waited, and
watched. Perhaps she knew the hidden burrows where
her quarry was wont to nest, he told himself, for she
concentrated intently on a large thicket. Still he did not
see how a mere female could be expected to shoot well,
no matter how impressive her musculature.

The thought made him turn away, and he studied his

surroundings in an effort to distract himself from Bethia's lean body. As a matter of course, he looked for signs of company, but he found none, only the sights and sounds of the creatures of the forest. He took a deep breath, enjoying the smell of earth and leaves. As it had once before, the chase settled a sort of peace upon him, and he leaned back, enjoying an ease that he rarely took at home.

After a while, his restlessness returned. Peace was fine in short doses, but he craved action. The afternoon was fading into evening, and he shot a sharp glance at his companion. She was still poised over the thicket just as intently as she had been before, and though he admired her strength and patience, Simon was losing his. He had just opened his mouth to call a halt to her futile efforts when she pulled back her arm and loosed the arrow, sending it straight and sure.

Simon felt as if someone had struck him, so stunned was he by her fluid movements. She was more graceful than a dancer he had once seen, her concentration so intense as to rival Geoffrey's. At first Simon could not see her prey, but to his amazement, she had, indeed, felled a rabbit, and with an expertise that vied with the best of archers.

Would she never cease to astonish him? Simon blew out a harsh breath. Although he had heard of ladies who kept falcons, he knew of none who could shoot and fence and lead others in the manner of this female. It was said that Geoffrey's wife was capable with weapons, but the very thought of Elene Fitzhugh made Simon wince.

The first time he had seen her, she looked a fright, her wild hair uncombed and her drab gown hanging upon her like a sack while she brandished her ever-present dagger, threatening all and sundry. Even though Geoff had cleaned her up a bit, Simon still thought her a bloodthirsty termagant.

Bethia was as different from that creature as night was from day. She might dress in men's clothing, but she was always neat and clean, her thick braid perfectly groomed, her face glowing with intelligence and beauty. Although her tongue was sometimes sharp, Bethia could just as easily coax a wounded man to her hand or call out orders while thinking on her feet. She was clever and strong and skilled nearly beyond his comprehension. Indeed, almost a match for a man…

The thought unnerved him, for Simon was unaccustomed to seeing women as anything other than weak and annoying. And Bethia knew it. The smirk she wore as she held up her prize almost made Simon regret his admiration for her, but she obviously expected her due. The silence stretched between them as she lifted her gaze to his own, until finally he gave her a curt nod. "Well done," he admitted gruffly.

"Come, then, let us eat," she said, ducking her head as if to hide her gleeful smile, but Simon was not fooled. He knew she relished her triumph, and he did not begrudge her. She had earned it, with her skill and patience. Simon's respect for her was growing, along with another sensation, that unfamiliar excitement she incited in him. Tamping it down, he turned to follow her, hoping that she did not intend to give their supper away to her ragtag band of followers.

Simon didn't want to share it—or her. Although he had no intention of losing his iron control in her presence, a sizzle of anticipation heated his blood at the thought of joining her in a simple meal. With a scowl, he told himself that he merely looked forward to the challenge of besting this female.

But did he want to best her any longer? The game had grown confusing, especially since he had heard Bethia's version of events. If, as she claimed, Brice was holding her father against his will, then he must do what he could to right the wrongs done her.

And yet there was the possibility that she was lying. Even though all Simon had learned so far pointed toward the truth of her story, he was not so foolish as to blindly believe her tale. Unlike some of his brothers, he took no leaps of faith but put his confidence in cold, hard facts. The thought that she might be playing him false even now made Simon frown, and he grunted impatiently. "Where are we going?"

"To a safe place I know where we can camp."

Alone? Simon wondered. At her words, he was battered by conflicting feelings, a heady elation that he promptly crushed, along with a strange wariness. Although he knew this woman could not trick him again, still he felt as if she represented a danger to him. To his very way of life. Perhaps even to a part of him of which he was barely aware.

Bah! The day he could not take on a mere wench was the day he gave up his knighthood! Simon decided angrily. He stomped forward, certain that he was thinking entirely too much. Had he become his brother Geoffrey, to waste his time musing when action was what was needed?

"Here, we can use this old fire ring," she said, shoving aside a familiar-looking rock. With a flicker of surprise, Simon realized that they were back at the camp he had found his way to earlier, the clearing that they had apparently abandoned after his escape. Did she not trust him enough to take him to her true haven? Simon found the notion oddly disturbing.

Although he was not certain he believed her, that was *different*. She ought to know that he was a knight and a man of his word. He grimaced while he watched her gather wood just as if he were useless—or not even present. "And what if you draw unwanted attention with your little blaze?" he asked.

She gazed up at him with a wry look that managed to make him feel foolish. "I will know if anyone enters the chase."

Simon grunted in disbelief. Did she think him so gullible as to believe she had men stationed at every corner of the forest, waiting to report to her each movement within the vast expanse? He would have laughed aloud at her boast, but she only shrugged at his amusement and continued her task, building a neat pile of kindling and catching a spark against a stone she had carried at her waist. As her small fire came to life, Simon shifted on his feet, feeling oddly superfluous.

"I'll see what else I can find to eat," he muttered, and stalked back to where he had noticed some fat mushrooms popping from the undergrowth. He harvested them quickly, then hunted around until he found wild leeks. When he returned to camp and dropped his bounty at her feet, she glanced up in surprise, studying him with an intensity that made him uncomfortable.

"You cook?" she asked, as if in disbelief.

Simon narrowed his eyes, uncertain whether she was taunting him or not. "I can manage for myself," he grunted as he crouched beside her and swiftly prepared a spit for the food. As he cut the outside stalks, Bethia leaned against one of the stumps that littered the clearing.

"I am impressed, my lord, for I would have not thought you skilled in the culinary arts."

Simon felt his temper snap. "Do you mock me?" he snarled, whirling on her.

"No," she said with a smile that struck him in the chest—and elsewhere. "I was just admiring your skills, Simon. 'Tis not every man who could prepare such a meal."

Simon grunted, still wondering if she were baiting him. "My father taught us all to fend for ourselves."

"Hmm. The great de Burghs don't have servants enough for such?" she asked, settling back but continuing to watch him.

He was absurdly aware of his movements as he readied the food for cooking. "I have spent a great deal of time on the road," he said.

"A warrior," she said approvingly.

"Yes." Once the meat was roasting, he too leaned against an oak, though he kept a distance from her. He studied her relaxed position, one leg crooked upward, and his mouth grew suddenly dry. "Won't your men wonder where you are?" he asked.

"They will see the smoke and mark me here," she said, seemingly unconcerned, but Simon was not so blasé. Others might notice the fire also, for there were outlaws who roamed the countryside besides her own, and any fool would easily divine her sex despite her odd clothing.

"Do you make a habit of going off alone?" he asked, angry at her heedlessness.

She shrugged, and her indifference irritated him further. She should not be out here by herself—or in these woods at all! Her band was naught but a motley bunch of thieves and outcasts, and he had already seen how poorly some of them followed orders. What if one were to take it into his head to have her? Who would stop him? Yes, he had come to appreciate her strength and skill with weapons, but against a determined man even the most able of females…

"Tell me of all the time you have spent on the road," she said with a wistful air, and Simon grunted, dragged from his unsavory thoughts. He opened his mouth to tell her what he thought of her heedless behavior, but somehow instead he found himself discussing the trip south when they had found Marion, heiress to Baddersly, with her memory lost and her train slaughtered.

And that led to the tale of how he and his brothers had freed Dunstan from his own castle, Wessex, and routed Fitzhugh's forces. Pausing only to tend to the cooking, Simon began to speak freely, as if he were talking to one of his siblings, for Bethia did not constantly interrupt or question or bemoan that which did not please her. Like most women would.

When she did pose a query, it was something one of his brothers might have asked. *But how did you judge the size of his force? Are cavalry or foot soldiers more important? What kind of longbow did they use?* And Simon was glad to answer, for it had been a while since he had shared such conversation.

Unlike his gregarious brother Robin, Simon never had made friends easily, nor did he see the use of them. More often than not he kept to himself, especially on the road, for he believed in maintaining a certain distance from his men. Even before Dunstan's betrayal at the hands of his old companion, Simon had been wary of friendships forged on the field.

But Bethia was different, because, like his brothers,

she was not under his rule, or even one of his household. And whatever wariness stood between them
seemed to have relaxed with the onset of the evening.
More than once he found himself leaning close, while
she bent forward, concentrating intently as he explained
using a spanning belt on a crossbow.

And she understood. No matter how detailed the discussion of weapons or tactics, she followed him wherever he would go. She was so clever that she reminded
him of Geoffrey, and it was only when he paused to
actually look at her that he was reminded she was not
one of his siblings.

In fact, she was not even a man. That realization was
brought home when the food was ready, and Simon
watched her reach for a piece of roasted hare, her
breasts straining at the tunic that covered them. *She
does not bind them,* Simon thought, his throat suddenly
dry. Blindly he grabbed a piece of meat and promptly
burned his fingers. When he swore long and low, he
was annoyed to hear her soft laughter.

"Greedy wretch, aren't you?" his companion ob-
served, and Simon wondered if she had any idea how
seductive she looked as she smiled over her food. At
first glance, a man might mistake her for one of his
own sex, but Simon was much too close to make that
error again. Even though her thick braid fell into the
darkness behind her, the firelight played on her bold
features, highlighting that wide mouth as she ate with
a grace lacking in any male.

Simon held his breath as her long fingers were poised
over her lips, and then, having finished her bite, she
slipped one into her mouth, sucking on it gently. He
felt himself grow hard and numb, as if his heart no
longer pumped blood to any part of him except his

nether regions, and with a harsh exclamation, he turned away, struggling for control over the body that would betray him.

He was unaccustomed to being alone with a female, Simon told himself as he chewed angrily. His body was reacting accordingly, not recognizing the difference between a paid consort and this outlaw, but he did, and he was not so foolish as to be ruled by his urges. No matter what a tempting sight she might be, her golden skin gilded by firelight, Simon was not about to break his self-imposed rule for this female rogue.

He glared at her, blaming her for the enticement she presented, and worse yet, he knew that even if he would be so reckless as to abandon the personal code that covered his dealings with women, Bethia would not welcome his advances. She had made that clear enough before when they had tussled on the ground, when he had discovered her muscles...

Swearing again, Simon wrested his thoughts from that direction, concentrating instead upon the silence that surrounded them. Eyes narrowing, he searched the area for signs that they might be watched, and though he could find none, he remained uneasy. This was her domain, not his own. He had confidence such that he did not fear anything, but he also had enough sense to know that he could easily find himself surrounded by archers again.

And that, more than all the other excuses he had conjured while eating, made his decision for him where Bethia was concerned. For, above all, he hated being robbed of his dignity—something this woman had stolen from him once already. And he refused to contemplate the possibility of earning an arrow in his back while his braies were down around his ankles and his bare ass hiked in the air.

With a grunt of disgust, Simon dismissed his baser urges with grim finality, and surprisingly, he was able to relax once more. The rabbit and mushrooms were well flavored and crisp, and Simon found himself enjoying the simple fare. As they ate in silence, he began to know an odd contentment.

Not for the first time he noticed the peace of the forest, its air rich with the scents of leaves and moss and earth. He was accustomed to the clash of swords or the daily noise of busy Campion, but here, the only noises were the crackle of the fire and the soft rustle of small creatures. He had never spent much time in the wood near his home, but now he began to wonder if all were like this one or if Burnel Chase was somehow different. Special. Like his companion.

As if drawn to her against his will, Simon turned, cursing his timing, for she was licking her fingers again, and he felt himself swell and harden, imagining her mouth upon his fingers and...elsewhere. How Stephen would have laughed, for they all knew that Simon took his pleasures swiftly and in the most basic of fashions, disdaining the more exotic satisfactions of which his brother boasted.

But now...now Simon felt the tug of the unknown, the untried, like a physical pull, luring him into the hold of unfamiliar ardor—and Bethia. Abruptly he tossed away a bone and stood, walking uncomfortably toward the trees and staring into the darkness.

Suddenly the forest seemed a dangerous thing, a place of dark attraction and uncontrollable passions. "Tomorrow, we go to Baddersly," he muttered. There, in the relative familiarity of his brother's castle, he would lose this strange edginess that plagued him. There he would draw out Brice and find out, once and for all, the truth of this woman's words. And then he would know...

"No." The husky sound was so low that Simon nearly missed it. And he turned, startled.

"Did you speak?" he demanded, refusing to believe his ears.

Bethia had stretched back again, apparently at ease upon the grass as another woman might be lounging in the softest of beds. Her lips twitched, drawing his attention once more to that mouth of hers. "I realize that you are not used to hearing that word, but *no,* I will not be going with you. My place is here."

Her place was with him. Simon nearly growled out the words, though he could make no sense of them even to himself. "If the situation is as you have explained, you will want to return to Ansquith as heir," he said.

"Yes, but not until Brice is gone."

Simon opened his mouth to snarl a response, then closed it abruptly. He had learned long ago that he was not as clever as Geoffrey, that his sword arm and his understanding of warfare were what made him superior. Yet it surprised him when he realized just how long it took him to understand what she was saying.

When he did, he stared in amazement. *She didn't trust him.* He could not remember anyone in his long life doubting him. He was a de Burgh, and his honor was not suspect. Ever. He felt a surge of frustration. How would he gain her faith? He had only his word, and none had ever questioned it.

Nor did anyone refuse him. At Campion, his word was law, and so he lashed out at her, angry at both her denial and her disloyalty. "You *will* come with me, for as your liege lord, I command it!" he snapped.

"You are not my liege lord," she said dryly. "'Tis my father who owes your brother allegiance."

Her calm manner, more than anything else, set off his temper, and Simon slammed a fist against his hand. "By faith, you will obey me, or I will toss you over my shoulder and carry you there, mile by mile!"

Her hoot of disbelief made him take a menacing step toward her before he caught himself and attempted to reason with her instead. "You must realize that this…life you have fashioned here is foolhardy and dangerous. Come with me, and you will be safe and well attended."

"And I am to do so solely upon your word? I don't think so, my lord," she said, rising to her feet in one swift, graceful motion. "You came here not at my invitation, and yet, like all men, you seek to have dominion over me, my people and my forest," she said in a low, even voice. "Well, you can take your lordly ways and begone!"

Simon stared at her, stupefied. "What are you talking about? I would aid you, you foolish female!"

"I need not your aid!" she responded, and she faced him with an expression that both challenged and infuriated him.

"You begged me for it earlier this day, or have you forgotten your wish for me to oust your betrothed?"

"He is *not* my betrothed," she answered heatedly. "And I would never beg *you* for anything, you arrogant oaf!"

Raising his fists to the heavens, Simon swore low and long. Had he thought this woman different? She was just as unwise and annoying as any other female, more so, in fact! Turning away, he sought to rein in his temper before she incited him to violence. It was full dark now and too late for traveling. Rather than continue making enough noise to alert both her men and any others that might be about this night, he must put aside his argument...for now.

There would be time enough to resume it upon the morrow. And if he met too much resistance, then he might just have to drag her by that fat braid of hers. Once at Baddersly, she would know the way of things. Then she would know better than to disbelieve him.

"If you would not go with me, how am I to contact you?" he asked, turning her attention from their dispute. "I can hardly roam the forest in search of you and your outlaws every time I wish to get a message to you."

When she hesitated, as if reluctant to answer, Simon's ire roused anew. Filled with frustration and disappointment, he wanted to take her and shake her, to bind her to him somehow, but instead he turned away.

"Leave a message in the village. I will get it," she said softly.

Whirling to face her once more, Simon studied her through narrowed eyes. How did she expect him to answer that? Was she implying that every villager and freeman was in league with her? Bah! More the fool he for expecting the truth from a thief and liar in men's clothing.

If she would speak only falsehoods, there was no point in further discussion, so without another word, Simon stalked to the other side of the fire and stretched out. Keeping one hand poised on the hilt of his sword, he laid his head upon his arm. It was a warm night, and he needed no covering but for his own garments, his heavy mail and the anger that clung to him.

He heard her take her own spot not far away, but he was too enraged to admire her adaptability. In the morning, Simon vowed, he would finish his dealings with this outlaw once and for all. Then he would set her to rights, he swore, one way or another.

As he settled down to rest, Simon realized that his body was again under his control. He was relieved to no longer be plagued by unwelcome desires. Indeed, all he wanted to do to the wench now was throttle her, and the notion made him smile slowly into the darkness.

The battle was joined.

Chapter Seven

Simon awoke in the gray light of early morning to a misty rain. Blinking away the moisture, he saw the fire was out and sat up swiftly, wiping his face with one hand while the other went to his sword hilt. But his vigilance was unnecessary, for nothing stirred among the abandoned tree stumps, and he grunted in satisfaction, anticipation warming him.

Today he would talk some sense into his companion, take her back with him to Baddersly and then— His pleasant musings halted abruptly when he saw no sign of life on the other side of the clearing. Rolling to his feet, Simon stood quickly, raking the area with his gaze even as his blood roared a denial.

She was not there! Although she might simply be attending to her needs, Simon knew instinctively that she was not nearby. She was long gone, and he wanted to bellow his frustration to the skies. He could not believe that the wench had managed to steal away from him, not once but twice! Did she sprout wings and fly off during the night? Raising his fists into the air, Simon swore low and long at his seeming ineptitude.

By faith, he should have secured her to him, her

claims and wishes be damned! After all, she was nothing but an outlaw. She had woven a fine tale of injustice, but he should not have let her words sway him! He ought to have taken her, like the petty thief she was, back to meet her fate in the court where he ruled!

For the first time in his life, Simon cursed himself for a fool. How his brothers would laugh to see him cozened by a wench! Unlike the rest of them, he had never fallen prey to a pretty face. He could not even understand such nonsense! And yet, he had let this woman spin him a story of needing his aid, only to disappear at dawn. More than likely, Bethia Burnel was dead and gone and this opportunistic tart had taken her place.

The other possibility, that Bethia was exactly who she claimed to be and had fled because she did not trust him, was something Simon refused to consider. *Everyone* trusted him. He was a de Burgh, and his name stood for itself. Besides, the wench who taunted and goaded him would not be so cowardly.

Nay, she was playing with him, and the knowledge was infuriating. Never had he been so disgusted—at her disappearance, at her seeming talent for besting him nearly every time he came in contact with her, and worst of all, at the way she had taken his warrior existence and upended it—sending him into a turmoil of seething passions and frustrations.

Yet, despite all, he was aware of himself as never before, filled with the pulsing of life and certainly more vital than when he had been kicking his heels back at Campion. Indeed, it was as if he were poised before a great conflict, with challenges to meet that tested his skills, intelligence and endurance to the limit, but through which he would emerge the ultimate victor. At the thought, Simon smiled grimly. The wench may have won this small skirmish, but she would not have the war. And the spoils would then be his.

As his tension eased, Simon searched the clearing, automatically eliminating all traces of his presence. Bethia had done the same, for not a scrap of cloth or strand of hair did he find to remind him of the night they had spent together in the makeshift camp. Ignoring an annoying sense of disappointment at the realization, Simon straightened once more, ready to decide on a course.

He could search for her again, naturally, but his instincts told him not to waste any more time among the trees. No doubt, she had set her men to watch for him, and this time, his element of surprise was gone.

Nay, before he spoke with the wench again, he would see this Brice and know the truth of what went forward at Ansquith. And, if the answers he received did not support Bethia's claims, then he would send a force into the chase to rout the outlaws for good. Simon grunted smugly, for he knew where to find her. She was bound to the woods.

And when the time came, she would not be able to hide from him, even if he had to take apart every inch of the forest.

Stalking toward the abandoned mine, Bethia barely acknowledged the greetings of one of her men. Apparently assessing her mood, John quickly stepped aside, but Firmin took his place, exclaiming loudly over her damp clothes. She waved him away, too annoyed to parry with the headstrong archer. Although she had left Simon de Burgh behind in the hour before dawn, her mind was still fully occupied by that arrogant bastard.

How dare he? She had asked herself the question over and over on her way back to camp, but could come to no satisfactory answer. How dare he barge into the chase and try to take over her life? Typical man! He had known her but briefly, and still he would tell her what to do, where to go, how to behave.

His arrogance be damned! Bethia and her followers had been doing fine without his high-handed interference, and they would do just as well without him. Even if he really was willing to help oust Brice, the price of his aid was entirely too high.

Bethia had spent years under the thumb of one man or another, and in the past few years she had taken her fill of orders from others. She had no intention of giving herself over to a short-tempered knight who could not speak without issuing a command. Stomping past a sputtering Firmin, Bethia seethed with indignation at the man's conceit.

When Simon de Burgh spoke, he expected all the world to listen—and obey! Ha! Bethia could not be so easily manipulated. She had a mind of her own. Had the man even bothered to ask her wish or her opinion? Nay. He was too busy spouting his own. And she was supposed to meekly acquiesce?

Bethia would have laughed had the situation not been so serious, for the clash of wills between them was only a part of the problem. Ruefully she acknowledged that even if Simon de Burgh had dropped to his knees and begged her, she could not have gone with him. Although the image was tantalizing, Bethia shook her head, for despite his claims of honesty, she would not so readily believe a stranger, no matter what his name.

Oh, she was tempted, Bethia admitted. Simon de

Burgh spoke with such authority that she could not help but be impressed. And she had always wanted to believe in the honor and goodness of those who took up the sword. But wants and wishes were one thing and harsh reality another. Bethia had given up those dreams long ago, along with the hope that someone would rescue her. She had learned to rely solely upon herself.

Her mood weighed heavily upon her as Bethia approached the opening of the mine, where one of the archers stepped forward to garner her attention. "We saw your fire, but when you made no sign, we kept away," he reported.

"Thank you," Bethia said, ignoring the odd mixture of embarrassment and gratitude she felt for last night's privacy. Although she had simply been doing her duty in treating with Simon de Burgh, she had to admit that she had enjoyed much of the evening—his stories of war and glory, his surprise at her hunting skills, his very presence....

"What's this?" Firmin asked. Planting himself firmly in front of her, he forced the other man to step aside. "Just where were you last night? This idiot would tell me nothing," he said, scorning the archer beside him.

Bethia took one glance at Firmin's red face and belligerent stance and had to struggle to maintain her composure. Her initial reaction was to tell him that her whereabouts were none of his business, but the last months of leading others had tempered her impatience, so she took a deep breath and responded evenly.

"I was meeting with someone who might aid our cause."

Firmin's brows drew downward. "We already have allies in abundance within the village and the countryside,'' he said dismissively. "Who was this person who would take you away from camp in the dark hours?" he asked, his voice rife with suspicion.

Bethia could hardly lie, for others who knew the truth lingered nearby, listening curiously. "I was with Simon de Burgh,'' she admitted, refusing to be cowed by yet another short-tempered male.

"Simon de Burgh! John, you allowed this?" Firmin raged.

Bethia felt her own temper stretch dangerously. "John is not my keeper. Nor is he my father. Nor is he the leader of this band. So why would he have any say at all in my whereabouts?" She spoke softly, yet with enough force that the others stepped back, leaving her facing an angry Firmin.

"He should have told me! He should make certain you are safe,'' Firmin sputtered.

"I think I can take care of myself,'' Bethia answered. "I have done so for quite some time.''

Firmin swiped at his wet hair, apparently willing to concede her the skills to protect herself, but still he stared at her with an accusing expression. "And did you take care of Simon de Burgh as well? Is that why you spent the night alone with him?''

Bethia felt an urge to slap his ruddy face but restrained herself. She no longer held to the constraints that kept other women in their place, and although she had little enough use for such rules, she realized that it was difficult for many of the men to ignore them.

"Are you insinuating something?" she asked. Turning to the others, who shuffled and dropped their heads, as if embarrassed, Bethia lifted her chin. "I camp with you and nothing is said. Why would you make so much of this?''

"Because he is our enemy!" Firmin cried.

"That has yet to be proved," Bethia said in an even tone as she swung back toward Firmin. "Meanwhile, if I wish to discover more about Simon de Burgh and his plans, I will."

Bethia held his gaze, as if daring him to say something else, and for a long moment, he looked like he might. Did he imagine her a whore to bed down with Simon de Burgh? Typical male thinking! They thought the whole world revolved around their nether parts, Bethia noted with a disgust she kept to herself. She had worked long and hard to overcome the prejudices against her sex and lead these men. She was not going to let a question about her sleeping habits destroy the respect she had won.

And, rebelliously, she could not help but wonder what business it was of theirs if she had bedded down with Simon. A bright spark of heat tingled through her at the very thought, though she would deny it. Lord de Burgh was already too arrogant for his own good; she had no wish to add to his conceit with her admiration.

Nor had she any intention of revealing her thoughts to these men. To them she must remain strong and untouched by unseemly desires, and so she met Firmin's gaze, unflinching, waiting for him to say something else against her.

He did not. With a few muttered oaths, he finally whirled on his heel and stalked away. And Bethia had too much else pressing her to waste any more thoughts on the unhappy archer. Putting her hands on her hips, she surveyed the makeshift camp, which would have to be moved yet again. Because of Simon de Burgh.

No matter what her personal feelings about de Burgh, Bethia remained determined to be wary of his sudden interest in her. He had already forced them to break camp once, and now he had found their new hiding place with little effort. He moved through the chase like a well-trained animal, avoiding with an uncanny skill, the men she had set to watch.

Yes, one thing was for certain: Simon de Burgh was a formidable knight. Whether he was trustworthy or not, Bethia did not like the idea of him sneaking around discovering their hiding places. Nor did she plan to wait for him to find them again.

"John, gather the men," she ordered softly. It was time for drastic action.

When Simon returned to Baddersly, he met each questioning look with a scowl, each sidelong glance with a grimace that sent its subject scuttling away. He was aware that news of his singular trip had traveled swiftly through the castle, but he was not accustomed to being the object of speculation.

At home it was Stephen they gossiped about! His escapades were legendary, as were Robin's amusing antics. If they spoke of Simon at all, it was in admiration of his skills in battle, as should be the case. Certainly no one had discussed his comings and goings before, and he found that he liked it not. For the first time in his life, he wondered if he truly craved the notoriety that went with Dunstan's accomplishments.

He had always wanted what his elder had achieved, success not only as a knight, but a demesne of his own. Yet a castle the size of Wessex or Baddersly now seemed too big, too full of people intruding upon him and too many tongues wagging. Although he had once disdained Geoffrey's manor house, now he began to see

the advantages to a smaller property, where fewer residents could talk about his business!

Gossip! He ought to forbid it outright, and he would
have, were it not for thoughts of his brothers' jeers at
such a ploy. Instead he chose to ignore the rumors, for
it was no one's concern but his own where he spent
his days—or nights. Suddenly Simon recalled his evening in the woods where a simple meal and easy conversation seemed strangely preferable to the large, lux-
urious castle.

Cursing under his breath, Simon told himself that
kind of life was impractical, the existence of fools who
would freeze to death come winter. Then he paused at
the dismaying thought. Where *would* Bethia go when
it grew cold? Would she continue to refuse his offer of
hospitality? Simon imagined her in the arms of some
skinny archer and grunted his displeasure, annoyed at
both the image and the train of his thoughts. Lately they
seemed to flow inextricably toward that wretched female.

Simon had decided before he even reached Baddersly that instead of struggling against such inclina-
tions, he would face them without flinching. And he
reasoned that the easiest way to banish Bethia from his
mind was to unravel the truth about her identity. With
that in mind, he hurried past the whispers in the great
hall and headed toward the solar, roaring for the steward.

Simon had retained Florian during his last visit, for
the man had come highly recommended by one of
Campion's friends, and he had proved to be a loyal and
able steward. However, Simon found his talkative manner annoying, and so he had avoided as much speech

with the fellow as possible since his return. Now, though, he had need of his skills.

"My lord! You are back!" Florian began, as if he had every intention of rattling on indefinitely about Simon's absence.

But Simon was equally determined not to allow it. "I wish to issue an invitation. No, a command," he said as he stalked across the room. When Florian raised his brows, Simon scowled. "Phrase it properly, but I want it clear that the man is ordered to come here to attend his liege lord."

"And who would you have attend you, my lord?" Florian asked with a look of bewilderment.

"Brice Scirvayne is his name, and he is in residence at Ansquith."

Florian hesitated, as if unsure whether to comment, which was so unusual that Simon snapped at him. "Well, what is it?"

"I mean no disrespect, my lord, nor would I question your command. However, as far as I know, that man is not sworn to Baddersly," Florian said.

"No, but he claims to hold Ansquith in the stead of its rightful owner, Sir Burnel. He represents himself as the head of the household and the demesne. Therefore, he must assume Burnel's loyalties, as well." Or face war, Simon vowed silently. Even if this fellow proved to be the most honest and worthy of men, he had slighted the de Burghs badly when he had refused Simon admittance to Ansquith. And for that alone, he would pay.

"But is he not just a visitor there?" Florian asked.

"If he is, then he has taken liberties no guest should be allowed. As my brother's vassal, Sir Burnel is under my protection, and if he is being threatened by this

Brice, then I would intervene,'' Simon said. He paused uncomfortably and gazed out the window before deciding to take the steward into his confidence. "There is also some dispute about Sir Burnel's daughter. I have reason to believe that she might still be alive, through no plan of Brice's.''

Florian did not bother to hide his surprise. "I've heard little of this Brice and most of it ill pleasing, but would he really hold Sir Burnel prisoner in his own home and declare the man's daughter dead?''

Simon glared at the steward. "I have spoken with her myself,'' he snapped. Florian bowed his head in acknowledgment, yet his gaze held a skepticism that made Simon bristle. "Of course, it is possible that this woman is lying,'' Simon admitted. "That is what I am trying to determine—the truth.''

Eyes narrowing, Simon dared Florian to gainsay him, but the steward only studied him surreptitiously. Simon would have snorted at the ploy except that he began to get the uneasy feeling that the steward was seeing more than he ought. Muttering an oath, Simon turned away to scowl out the window.

"And what if the truth is not to your liking, my lord?'' Florian asked.

"What do you mean?'' Simon asked, whirling on the man. The de Burghs had never condoned falsehoods.

"Well…'' Florian paused, as if to choose his words carefully. "What if her father is not endangered? From what I heard, she was to marry this Brice. What if her father commanded her to marry, and she has disobeyed? She wouldn't be the first maid who did not want the man her father had picked for her.''

Simon stared at the steward, stunned. Whatever he had thought of Bethia, he certainly had not imagined her to be anything as simple as a runaway daughter. "And they would kill her for that?" he asked with a snarl.

"I would hope not!" Florian said. "But she would not be the first to fake her own death, either. If you restore her to her family, will you see her wed, as well?"

Wed? Bethia? Simon would have laughed but for a sudden rush of dismay. He lifted a hand and rubbed at his chest even as he denied the steward's words. No matter what the truth might be, Bethia was not going to marry anyone. She was not the type. Indeed, he could not imagine a wench less suited to the role of wife.

Bethia was too much like a man to please one. No simpering, fainthearted flower was she, but strong and bold and brave and not likely to settle well into an institution where she would be relegated to sewing and housekeeping. Simon could imagine her turning a well-aimed arrow upon anyone who would try to put her in her place, and he bit back a grin at the thought.

Dismissing the very notion of such nuptials, Simon nonetheless gave the steward a sharp look, for there had been something odd about the man's tone. "Do you know something I do not?" he demanded.

"Nay, my lord. I was simply presenting you with all the possibilities," Florian said with an air of innocence.

Frowning, Simon studied the man with narrowed eyes. "Well, there is no use speculating until we know more, and we won't know more until I talk to Brice." The impatience in his voice had Florian up and moving immediately.

"Aye, my lord. I will see to it at once."

"Good," Simon said, staring after the steward in annoyance. It appeared to him as if everyone at Baddersly was determined to turn a blind eye to the doings at Ansquith, and though Simon could see nothing sinister in their neglect, it was all to the good that he had returned here to take charge.

But the assurance did little to settle Simon's mood, for the steward's suggestions lingered, like the stench of bad meat, in the air. What if Bethia were simply defying her father? Simon could not countenance it, and yet the thought of her marrying a man about whom he had heard nothing but ill filled him with unease.

She would not be bound to any man, Simon vowed, whatever her father willed. He was a de Burgh, and he would not allow it. Slowly a smug smile came to his lips. If anyone sought to marry Bethia, then he would simply have to intervene.

As liege lord in Dunstan's place, his opinion could hardly be ignored, and he refused to allow any nuptials. Feeling better already, Simon chose to ignore the attendant questions, such as how he was going to do it, or more important, why?

Although Simon knew that a messenger had been dispatched immediately to Ansquith, he felt a restless impatience that would not leave him. He was not accustomed to sitting and waiting. He was a man of action, and as the hours began to chafe on him, he finally stalked through the bailey to the mews, determined to put the outlaw wench and her mysterious doings out of his mind.

Once his eyes adjusted to the semidarkness of the building, Simon studied the various hunting birds on their perches. Goshawks, sparrow hawks, gyrfalcons and merlins lined the long room in impressive array.

And he was pleased to hear the low voice of the falconer behind him, attentive to his charges.

"My lord, I give you good greeting. Is there aught I might do for you?" the man asked.

Swinging toward the short figure, Simon grunted his assent. "Aye. I would test your birds," he said. "Let us hunt."

But even the fine specimens available at Baddersly did not hold Simon's attention for long. Instead of the graceful, soaring bird diving for the kill, somehow he kept seeing a lone woman with a bow and arrow, her aim true, her body flexing with strength. Muttering an oath at his preoccupation, Simon finally called a halt to the hawking and urged his mount back to the castle.

When he found that the messenger still had not returned, Simon stalked impatiently through the bailey, checking the dairy, the brewery and the various enterprises and leaving anxious workers trembling in his wake. All seemed to be in order. Although he had not the head for business that his brother Geoffrey did, Simon gave all at Baddersly a cursory study and found them thriving.

He was on his way to the kitchens when the steward hurried toward him, and Simon grimaced, tempted to duck into the garderobe rather than face the man. But it was too late. Already Florian was nearly to his side, bowing and grinning delightedly.

"I was not aware that you were going to view our operations today," the steward said. "What did you think of the brewery? May I tell you how we have increased the production of ale in the last year?"

Without waiting for agreement, Florian began explaining, going into such detail that he swiftly lost Simon's interest. No doubt Geoffrey or even his father would have been delighted to learn of these new methods, but Simon chafed at the talk. "Enough," he said, waving a hand in dismissal. "Prepare a report, and I shall look it over before I send it on to Dunstan," he said, striding away from the man of business with haste.

Is this how his eldest brother spent his days? Simon wondered sourly. Assessing the ale? Overseeing the dairy? Even as he wanted to deny it, Simon sensed the truth of the matter, for Dunstan's fighting days were over. Although the elder de Burgh brother rarely spoke of his duties, he had told Simon to make certain that the growing fields were cleared and the crops doing well. At the time, Simon had merely nodded, eager to get on his way. But now the message dismayed him. His father attended to such matters at Campion. Not Simon.

During his last visit to Baddersly, Simon had ousted the corrupt knights who had served the wrong master, organized a new army, employed a new steward, shored up defenses and recovered his sister-in-law's rightful property. But now there was naught to do but oversee a well-run castle. No wars to fight. No new men to train. No challenges.

Except for a certain band of outlaws...

Grunting in annoyance, Simon refused to pursue that line of thought. Until the messenger returned, he would waste no more time upon that wretched Bethia. He could not resist a glance toward the gate, but the road beyond lay empty and the sun was sinking low.

Remembering his own camp in the woods, Simon decided to wash himself before supper. His father had been much for cleanliness and instilled it all his sons, though some, namely Stephen, took his grooming to extremes. Striding swiftly to the hall, Simon called loudly for a bath before heading toward the great chamber.

His squire arrived shortly to remove his mail. "Shall I polish it?" the boy asked.

"Nay," Simon answered, frowning at the youth's surprise. "I do not intend to be without it for long," he muttered. Back at Campion, he would not take his evening meal while wearing it, but he was at Baddersly. And even though the castle had been at peace for years, he was alert. There were always enemies waiting to catch one unawares.

Like Brice. The man would have to be an idiot to challenge Baddersly, but in Simon's experience, most people didn't have a lot of sense. And so far Brice had not acted very intelligently. So Simon simply laid his sword aside for now and sent his squire away with a grunt. He dismissed, too, the servants who had carried in a round wooden tub and partially filled it with warm water. All of them hurried to leave except one—a young, delicate woman with long black hair. Simon lifted his brows in question when she alone remained.

"I am Ida, my lord. Master Florian, the steward, sent me here to bathe you." She folded her hands in front of her and cast her eyes down demurely.

A woman to bathe him. Simon grunted in disgust, for he had never engaged in that ritual. His father had never approved of it, especially with seven young males in the household and a yearning for legitimate heirs. And Dunstan, who was fiercely protective of his wife, did not allow such practices at Wessex, either, even if Marion was like a sister to his siblings.

During his travels, Simon had been offered the service more than once, but had rejected it out of long habit. He had but one use for women, and that did not

include having them wash him. And yet, he was aware
of a deep, simmering frustration that such attention
might assuage. He hesitated, ready to dismiss her just
as easily as her fellows, but something stopped him.
Giving the girl a curt nod, he stripped off the rest of
his garments and stepped into the steaming water.

For a moment, Simon closed his eyes, allowing himself the pleasure of the hot moisture seeping into his
muscles, but then he remembered the servant, and he
tensed again, wary. She had not moved, he sensed that,
and when he glanced over at her, she was staring at
him with rounded eyes, her tiny mouth drawn up in
an O.

Simon scowled, displeased with the results of his
plan. He had thought to refresh his sorely battered
pride, and instead, he was faced with a girl who saw
little to admire in him. He had never been aware of his
body before, but now he wondered if he had some lack.
Something that had made Bethia turn away from him...

"Well? What is it?" he snapped.

"I beg your pardon, my lord," the servant said.
"You are so...big, my lord. All over. And scarred,"
she admitted, red faced. "You must have been in many
battles."

Scars. Well, there was precious little he could do to
improve the appearance of his skin, which bore the
marks of his knighthood and an active life. There was
the time when he was six and an ax had slipped, slicing
his arm, and he carried with him various small remind-
ers of bouts with his brothers, plus a few rather nasty
looking battle wounds. Was he so repulsive? Simon had
never considered it. All the de Burghs were accounted
to be handsome, though he perhaps less than the others.

And women had never made any complaint. Indeed,

Simon had often ignored the flirting of noble ladies, while the women he had paid for their services seemed enthusiastic enough. But, then, none of them had seen him naked either. The thought was suddenly jarring.

"Get out," he said.

"But, my lord, I would—"

Simon cut the girl off with a fierce growl, and she dropped her cloth and fled. When the door closed behind her, he sank in the enveloping liquid and stared at his knees. For the second time in his life, he felt oddly vulnerable. And he didn't like it.

But what he liked even less was the knowledge that somehow Bethia Burnel was responsible. Again.

Chapter Eight

After a hasty bath that did little to improve his spirits, Simon strode toward the hall for supper. He realized that the messenger, having not returned, must be staying the night at Ansquith. Although an encouraging sign for relations between the two demesnes, the knowledge did little to improve Simon's mood.

A lavish meal was wasted upon him, as well. Although Florian obviously had spared no expense on delicacies to welcome him to Baddersly, nothing tasted as good as the wild rabbit on which he had dined the night before. And that annoying discovery made the food stick in his throat like so much bad meat.

It didn't help that those around him were so obviously enjoying the feast. "My lord," said Leofwin between loud gulps. "'Tis most delicious the ducks you brought down today." He pushed the platter toward Simon, who nodded but said nothing. His silence was a mistake, he realized, when he saw the looks those seated nearby were sending his way.

"You do not care for the food?" Florian asked, eyeing Simon curiously.

"I have had my fill," Simon snapped, deeming his

habits none of the prying steward's business. With six brothers and his father to attend, the servants at Campion had been too busy to notice what Simon did or did not eat. Did they trouble Dunstan so at Wessex? If so, Simon found much to dislike in being the focus of so many eyes and interests.

Ignoring his forbidding frown, Florian studied him carefully. "I do hope you have not been stricken with some illness after your stay away from the castle. The cold night air is most unhealthy and as for the accommodations elsewhere…" The fastidious steward shuddered.

"What's that? Is someone sick?" Leofwin asked, pausing to lick his fingers. "Why, my squire suffered a most debilitating malady most recently."

"Did it take away his appetite?" Florian asked.

"Aye!" Leofwin answered as he broke off a generous hunk of bread. "He was laid low by a diarrhea and spent two days in the garderobe. Came out smelling like a dung heap!" Taking a big bite, he chewed noisily as he turned to Simon. "I hope you are not coming down with that, my lord," he added, although from the enthusiastic way he was eyeing Simon's trencher, his true sentiments were in doubt.

It was time to call a halt to this nonsense. "I am never ill!" Simon said. Suitably chastened, Leofwin turned his attention back to his food, but Florian studied him speculatively. Having had his fill of the steward, Simon glared at the man, until he too turned away.

"'Tis to my thinking that some here are eating too much," Simon muttered with a glance toward Leofwin. The hefty knight had the grace to look chagrined for a moment, before burping loudly.

With a low grunt, Simon pushed his trencher aside.

Suddenly the company that had always satisfied him before seemed lacking, the rough warriors intrusive and uncouth, the vast hall with its luxuries and its crowded trestle tables stifling. Although smaller than Campion, it was too big, too crowded, too noisy. Unable to make sense of his restlessness, Simon shoved back his chair and stood. Without a word to his fellows, he stalked from the hall.

Outside in the bailey, he breathed deeply of the many scents—wood smoke and dung and horse and cooking. All were familiar, but none bore the fragrance of the chase—or a certain female. Closing his eyes, Simon tried to recall the very smell of her until he realized just what he was doing.

He was not some lovesick lute player. He was a de Burgh, a skilled knight, a warrior! And the only reason the wench lingered on his mind was because she presented a problem. Just as soon as it was solved, he would be rid of her for good. Although the knowledge failed to please him as it should, Simon told himself all would soon be back to normal and the strange feelings coursing through him would cease.

Ignoring the questioning eyes of his brother's subjects, Simon strode back through the hall to his chamber, suddenly weary of his own company and eager for his rest.

Although he took to his bed early, Simon lay awake until late into the night, and when dawn arrived, he was bleary-eyed and prickly. Shouting for his squire, he wondered what the devil was the matter with him. He always slept like a rock on all kinds of berths, including the hard ground, and in every type of weather, even rain and sleet.

Pausing abruptly in the act of dressing, Simon considered the possibility that Florian was right. Perhaps he had some malady. Taking a deep breath, he rubbed his hard stomach, as if searching for some sign of illness. Obviously he was not suffering from what had struck Quentin's squire, but had his long night signaled the onset of some other ailment? Running a hand over his chest, Simon wished for Geoffrey's expertise.

Although annoying at times, his learned brother might be able to shed some light on his condition. Simon had never paid much attention to such things, having boasted of perfect health his entire life. Certainly he had seen his share of deaths on the battlefield and a few from strange sicknesses that wasted and killed, but none had ever dared to strike the de Burgh men.

Nor would it now, Simon told himself with the innate arrogance of his family. Briefly he stretched his arms and legs, assured of his own vigor, and strode to the hall in eager anticipation—only to find that the messenger had not yet returned.

"But 'tis early yet, my lord," Florian said when Simon uttered a grunt of impatience. The steward gestured toward the high table with a soothing smile. "Come, sit, and have a cup of ale and bread."

Florian's pointed efforts to get him to eat did not strike Simon well since he always waited upon dinner as did the rest of the castle residents. He demanded no special treatment, especially where food was concerned, and he opened his mouth to tell the steward so in no uncertain terms. Before he could speak, he was hailed loudly by Leofwin.

"My lord!" the knight said, huffing as he reached Simon's side. "I spoke with my squire, and he said that the first sign he had of foul humors was a sudden seiz-

ing up of his belly, followed by the release of loud and
noxious gases.''

Simon's eyes narrowed at the recitation, his temper
chafing as Florian stepped closer. Putting a finger to his
lips, the steward studied Simon in a pensive manner.
''I have noticed no such odors, but you do look pale,
my lord. Did you sleep well?'' The barb made Simon
flinch, but just as he would have told the meddling
steward to mind himself, Quentin approached.

''My lord! Did I hear aright? Are you having trouble
sleeping?'' Without pausing for Simon's answer, the
knight gave them all a significant glance. ''I heard that
there is illness in Cobbington. A passing carter told me
that he suffered most frightfully from a bout of sleeplessness. Of course, that was just the beginning. Even-
tually his hair fell out, and he grew a thick, white paste
upon his tongue. Here, let me see,'' he said, reaching
upward to grasp Simon's chin while squinting at him.

Simon was so stunned by the man's gall as to be
speechless, and when the old knight actually tried to
pry open his jaws, Simon shook him off. ''Let go of
me, you idiot,'' he snarled, knocking Quentin's hand
away with a fist. He was so enraged that he nearly
shook with the force of it as he whirled to face them
all. How dare they put their hands upon him? And in-
sinuate that he had some hairy growth upon his tongue?

''There is nothing wrong with me, do you hear?
Nothing!'' he roared. And ignoring his steward's bale-
ful look, Simon stalked out of the hall.

The messenger had not returned by dinner. Nonetheless, Simon forced himself to eat heartily of the elaborate meal. He had never been one to appreciate fine
food. Burned or nearly raw, it mattered little to him,

but now he found that bread and ale, goose and herring, all tasted of naught. He rolled his tongue tentatively around his ale, testing for any fur that might be growing there.

Bah! These idiots at Badderly had him behaving like an old woman. Despite his slight appetite, he was well and good. It was simply the wait that chafed at him, and as he chewed loudly, glaring all the while at his companions, Simon wondered if he ought not to go into the chase and check on Bethia. Perhaps the absence of the messenger boded ill for the female outlaw. Had Brice sent his men into the forest for her? Simon gulped hard, frustrated and impatient, for he was ill accustomed to kicking his feet.

Mayhap he should ride into the village this afternoon and see if anyone there could reach her, Simon thought, even as he choked on the notion. He cared not to leave a message at the smithy like some errand boy! Pushing aside his trencher, he vowed to find her himself, to assure himself that all was well, that she was all right. *To see her again.*

Even as his pulse pounded in anticipation, Simon frowned, for what would he tell her? He felt the hot rise of blood in his neck at the thought of facing her without good reason. She would look at him with those hazel eyes, *knowing* eyes, and he would feel the fool yet again.

With a grunt of disgust, Simon rejected that vision, for he would not be laughed at once more by the wench. Besides, he had sworn to discover the truth from Brice and he was bound to it. Nevertheless, this constant delay was grating—enough to make anyone restless. Lost as he was in thought, Simon did not heed the conversation that flowed around him until the voices lowered significantly. Then his warrior's instincts were all attention, and he remained still and listened.

"But he was pale this morning. Lack of sleep, I'll warrant. That's what I asked him, though he would not admit it, of course." Simon ground his teeth at the sound of Florian's voice, for he could easily guess just whom the steward was discussing.

"Pale? But he is flushed now. A fever perhaps?" Quentin suggested.

"He doesn't eat enough," Leofwin muttered.

"Ah, but perhaps that is part of his condition, this lack of appetite," Florian said. "As your friend, the carter, attested."

"If you ask me," came the voice of one of his own knights, "he suffers from an excess of choleric temperament, especially since arriving here!"

"Ah, that might well be it, caused by an imbalance of humors, of course," Florian said in a thoughtful voice. "I have heard that an excess of any of the four bodily humors—blood, phlegm, yellow bile and black bile—can cause an imbalance in temperament, resulting in illness."

Unable to contain himself, Simon glanced up to confirm his suspicions. Every eye nearby was focused upon him in a furtive manner that made him roar with outrage. Rising from his chair, Simon swept the table with a ferocious glare.

"What *condition?*" he bellowed in a voice that would have done his elder sibling proud. "I am not flushed. Nor am I pale. Or queasy. Or sleepless. Or growing fur upon my tongue. *I am perfectly fine!*" Simon roared. "And the next man who suggests otherwise will find himself facing my wrath!" Tossing aside the linen cloth that he had bunched in his fist, Simon strode toward the doorway just as the messenger appeared, looking harried. And alone. Simon's temper snapped.

"Where is Brice?" he roared.

"He would not come, my lord," the man answered, falling to one knee in supplication.

"Get up!" Simon snapped, aware that Florian and several knights had quit the table to crowd around, their curiosity whetted. Although he would rather have learned this news without an audience, Simon was too impatient now to go elsewhere. "Well?" he prodded.

"They would not even let me in the gates at first," the messenger said, visibly trembling. "They made me sleep upon the ground outside while awaiting Brice Scirvayne's leisure. And this morning they only allowed me a short way into the bailey, without my dagger or sword, which they returned to me when I was once again outside the gates!"

His eyes narrowing at the insulting reception given his messenger, Simon forcibly reined in his temper. "Go on."

"Inside the bailey, I again waited until several knights rode forward, led by Brice Scirvayne."

"Did he wear a knight's mail, as well?"

"Nay," the messenger replied with a shake of his head. "He was very richly dressed, in fine colors."

Simon frowned in disgust. "Go on."

The messenger looked down at his feet, as if afraid to continue. "I delivered the message," he said, wiping his palms upon his tunic.

"And?" Simon asked, impatient.

"And he gave his…apologies, my lord," the messenger replied, darting a quick, fearful look at Simon.

"Apologies?" Simon wondered if something really might be afflicting his well-being, for surely he had not heard the man correctly.

The messenger trembled under the force of his stare. "He said that he must decline your kind invitation."

"Kind invitation?"

"Is there an echo in here?" Florian's voice rang out, followed by a few rumbles of laughter that turned into coughs when Simon whirled to glare at his audience.

Turning back to the messenger once more, he tried to curb his rapidly growing fury. "What did he say exactly?" Simon asked through gritted teeth.

The man looked thoughtful, then somber. "'Please extend my regards to Lord de Burgh and thank him for his kind invitation. However, I must regretfully decline at this time. My apologies, of course.'" The messenger paused. "Scirvayne said that real slippery like," he added before continuing. "'But since Sir Burnel is ill, I feel that my place is with him, for I am certain that Lord de Burgh would not wish the old man to take a turn for the worse while unattended.'"

Simon stared at the messenger in astonishment. Was this upstart Brice actually threatening Sir Burnel? He heard the gasps and low murmurs of those around him as others similarly interpreted the man's words. How dare he?

The messenger gazed about him with a look of chagrin. "So I reminded Master Scirvayne that his lordship was most insistent, and then..." He hesitated as if afraid to proceed.

"Go on," Simon urged through gritted teeth. His blood was already boiling, his fingers itching to thrash Brice Scirvayne with his bare hands.

"Then...then he asked me..." The messenger wiped

his palms upon his tunic once more before rushing on, as though eager to finish. "'Is it not the Baron of Wessex who is rightful lord of Baddersly and therefore only he who can summon his vassal?'"

Rage raced through Simon so overpowering that he could not speak for a moment. How dare this insolent nobody question his position? His command? Everyone knew that the family stood together, and no one questioned the word of a de Burgh. As if well aware of his growing fury, the messenger backed away and some of those who had watched with interest now shot him fearful looks as they, too, returned to their tasks.

But Simon had no quarrel with these people. They all knew of Dunstan's letter giving him full control over the castle—Florian had seen to that—and he suspected that word had traveled into the village and beyond—certainly to Ansquith. Even those unfamiliar with the de Burghs would not refuse a summons, so Simon could hardly excuse Brice for simple ignorance. Nay, his insult was calculated, a move not unlike that made in a chess match. Unfortunately, Simon had never been one for games.

He usually upended the board.

Florian's quiet cough broke the tense silence. "It does appear that something is amiss at Ansquith."

"Aye. Something is ill there, and 'tis not only Sir Burnel," Simon said, turning on the steward. But just as he lifted a fist to smash against his palm, something penetrated the heat of his anger.

Bethia. However loathsome Brice's actions might be, he was bearing out her story with his misdeeds. The pleasurable thought seeped through his rage, tempering it, for he realized that Bethia might well be telling the truth. The knowledge both heartened and excited him, for if her tale bore out, then he must surely aid her.

Bethia. Dropping his fist to his side, Simon grinned suddenly, startling his steward and the knights who stood nearby. "I must go," he said, already seized with urgency for his quest.

"But surely you do not plan to go to Ansquith alone!" Quentin protested.

"Would you have us attend you, my lord?" Thorkill called.

Shaking his head, Simon ignored them all, leaving the protesting group of warriors in his wake along with a curiously quiet Florian, who put his finger to his lips and studied his lord with a speculative gaze. Simon hurried by them, oblivious, for he was on his way to the village. To Bethia.

Simon frowned, slowing his destrier as he approached the smithy. He had left Baddersly in a rush, disregarding his knights, but now as he rode into the village alone, he wondered at the folly of his trip. What if the wench were leading him a merry chase yet again?

He scowled at the thought of her laughing at him while he roamed among the cots and huts searching for some means of contacting her. The idea set his mouth into a deeper grimace, but his only other option was to search the chase, and her men would be alert for him. He had no wish to be caught in another trap of Bethia's making.

Simon's eyes narrowed as the smith stepped out of the shadows. Swinging down from his mount, he handed over his reins and stood, suddenly uncomfortable, for he had no idea what to say. And the foolishness of his errand became apparent as he met the oaf's expectant gaze.

"I'm looking for someone," Simon muttered.

Instead of staring back at him blankly, the smith nodded his big head slowly. "You're to go to the alehouse, m'lord."

It was Simon who now stared blankly at the slow-witted fellow. "The alehouse?"

"Aye. You'll be met there." With that, the man led Simon's horse into the shadowed interior, leaving him standing outside alone.

Feeling as if he had somehow exchanged places with the smith, Simon glanced down the rutted road toward a small building where a pole hung with bushy green branches stuck out over the door. Although often such places were unsavory, from his prior visit Simon knew this alehouse to be cleaner than most, and he was not wary of trouble. If Bethia sent her bowmen to trap him, she would be disappointed, for without trees to hide them, they would pose little threat.

Confident of his own abilities, Simon strode toward the alehouse. More than likely, no one at all would appear, and Bethia would have another good laugh at his expense. Frowning at the thought, Simon stepped through the open door of the building. Little more than a hut, it was dark and strong smelling with a few benches for weary travelers to take their ease upon while they quenched their thirst.

Two men were there already, and Simon eyed them carefully before taking a seat with his back against the wall so that he might watch all who entered. It was getting late, and the two called for bread to go with their drink. Simon suspected the tiny business could offer little else. He took only ale and sipped it while he waited.

The two opposite him were obviously packmen, for they kept a wary watch upon their carts outside. When they tried to engage Simon in conversation with a friendly greeting, he grunted in response, glaring them into silence. He would not waste his time thusly. He wanted Bethia, and each minute that passed without news of her annoyed him.

What if something had happened to her? Despite all his efforts to quell it, agitation rose in his breast, and he felt a restless need to get up and look for her. But he retained enough discipline to stay where he was for now. He would give them until the sun dipped low. And then…

Someone appeared in the open doorway, and Simon tensed, prepared for anything. But the newcomer was only a man dressed in dirty garments, mud-splattered boots and a hat slung low over his forehead. Simon took quick note of the fellow's scraggly beard and knew a sharp stab of disappointment. Although he certainly had not expected Bethia to walk into a public alehouse, still he could not tamp down his impatience. He told himself that such a place was not fit for her, and yet where, exactly, she belonged was something Simon had not determined.

He kept his attention on the newcomer, hoping that the man might have a message for him, but the fellow kept his head bent. He moved with the stiffness of age and Simon would have dismissed him outright, except for his voice. When he called out for ale, the husky sound was vaguely familiar. Leaning against the wall in a deceptively casual pose, Simon studied the figure more carefully, his gaze dropping low to the man's backside. Was it his imagination, or did it sway slightly?

The stranger turned then, stepping closer, and the two travelers shied away as Simon, too, got a whiff of him. Fie, the old fellow smelled awful! And that unkempt beard, stringy and mangy, probably with the remains of his last meal, bobbed forward nearly into his cup. Grunting, Simon slid to the end of the bench as the man sat beside him.

"Good eve, sir knight," he said, and Simon stilled, his body tensing further, for something in that raspy voice struck him more fiercely than any blow. Warily he lifted his gaze to the stranger's, only to find himself staring into hazel eyes that looked an awful lot like a certain outlaw's. And, as if to confirm his suspicions, one eyelid dipped low, giving him a conspiratorial wink!

A startled growl broke from Simon's throat, causing the travelers to glance his way, and he bit back an oath. "What are you doing here?" he snarled, lowering his voice to avoid being overheard.

"Did you not send for me?" she whispered. Her response, so calmly uttered through the dirty beard, made his hands itch to throttle her.

"What are you doing here—dressed like that?" Simon asked through gritted teeth. She leaned closer, giving him a hefty dose of some pungent odor and had the audacity to grin at him, revealing that she had blackened one of her teeth. Was she enjoying this? Did the fool wench thrive on putting herself in danger? He wanted to put his hands on her and shake her until she came to her senses—if she had any.

"I couldn't very well come as I truly am, could I?"

she asked, just as though she were being quite reasonable.

But who was she, truly? The question jarred Simon from his fury. Here was a woman who was always surprising, interesting, baffling…and yet cloaked in disguise, a mistress of deception. It was the last part that did not sit well with him. Simon was not accustomed to trickery and lies and playing at being someone else. He liked things straightforward, enemies and allies alike easily determined.

Eyes narrowing, Simon turned away from her, unsure. Suddenly the small hut seemed too close, too dark, too stifling. He drew in a deep breath, but his lungs needed fresh air to think clearly—to decide the truth of the woman beside him.

"Well? What did you want?" she asked, her low voice a feast for his starved senses. *Want.* The simple word took on new meaning as Simon swiveled his head to look at her once more. Even costumed as she was, she had the ability to affect him, for he knew the slender form beneath the bulky clothes, the subtle scent that lay under the foul stench. In any guise, Bethia was exciting beyond anyone he had ever known, and Simon felt a flush crawl up his neck, a heat that only she could rouse in him, as he stared down at her thick-lashed eyes, golden dark and gleaming.

A noise from across the small room drew his attention, and he noticed the two packmen watching them with no little interest. He scowled until they bent their heads together, but even he realized how strange he must look, sitting far too close to what appeared to be a smelly old beggar man. He knew it was Bethia, yet even he found it disconcerting to be seated so cozily with someone dressed as a man. He slid a few inches away, doubly uncomfortable because of the feelings she stirred in him—feelings that had to do with *want*.

As if aware of his discomfort, his wretched companion only leaned closer, putting a grubby hand on his arm in a far too intimate gesture. The sensations she evoked by touching him, even in this noxious guise, made him hot and cold inside, and he scowled at her in warning. But she simply stared back, eyes wide, as if taken unawares herself.

"Here, now, none of that, gentlemen." The burly fellow who ran the alehouse banged a cup against the wall. "Take it outside, if you're so inclined."

Simon shot to his feet in an instant, hotly aware that the man thought he and his smelly companion were…involved in something illicit. For a moment, his fingers curled into a fist to answer the insult with a blow, but the knowledge of Bethia's identity stopped him. He could ill afford drawing any more attention to them, and while he hesitated, she was already moving toward the door.

Swallowing his denial, Simon swept the room with a fierce glare and followed her, his body relaxing slightly as they stepped from the close hut into the soft glow of twilight. He hated being confined in small spaces like the dingy alehouse, and he straightened, drawing several deep drafts of air to cleanse his lungs. The breaths steadied his taut nerves but did little to assuage his anger.

In fact, when he realized that the source of his fury was moving down the road at a goodly pace, despite affecting the stiffness of age, he grunted his displeasure. In the space of two long strides, he was reaching for her, intending to shake her soundly for giving such an impression, for perpetuating a lie, for making him so obsessed with her.

But she was quick. Easily evading his touch, she bent over to take up a stick. "Ah, there you are! Now, son," she rasped out. "Help me down the road a piece." Then, using the wood as a makeshift cane, she began hobbling down the side of the rutted way like an old man, leaving Simon standing dumbfounded in her wake.

It took him a good minute to collect himself, during which time his ragged companion had made surprising progress, but Simon caught up with her swiftly even as he reined in his temper. She was right to continue her pretense, of course, and to avoid any kind of confrontation, even here. Some of the villagers still lingered out of doors before settling in for the night, and the voices of men herding their stock back from grazing could be heard.

Gritting his teeth, Simon kept silent with an effort, for Bethia had made him look the fool again, and he was certain that she reveled in the accomplishment. Even worse than the scene in the alehouse, however, were the moments afterward when she had kept her head while he had not. Silently defending himself, he wondered what man could keep his head when goaded on by such a wretched wench?

None, Simon vowed as he walked stiffly alongside her. He refused to pretend to help her, and firmly ignored her ridiculous gait while moving past the clustered huts to the end of the village and beyond. There, in the murky evening of the countryside, far from prying eyes and listening ears, he would confront her at last, but what, exactly, he would do with her, Simon had yet to decide. Nor had he decided when her voice rang out, deep and distinct, in the quiet.

''Well, what is it?'' she asked, and Simon turned to face her, seized by a wealth of conflicted thoughts. Before meeting Bethia, everything had always been clear to him. He had grown up to be a warrior, like Dunstan, and that was the way he lived. When someone threatened his lands or his family, he fought for them. If there was injustice, he fought against it. It was all very simple.

Unlike Geoffrey, he had never believed in anything that he couldn't see. He could read, as could all the de Burghs, but he had never acquired a taste for it because to him the writing on the page was not real. Unless he could see it with his own eyes, he remained in doubt about what the writer professed. Nor was he one to be swayed by feelings, as were some of his siblings. As far as Simon could tell, he had no emotions, except for the respect he held for his family.

Hard facts were what he lived by, yet how could he apply that measure to this woman who stood before him in filthy men's clothing, a ragged beard clinging to her chin? Simon glanced away, suddenly unsure. ''Brice would not attend me, so I am no closer to the truth than before,'' he muttered.

''Ha! I knew it! The bastard!'' His ragged companion ran through a string of foul oaths that should have blackened the air, before pausing to stare up at him. ''But surely, you cannot believe him to be in the right when he flouts your summons!'' she said, as if suddenly realizing the significance of his words.

Simon didn't know what to think. What precious little information he had pointed to Bethia as the rightful heir of Ansquith, but he had no real facts. And how could he trust a fanciful female, especially one who dressed like the lowliest beggar man and smelled worse? Grunting, Simon whirled on her. "What the devil is that stink?" he snarled, taking his frustration out upon the source of it.

She grinned, revealing the blackened tooth, and as he glared at her, she reached up and yanked down the straggly beard. "Sheep dung mixed liberally with soured milk," she said, as if sharing some great secret with him. He had no idea what sort of animal hair the mangy beard was made of, but it was somehow attached to a string, and when she pulled it down, revealing the smooth, clean line of her stubborn chin, Simon flinched as if she had struck him through the heart with one of her well-aimed arrows.

Lifting a hand, he swiped at his chest while staring at the face that peeked up at him. Perhaps it was the conspiratorial whisper or the tilt of her head cloaked in the absurd guise, but in that single moment, all his waffling and struggling ended, for the truth no longer was a question. In that instance, he looked down at Bethia, and he knew that she was who she claimed, despite the lack of proof. Despite everything.

He believed her. He *believed,* and it shook him to the core, more fiercely than any blow. Geoffrey had once talked of religion as a leap of faith, and though his quandary had more to do with earthly concerns than those of the heavens, Simon felt himself taking it. With a giant jump, he accepted her story, her identity, and all that she was—everything about Bethia Burnel—deposed daughter, thief, trickster, warrior and woman.

"Now what shall we do?" she asked. She was oblivious to his epiphany, and Simon wanted to shake her with the strength of his newfound convictions. He wanted to take her in his arms and swing her around in celebration of his freedom from doubt. He wanted to tear off that hideous beard and kiss her mouth, defying dirt and stench. But other uncertainties kept him still, so he simply stood there, scowling at her.

"We think of some other way to get to him," he said finally, his voice harsh from the strain of his own inaction. Turning away from her, he stepped off the road into the long stretch of grass that disappeared into the chase. "There must be a way," he muttered.

A year ago—or even a week ago, he might have marched on Ansquith without a second thought, the life of one old man be damned. But now he hesitated. For the first time in his warrior's existence Simon realized that brute force might not win out, especially for Bethia. But what else was there?

When she said nothing, he glanced back, and saw her shoulders slump in defeat and felt her loss as if it were his own. In the long silence that followed he lifted his hands toward her shoulders, only to drop them, staring stupidly at her back, uncertain.

"No," she said. "I had thought that might was the answer, that if we could only sway enough people to our cause, that we could prevail, but I was not thinking…clearly. You have shown me that a battle would defeat our purpose, as would a siege."

"Aye," Simon answered thoughtfully. "A long siege lays waste to the countryside, starving the innocent. Those who already suffer under Brice's hand would feel it even more cruelly." But even as he dismissed such a plan, Simon began to consider other methods of attack. Above all, he was a warrior, and he was not about to admit defeat before he had even begun. As he studied the problem, he wished briefly for his brothers, especially Geoffrey, whose intelligence and negotiating skills might resolve the dispute without bloodshed.

Smiling grimly, Simon rejected such a course, for he could not wait to shed the blood of a certain Brice Scirvayne. Nay, the time for parlaying was past, thanks to Brice. Instead of Geoffrey, perhaps Dunstan would be of help. Although Simon once would rather have died rather than ask for his brother's aid, now he wondered if his elder sibling could contribute any ideas. After all, Burnel was his vassal.

But Simon had no patience with awaiting Dunstan. Instead, he considered all the devices he knew to gain entry to a fortified building, but most were far too slow and obvious to the defenders, and he swiftly rejected them. When Dunstan himself had been taken, they had entered Wessex through a secret passage to retake the castle. "Are there no hidden entrances to Ansquith?" Simon asked.

"No. None that I know of, and I would know all," Bethia answered. Watching her stoop low over the makeshift cane, Simon glanced quickly down the road, his eyes narrowing in the growing darkness. A single figure walked from the village into the woods, disappearing under the trees.

"A miner," Bethia said, straightening once more, and Simon dismissed the man from his mind, only to grin suddenly.

"A miner?" he echoed.

"Yes," Bethia answered, turning toward him with a curious look.

"And are there many miners who are sympathetic to your cause?"

"Yes, those who work the chase hate Brice, for he

has…'' Her words trailed off as she stared at him. ''You are smiling.'' She whispered the observation in such a strange tone that Simon felt his mouth go slack. He looked away hurriedly.

''Aye, I am smiling,'' he said, ''for I have thought of a way, just as I told you I would.'' He returned his gaze to her, enjoying the brief flash of hope in her eyes, quickly shuttered. ''We undermine the manor house.''

''Undermine?''

''Aye,'' he said, anticipation surging through him. ''We dig a tunnel under the curtain wall and into the bailey, where we emerge to retake the house before Brice can do aught. 'Tis a common enough practice when laying siege to a castle, though few could claim to have as skilled workers as your miners.''

''It could work,'' Bethia said cautiously. ''It could work!''

And then, before he had an inkling of her intention, she was launching herself at him, her arms closing around his neck as she hugged him close. The stench at first was overpowering, then it was her body he noticed, slender and firm as she pressed against him. Awkwardly he encircled her, holding her for a moment in an odd sort of communion that he had never known before.

When she pulled away from him, as if remembering herself, Simon felt bereft, as though something had been stolen from him. Drawing in a deep breath, he caught the smell that now clung to his own clothes and choked.

''If you get some of the miners together, we can begin tomorrow at the edge of the chase nearest Ansquith,'' he muttered. ''You say that Brice never leaves the gates, but does he send out soldiers to look for your band?'' Already Simon was focusing on the best location, which would be determined by both distance and the need for secrecy. When silence met his question, he hesitated, turning to see her open smile replaced by a cautious frown.

''I am sure you have other business that requires your attention,'' Bethia said, evading his gaze.

Aye, he had the business of Baddersly, but naught seemed more important now than this. Nor would he choose to pore over boring accounts or rule on the squabbling of villeins when a fight lay ahead. ''I have things I must do, yes, but this takes precedence,'' Simon answered.

''But I thought you didn't like mines,'' she said softly, suspicion coloring her voice in a way that made him furious.

''I don't, but I would see it done correctly, else you will lose your advantage,'' he said tightly. Although he held her capabilities in respect, Simon did not trust this operation to her motley band of archers. ''Where are you staying? I will go with you now.''

The usually unflappable outlaw looked positively flustered by his intention, and Simon realized that she still did not trust him. The knowledge disgusted him, for had he not taken a leap of faith to believe in her? He expected no less from her, and his mouth hardened into a grim line as she kept her distance. He was aware of the deepening dark and the nearby trees, and he put a hand to the hilt of his sword, lest her minions catch him unprepared.

''I would supervise this myself, wench, if not with your miners, then with men of my own choosing,'' he said through gritted teeth. He would take Ansquith for his brother and fie on the wretched female!

His threat obviously alarmed her, though she was swift to hide it, the deceitful creature. "Tomorrow," she said, backing away toward the forest. "Meet me in the glade."

Annoyance at this constant skulking and hiding made him reach for her, but she moved too swiftly, disappearing like a dream beneath the darkness of the trees. Startled by the abruptness of her departure, Simon grunted in disappointment at her defection. He would share no rabbit or berth with her tonight.

"Fie on you, then! You will get yourself killed!" he warned, for the chase held myriad dangers to threaten one lone female in men's clothing. For a moment, Simon considered going after her, but his pride protested loudly. Bah! What did he care what happened to her? he thought, turning back to the road. Annoying, feckless female! He should not be concerned about her or her lost heritage or the reckless risks she took parading about in disguise and wandering through the night woods.

Striding away determinedly, Simon vowed to ignore the pain in his chest, which had naught to do with his frustration. Undoubtedly, as Florian would confirm, it was caused by his poor eating habits. And not Bethia.

Chapter Nine

Frustrated and angry, Simon returned to Baddersly, though it was late and the gates were closed by the time he reached the castle. The guards knew better than to deny him entrance this time, but he could see their strange looks in the torchlights and guessed they thought him mad for riding out alone at night.

Let them think what they pleased, he vowed, his foul mood blackened further by the arrival of Florian, fussing over him as if he were a babe in swaddling the moment he entered the hall.

"My lord! Look at you! Soaked to the skin. I'll have a hot bath prepared at once." It had begun raining during the ride back to Baddersly, and Simon had nearly turned around several times, stricken with disquiet over Bethia. Was she all right? Had she found proper shelter? Of course, it was not his fault if she found herself drowning under a bush. Fie on the wench for not returning with him, or at least accepting his protection!

She did not trust him, and as much as Simon tried to shrug off the slight, it stung. He was a knight and a de Burgh, but above all things, he was honorable, and to have anyone impugn his good name was unthinkable. Yet Bethia continued to look at him with wariness, her golden eyes cold and shuttered as she kept the distance between them.

Simon shook off the unsettled feeling that clung to him while he waved Florian and his minions away.

"But, my lord, you missed supper!" the steward protested. "You must eat!"

As if the very mention of food drew him, Leofwin appeared, followed by several knights who were sharing ale near the fire. "Baddersly's cooks are among the finest, my lord. You have to taste the lamb! I know they put some by for you."

Simon eyed the portly knight askance, but before he could comment, Florian threw his hands into the air. "He won't eat. I fear he's suffering some malady."

"Perhaps he needs a purgative to rid himself of noxious humors," Quentin said. The knight had ambled over to study him curiously before taking a hearty swig from the cup he carried.

Simon glared at the older man. "I have no noxious humors!"

"Aye, perhaps hyssop or wormwood," Florian said, just as though Simon had not spoken.

"I have no worms!" Simon growled. "There is naught amiss with me."

Florian sighed loudly, as if *he* were beleaguered. "My lord, I have made some study of such things, and 'tis well-known that the six 'non-naturals' influence bodily well-being," he explained. "You are being ill affected by at least two of them—sleeping and waking, and food and drink. I understand that you have not suffered any unusual secretions and excretions, but what of the surrounding air? Take a good breath and tell me if it bothers you," he suggested.

Simon inhaled deeply, but it was to maintain control of his temper, not for the benefit of testing the air. The smells that assailed him were the usual scents of cooking and smoky fires and dogs that roamed the hall, and he grimaced, prepared to strangle the vexatious steward.

"Nay?" asked Florian, oblivious to his growing fury. "Then mayhap it is motion and rest. It could well be that you are too much in the saddle, out riding about day and night by yourself! You should sit more, my lord," he said. Hurrying to the nearest bench, he dragged a corner forward and motioned for Simon to take a seat.

When Simon remained standing while glowering ominously at the steward, Florian put a finger to his chin in a pensive pose. "There is the other, of course," he said. Then he walked slowly around Simon's taut figure as if in deep study, while several knights gathered around to watch the proceedings with interest.

Even though he had little faith in the steward's medical knowledge, Simon found himself awaiting this final verdict, but Florian made no further comment. "Well?" Simon finally roared. "What is the other?"

"What?" Florian asked as if roused from his thoughts. When Simon glared at him, he recovered himself quickly. "Ah, the remaining non-natural? Why, that, my lord," he said, smiling slyly, "has to do with the passions of the soul."

For a moment Simon could have sworn he saw knowledge and amusement flicker in Florian's steady gaze, and his eyes narrowed. Was the steward amusing himself? An innocent expression met Simon's fierce stare, and with a grunt of annoyance, he swept away from them all.

Passions? The only thing troubling him was a castle full of pestering, gossiping fools! Striding swiftly toward the great chamber, he considered tossing the worst of the lot, that irritating steward, out on his ear.

Passions! Simon felt his neck heat as he imagined how his brothers would laugh, for it was well-known that he had none, save his devotion to warfare. And if Florian thought that was what ailed him, the steward was the one who needed help.

Watching from her perch in a tall oak, Bethia didn't know whether to hope that Simon de Burgh would appear or not this morning. Some small, uncontrollable part of her wished that his suggestion was all a hoax or a trap even though it represented the best chance she had of saving her father. It wasn't logical, that wild wish, but it sprang from some deep-seated sense of self-protection.

Simon de Burgh was a danger to her even if he was telling the truth, and Bethia knew it on a level stronger than logic. Instinct had pulsed a warning insistently since the night before when she had hugged him. A foolish reaction born of hope, the embrace had been a mistake, for it had made her aware, more than ever, of his maleness, his power and his appeal.

No man had ever tempted her before, but now Bethia found herself wondering how it would feel to touch him in more than innocent happiness. With intent. She sucked in a sharp breath. Would the coiled intensity within him unleash with frightening speed or would he temper his strength with his usual control?

As if in concert with her thoughts, the subject of her musings appeared on the other side of the clearing, and Bethia released the air she had been holding in a silent rush. Simon moved with great stealth, but she knew that if he had brought others with him, her own men would have alerted her. He was alone, and Bethia took the opportunity to study him.

What a fine form! Tall and wide shouldered and rock hard with muscle, he was the measure of any man. He wore no helm, and his dark hair fell to his shoulders, glossy as ebony and nearly as black. His face was lean and grim, and yet Bethia had seen no evidence of cruelty.

If only she could be certain of his motives. Even now Bethia wondered, with the practice of long habit, if he planned to herd them all into his tunnel to trap them. Deceit was too much a part of her life for her to disregard the possibility. Indeed, Firmin had been against allowing him access to the area at all. He wanted to start another passage unseen by Simon. Only Bethia's argument that if he truly wanted to capture them, he could have done so already, kept them from wasted efforts.

To her men, she tentatively offered Simon up as an ally, but Bethia fully intended to keep her wits about her—in more ways then one. Drawing in a shaky breath, she realized that her fascination with the hard knight was one she would have to ignore. Simon de Burgh was not for her. Nor was any man. She had made that decision long ago, and her current situation only made it more crucial.

With silent resolve, Bethia swore that she would take Simon de Burgh's strong arm and battle advice and fight alongside him, if need be, but that was all she could ever do. Untroubled by her choice, she nonetheless lingered for one more look at the only man who had ever intrigued her.

* * *

Simon eyed the empty clearing and wondered if Bethia would leave him dangling here alone for her amusement. But something, his warrior's awareness or the scent of her caught on a breeze, told him that she was nearby. His taut stance relaxed slightly at the knowledge that she had made it through the night, unharmed, despite his absence.

He frowned, uncertain whether to be pleased or chagrined. Although he admired her skills, Simon would have preferred protecting her himself. Perhaps today he could convince her to return with him, he thought, scowling deeply. If not, he was determined to stay. This undermining operation was his, and he had no intention of handing it over to a bunch of archers and oafs.

Besides, he had taken his fill of questioning glances from Florian and the rest of the rabble at Baddersly. He had managed to evade the intrusive steward this morning by slipping out before dawn, but the attention was grating on him. The promise of a castle of his own now seemed burdensome and confining instead of the rich reward that he deserved.

But what would he seek instead? Simon grunted in dismay as a vision of Bethia Burnel appeared in his mind before Ansquith. Bah, he had no use for a woman! And the fortified manor house, though prosperous, fell far short of his previous expectations. He paused, taking in the pleasant appeal of his surroundings. Still, the chase was a nice piece of land, rich in wood and iron and...

An amusing thought, but he was here to save this demesne for Sir Burnel, not himself. And undoubtedly, he would quickly grow tired of one place, even if the maddening Bethia were there to entertain him. Without pausing to pursue that line of thought, Simon grunted low in denial. Nay, such a quiet life was not for him. He accepted the truth even though it sat uncomfortably upon him.

Simon lifted a hand to the mail that covered his chest only to drop it swiftly. Although he had no intention of staying in the area for long, he wouldn't mind slipping into the forest for a fortnight or so. He could rout Brice Scirvayne after enjoying a peaceful interlude without the harrying of his brothers or the annoying attentions of those at Baddersly.

Simon smiled grimly, for surely none here would question his business. His habits could hardly be of concern to the archers and miners who frequented these woods, and well pleased with that knowledge, he stepped into the clearing. Unfortunately, he was proved wrong all too quickly.

When Bethia's men eyed him with varying degrees of hostility, Simon welcomed it as preferable to the kind of close association that allowed others to discuss his health at will. He simply ignored the brooding looks and headed toward the edge of the chase to find a likely site for the tunnel. After conferring with one of the less taciturn miners, he settled on an old smelting site inside the concealing woods that rose behind Ansquith. Brice's men avoided the chase and its outlaws as much as possible, and the area they chose was well away from the road. It would require a lot of digging to tunnel beneath the grass slope that led to the manor, but the men set in at once without complaint.

His satisfaction at that good beginning did not last long, for immediately Bethia was at his elbow, questioning him. "What do you think you are doing?" she asked, folding her arms across her chest in a combative stance.

She was dressed as a male again, but this costume was such an improvement over the smelly, bearded one of the day before that Simon eyed her with something akin to pleasure. A shaft of sunlight through the trees glinted upon her wheat-colored hair in its long braid, and Simon's attention was caught so well that he found it difficult to concentrate on her words. What was he doing? "I am directing the undermining," he answered, his gaze lingering on a stray strand of pale gold.

Forcibly she dragged his attention back to her speech when she yanked on his sleeve, pulling him away toward the shelter of a thick oak. "And what makes you think that you can just march in here and take over?" she asked, crossing her arms once more. The motion made her breasts beneath the heavy tunic more prominent, and he was hard-pressed to focus on anything else.

"Because it was my idea, and I'm the only one with experience in siege warfare?" he muttered, jerking his gaze upward to her angry scowl.

She did not back down but glared at him fiercely. "Yes, but I am in command of these men, and you cannot expect me to maintain my position when you circumvent my authority."

Her *authority?* Simon stifled a laugh. "I am accustomed to being in charge," he said, trying, with difficulty, to keep his expression blank.

"Perhaps elsewhere, but need I remind you that here you were once tied hand and foot by my orders?" she asked coolly.

Simon cursed the flush that rose in his neck. "And

this is my operation, wench, or would you have me bring in my own men to do this work?''

She gasped softly. ''You wouldn't dare!'' she protested, facing off against him without hesitation.

''I have jurisdiction over this dispute,'' he answered.

''And how did you determine that, when it is my home we are talking about?'' she snapped.

'''Tis a matter for the lord of Baddersly.''

'''Tis my father in there, you lout!'' she said, pointing furiously toward the manor house.

''And I am going to get him out,'' Simon said, his face unyielding. He would not dance attendance on any female, even one whose abilities he respected. Whether she cooperated or not, he would bring down Brice and return Ansquith to its rightful owners.

With a low huff of exasperation, she ducked her head and pressed her hands against her legs, drawing Simon's attention there against his will. Muscles. He thought of those he had discovered and those he had not, and imagining hard thighs encased in smooth skin, he flushed again and glanced away.

''Very well,'' she said. ''I will accede you control of the undermining, but I must insist that you do not bring your own people into this!''

Simon frowned. ''And what of countermining?'' he asked, with no little impatience. ''What if Brice sets his men to digging into our tunnel and engaging ours in combat? These fellows are miners, not fighters, by trade, and I do not want them battling underground.''

''And why should they? If you do not bring your men here, how will Brice ever discover our plan?'' Bethia countered. ''So far all he knows is that you have summoned him to Baddersly. He has no idea that I still live, does he?'' She eyed him with suspicion that galled Simon.

"How would I know? You are the expert on the man, your former betrothed.'' He spat out the words with a bitterness that startled them both, and they stood at odds for a long silence before Simon acknowledged the truth of her words.

Since Ansquith was not under siege, Brice would hardly be expecting an attack of any kind. And only someone well versed in such techniques would guess that water quivering in a jug upon the manor grounds meant there was digging below. Later, when they were ready to break through, Simon would bring in a hand-picked group of soldiers. In the meantime, Bethia was probably right. The fewer who knew of the tunnel, the better their chance of maintaining secrecy.

"All right,'' he said, giving her a gruff nod. "For now we will use your workers, but when the time comes, I will lead my own skilled swordsmen into the bailey, not miners.''

Looking decidedly displeased, despite his capitulation, Bethia lifted her chin. "And I will lead my archers,'' she said, visibly squaring her shoulders.

Simon scowled. He did not like the idea of Bethia being involved in any battle, but there was time enough to persuade the obstinate wench otherwise. He smiled. "First your miners must open a passage for us.''

She gave him a chary look, as if noting his lack of agreement, and nodded. "So we are in accord?''

"As well can be,'' Simon answered, though he was not usually one to prevaricate.

With a quick nod, Bethia stepped away, and Simon felt a pang of regret that their heated argument had ended so swiftly. "Excuse me then, for I have matters to attend to," she said, her expression cool once more. For a moment, he longed to shout at her, just to catch a glimpse of the passion banked behind that controlled demeanor.

Instead Simon watched her go, wondering, if she did, indeed, have tasks elsewhere or if she was simply fleeing his presence. Then he grunted in annoyance at his own thoughts, for there was no reason she should avoid him. No reason at all, he told himself, even as his gaze lingered on the slight sway of her hips and the long stride of her legs as she disappeared among the trees.

He turned only to find himself facing a much more unpleasant sight, for a grizzled fellow with a short, graying beard was standing directly in his path. Despite his age, the man had hefted a heavy shovel over his shoulder, though he did not seem intent upon digging. "A word, if you please, my lord," he said.

Although he would much rather have followed Bethia, Simon inclined his head slowly even as the fellow heaved the shovel to the ground. "Grateful we are for your help, if that's what it is, my lord," the man said, leaning on the tool. "But, along with my thanks, I would tender a warning to you."

Simon's eyes narrowed as he tensed for a possible assault, but no one else approached the secluded spot under the oak. "No, I'm not seeking to fight with you, my lord," the man hastened to add. "But I'm advising you to watch your step with Bethia. Her father may not be here, but she has plenty of friends—and champions."

Simon wanted to ask just where all these brave fellows were when Bethia was traipsing around the village in a false beard and old braies, but he kept his reservations about her recklessness to himself. "Are you threatening me?'' he asked the fellow with no little astonishment.

The man loosed a brittle cackle of laughter. ''Nay, my lord, but I've seen the way you watch her. Just keep your mind on your business, that's all, and leave Bethia to hers.''

Outraged, Simon lifted a fist, but the fellow was already turning and walking away. Instead of striking the impudent oaf, he slammed the hand hard against his palm in mute fury. So much for his hope of escaping from meddlers! He seemed destined to be plagued with them, and he was more than weary of the intrusion.

''Go on, old man,'' he muttered. ''But as for Bethia, she *is* my business.''

Simon was still thinking the same by evening when some of the workers gathered together for a small supper. He had spent most of the day digging and whether due to the physical labor or the presence of Bethia watching him warily, Simon found that his appetite had returned full measure.

An older woman, hunched over a pot, passed out loaves of bread and ladled some sort of stew into the broken halves. Unlike the food that reached the great hall from the separate kitchens at Baddersly, it was steaming hot, and Simon inhaled the tangy scent of lamb. He ate three portions, followed by sweet pears, while Bethia, perched as far away from him as possible, on a low stump, picked unenthusiastically at her food.

''You should eat more. Your cook does well,'' he said, and she jerked her head, as if startled to see him.

''I am not hungry,'' she said, handing the remains of her meal over to one of the archers who sat nearby. For some reason, her lack of appetite amused him until he considered that she might be suffering the same malady that had stricken him—or so Florian might suggest. He frowned, uncertain, but she was already rising to her feet and turning away, so he followed, aware of the grim glances of her men as they walked from the clearing.

"I did not expect you to join us for supper," she said, crossing her arms over her chest in a gesture with which he was rapidly becoming familiar.

His mouth grew dry as he forced his attention back to her face.

"It is growing late," she said. "Do you need a guide to lead you back to the road?"

Simon stared at her. "I know my way well enough, but I'll not be traveling this night."

Her eyes widened, as if in alarm, and he knew a swift annoyance. Why couldn't she trust him? He wanted to take her and shake her and...

"But shouldn't you return to Baddersly? Won't your absence raise suspicions?"

"Of what?" Simon asked with a low grunt of disgust. It seemed to him that any suspicions were to be found here in a pair of golden eyes. He cared not what those back at the castle thought, for his business was no concern of theirs. Besides, he had no intention of riding back and forth to Baddersly each day, wasting most of his time in travel. Eyes narrowing, he studied Bethia with annoyance, for no doubt that was her hope.

Swearing harshly, he reached for her, gripping her shoulders in a sudden fierce grasp that startled her. All that he meant to say to her stuck in his throat as he stared down at her. Her form beneath the thick tunic heated his fingers, and his heart raced unaccountably at the warmth. "You must trust me," he muttered.

"It's difficult," she whispered back, and the curve of her lips seemed oddly enticing. Silence settled around them as they stared at each other in mute acknowledgment that something was growing between them in the gathering dusk.

"Bethia!" The charged quiet was broken by the sound of someone calling her name, and Simon bit back a curse as she broke away from him, whirling toward the speaker. It was that archer Firmin, the one who did not obey orders well, and Simon's hand shifted to the hilt of his weapon as he met the open hostility in the man's gaze.

"We are making camp for the night," Firmin said, pointedly ignoring Simon. "I have made you a place in the shelter of the mine."

"Thank you," Bethia said in a low, breathy voice. "Find something for Simon to bed down upon, will you?"

"We have no extra blankets," Firmin claimed, his dark eyes shifting toward Simon with surprising hatred.

Simon met his stare steadily, holding the black gaze until the shorter man looked away. "I need nothing," Simon said, but as he turned to watch Bethia walk from his side, he wondered at the truth of his own words.

While the miners labored during the weeks that followed, Simon joined Bethia in her watches on the forest road and sometimes in raids upon Brice's shipments, striking out against his men and the wealth he would covet for himself. Although Simon often stopped at Baddersly, he refused to stay, for he did not care to be long away from Bethia.

She was like no woman he had ever known, with a boundless strength of spirit and a powerful body, too.

Of course, she was no match for him, but she could hold her own against some of the smaller members of her band. She did not have a female's craven ways and did not weep and wail when presented with difficulties. With the cool intelligence of a man, she planned and plotted to achieve her goals, though she sometimes evidenced a recklessness that Simon frowned upon.

She used not her woman's wiles, flirting and flaunting herself, but kept her distance in a way that both reassured Simon and discouraged him. Her commands were clear and forthright, unmuddled by a woman's incessant prattling. Indeed, she spoke little and in that, as in nearly all ways, she was very much like a man— in a woman's body.

And Simon had been noticing that body more and more, his eyes following her, whether he will it or no, his own ironclad control betraying him at odd moments. The thought of her muscles made his mouth go dry and his body harden. If so sorely tested at any other time, he would have found a woman to allay his needs, paying her good coin to find quick release in her body.

But such a course no longer held appeal to him. Indeed, the idea seemed an affront to Bethia, as if her unique presence would be tainted by association. Even his past encounters, though nothing but straightforward business transactions, had taken on a stigma, and memories of those anonymous females left a sour taste in his mouth.

It was Bethia he wanted and yet Simon had to deny himself. Despite her outlaw existence, she was not one who took money for her favors. By all appearances, she was a decent woman whose displacement put her under the protection of Baddersly and its lords. More than that, she was the only female Simon had ever admired, and as such, ought not to be the object of his lustful urges. And so he took to a stream that ran through the chase, bathing in its chilly waters whenever he was plagued by untoward cravings, for what else could he do to assuage his aching body?

Unfortunately, despite his best efforts, Simon's escalating interest in Bethia came to a head when the two of them came upon a shipment of supplies meant for Ansquith. Quickly cutting off the route, they had taken precious spices and bolts of cloth from London, leaving several of Brice's men standing the road shaking their fists.

It had been a daring maneuver for just the two of them, but they had made a small strike against the enemy, and it was a heady feeling. Even headier for Simon was the sight of Bethia, flush faced and excited from her labors as they dragged their booty through the chase.

When they stopped to catch their breath under the safety of the greenwood, she was so close to him that a toss of her head snapped her braid against his chest. Staring at the long plait, Simon was seized by an urge to wrap the long hair around his fist and reel her in like a prized catch, to take her in ways he had never taken a woman before.

Unable to help himself, he reached out, his fingers closing around the smooth thickness, and he twirled it around his knuckle, a low hiss of satisfaction escaping from his throat. Lifting his gaze to her face, Simon saw her wide eyes, her flushed cheeks, and he pulled her toward him. She had the strength to stop him, and he would have honored her resistance, but she did not protest. And though she had a chance to tell him nay, her lips only parted as if in invitation.

So Simon took them with his own. He was not much for kissing, his experiences with women limited to the most basic of joinings, but Bethia was different. Her mouth was so lush and so supple and so much a part of her that he felt a roar of blood in his ears. It rushed through him so violently that Simon wondered if he could stay on his feet, but she slid her arms around his neck and her body pressing against his anchored him there.

With a low grunt of pleasure, Simon opened his mouth over hers, seeking, tasting, claiming her as his own, and she met his tongue boldly, joining him in hot exploration. He kissed her until they were both panting for breath, until his heart threatened to burst and his body screamed for release. Until he had to have more of her or die in the effort.

It was like the excitement of battle, only far better, for the war involved only the two of them, and it seemed that in this, at least, they were in agreement. But when Simon slid his hand down her back to cup her buttocks and bring her hard against his aching groin, she broke away, pulling her arms from his neck and her body from his grasp.

Caught in the throes of passion such as he had never known, Simon was slow to understand his loss. Bethia stood before him, her chest heaving, her lips swollen and moist and her eyes wide with unspent desire. Why, then, were they apart? Lifting a hand, he reached for her again, but laying her palms against his chest, she pushed him away and stepped back.

''No,'' she whispered, her soft voice shaky but resolute. ''That can never be between us.''

Before Simon could protest, she turned and disappeared into the forest, finding her own secret path and leaving him gritting his teeth in frustration, the heat of angry chagrin rising to stain his throat.

Chapter Ten

Although loath to admit it, Bethia was still shaken a full day after Simon had kissed her. Despite her best efforts to put the incident aside, when she least expected it a shocking heat would rush through her at the memory. Even now as she stuffed a tick with fresh straw, Bethia noticed her hands were trembling. With an angry sound, she stepped back, staring down at her betraying fingers in disgust.

He was affecting her still, but she could not allow it. If she weakened all would be lost, and she had fought too hard and too long to give up everything for the dubious delights of the flesh. She was stronger than that, Bethia told herself, and she had only to maintain that strength until the undermine was complete. Then she would vanquish Brice, liberate her father and enjoy her own freedom, without the constraints imposed by any man—including Simon de Burgh.

Releasing a low hiss of breath, Bethia placed her palms on her thighs, willing them to stillness. When, after a long moment, she lifted her hands to find them steady once more, she returned to her task with renewed vigor, certain that it would aid in her resolve.

She had decided, after yesterday's lapse, that raiding, eating and sleeping with Simon de Burgh, even if they usually were surrounded by others, was no longer feasible. And so she had taken over this abandoned miner's hut, adding thatch to the sunken roof and airing it out in the hopes that having her own place away from the temptation of Simon's tall, hard body would do much to return her to her purpose.

The privacy would be welcome, too, for the past few days in the company of her men had been strained. Although some accepted Simon, others did not. And a few, like Firmin, did not bother to disguise their disapproval. They closed ranks around her, as if to keep out the enemy, stifling her and raising barriers she had thought long broken down.

Thanks to Simon, her sex was an issue once more, eroding the respect that kept her in command. *You must trust me,* he had said. Ha! Bethia pushed down the straw with more force than necessary, assured that she could trust him to behave as any randy male and try to seduce her. The others dared not, fearing her fighting skills. Not Simon. He was afraid of nothing, including her, for he had proved he could overpower her. The thought made Bethia shudder with both abhorrence and excitement, and she sank down onto the lumpy tick in dismay.

She had to stop letting her mind wander to such things! Bethia had no delusions about what lords like Simon de Burgh wanted from women, and she had no intention of ending up as someone's leman—an object of derision, nameless and powerless. Independence and the wealth to keep it were all that mattered in this world, not the fleeting pleasure of a moment's passion!

The sound of footsteps outside wrenched Bethia

from her thoughts, and she swiftly rose to her feet. She was reaching for her bow when she heard her name called with a wary urgency. Moving cautiously to the open door, Bethia stopped on the threshold only to halt abruptly, stricken numb at the sight of Simon de Burgh slumped between two of her men.

With a low sound of distress, Bethia stared at the great knight's prone body, unable to believe that he had been struck down. The anger she had but recently been feeling toward him was swept away in a rush of other, indefinable emotions. What if he was dead? Or dying? The thought forced her to action.

"What happened? Where is he hurt?" she asked, her voice raw as she moved forward.

"Aw, naught but a bump on the head, I think," said Will, a large freeman who was aiding the miners. "He got hit by a shovel."

"A shovel?" Bethia asked in astonishment.

"He shouldn't have been standing so close to Firmin," the other fellow said with a negligent shrug.

Hot rage coursed through Bethia, steadying her frayed nerves as she stared long and hard at the two men. She suspected that Simon's injury was no accident, and if so, his retribution would be swift and sure. Indeed, one man's foolish, spiteful act might have endangered them all. Under the force of her stare, the two before her had the good grace to look away, and Bethia stepped back to allow them to pass. Other questions would have to wait. "Put him inside on the mattress, and help me remove his sword and mail," she said curtly.

"But I thought this was to be your place," Will protested.

"It is," Bethia said, meeting his gaze until he dropped it, a flush staining his already ruddy cheeks.

"He'll come around," the other man said, dropping Simon's heavy form onto the makeshift bed with a grunt.

"He had better," Bethia said, her temper in tight check as they stripped Simon of his knightly trappings. "For should the lord of Baddersly, brother to the Wolf of Wessex and son to the Earl of Campion, die here, you will find Brice Scirvayne to be the very least of our worries."

Paling visibly, Will nodded, while his companion turned and fled, probably to report to Firmin, as well he should, the cost of such thoughtlessness. Not for the first time, Bethia regretted that no one except herself seemed able to see ahead to the consequences of their actions.

With a shake of her head, she turned her attention to Simon and felt anew the shock of seeing the invincible warrior laid low. Although he had once been bound hand and foot by her order, even then his indomitable spirit was in evidence. Indeed, he had been like a chained animal, coiled and ready to strike at the earliest opportunity.

Not now. Now his powerful body lay still, his eyes closed, his dark hair tumbling about his face in an unruly fashion that made her draw in a harsh breath. With infinite care, Bethia laid a hand upon his chest and exhaled in relief to feel the steady beat of his heart. She hesitated then, noting the trembling of her hand before dismissing it. She would have to touch him; there was no other way to determine the extent of his injuries.

The knowledge freed her, and she lifted her fingers to his head. His hair was smoother than the finest of fabrics, rich and shiny, and Bethia shuddered in reaction. Drawing a deep, sustaining breath, she leaned closer, feeling gently for a wound. When her fingers brushed against a lump, Simon groaned, and she leaned back to look at his face.

''Simon, can you hear me? Were you hurt anywhere else?'' When he did nothing but groan again, Bethia's efforts to remain calm faltered in the face of his distress. Worriedly she ran her hands along his wide shoulders and down his arms, then pushed up his tunic.

His chest was wide and hard and topped by a patch of dark hair narrowing to a thin line that disappeared into his braies. Bethia skimmed the smooth flesh but could find no fresh marks, only a few old scars. Giving in to her fears, Bethia laid her cheek over his heart to reassure herself that it still beat only to discover that it thundered faster and louder than before under skin that seemed to be growing hotter. Had he a fever?

Lifting her head, Bethia tried to stem her panic, but it surged through her, making her hurry as she ran her hands down one of his muscular legs and up the other, searching for additional wounds. When Simon groaned and shifted slightly, she halted abruptly, looking vainly for the source of his pain.

''Where does it hurt?'' she asked, though she did not expect an answer. Her gaze roved over his splendid body frantically, only to pause upon the front of his braies, where a large lump seemed to have appeared most suddenly. Bethia's suspicion that her patient suffered no broken bone or loss of blood grew apace with the rise in the fabric, and frowning angrily, she looked at his face only to find him watching her with a particularly avid expression.

"Luckily, your hard head is the only part of you that was hurt," she said, glaring at him.

"But I'm in pain elsewhere," he said in a low voice that would have made her shudder if she were not so angry with him.

"Yes, Simon, you poor thing. I can see how swollen you are," Bethia said, half tempted to smash her fist into the area in question.

To her extreme annoyance, he let out a rasping laugh. Or was it a groan? "I know how you can relieve that," he suggested.

"And how is that?" Bethia asked, though she was fairly certain of the answer.

"Kiss me there, Bethia, and I guarantee you my ache will ease…eventually."

With a gasp that was part outrage and part amusement at the normally taciturn knight's audacity, Bethia tried to ignore the vision that leaped into her mind— of her leaning over, stripping him of his braies and touching him in ways she had never imagined possible. To do whatever she would to his splendid body. It had lured her from the beginning with its hard muscles and lean strength, but even more tempting now was the man who went with that fine form.

Over the past few weeks, Bethia had come to know and respect Simon de Burgh. Despite his arrogance and sometimes galling stubbornness, she admired his straightforward manner. A skilled fighter, he possessed a rare intelligence that made him all the more formidable, yet he was a true knight who fought for justice without seeking his own gain. He had not only joined her against her enemy, but had chosen wisely his method of attack, biding his time though it went against every urge of his warrior's nature.

You must trust me. Drawing in a sharp breath of startled awareness, Bethia realized that she did—that sometime over the long days and nights, she had begun to believe in Simon de Burgh and all that he stood for. The discovery was daunting and she rose to her feet hurriedly, as if to escape it.

Glancing down at him, Bethia felt her feelings expand and sharpen in a frightening manner, although Simon said and did nothing to encourage her. He lay there as she had left him, his tunic bunched up to reveal his beautiful chest, his expression cloaked as he watched her under half-closed lashes, and she knew a deep, intense desire to lie down with him.

A low sound of something like despair escaped her, for she suspected that inside that hard exterior was a man of great strength and goodness and passion. Unfortunately, she was not the kind of woman to give herself to any man. She would not relinquish her independence and risk pregnancy for a taste of pleasure, not matter how tempting.

Although it took nearly all of her will, Bethia forced herself to turn her back on Simon and all that he offered her. "I'm not some servant girl eager for a quick toss," she snapped, stalking from the hut without another glance.

Simon fell back against his odd bed and groaned. He wanted to get up and go after Bethia, but he still felt slow and dizzy. And what would he say? He had no idea what had possessed him to tease her in that fashion, while her response was certainly not what he had intended. What *had* he intended? Simon was too befuddled to answer.

Perhaps it was the head wound that made him say

things he had never said to any woman, *want* things he had never wanted from any woman. Grunting in frustration, Simon pushed himself up on his elbows only to groan again as his head throbbed. For a while, the aching of his groin had distracted him, but now there was no mistaking his injury. He lifted a hand to his skull, where he found a hard knot, along with a little blood.

Simon had suffered worse, and so he gritted his teeth and rose to his feet. The room spun, but he put out a hand to balance himself against the wall until the wretched place righted itself. He felt bad. Not the kind of feeling that came with a great loss of blood or a dangerous blow, but some new sensation that settled inside him like air that had gone foul. He rubbed his chest as if searching for a wound, but finding none, he pulled down his tunic and moved to the doorway. Bethia was nowhere to be seen, and a now-familiar flush climbed Simon's throat at the realization that she had left him.

He had been rejected.

It was a new experience, because he had never offered himself to anyone before. Unlike some of his brothers, Simon never had flirted, never had wooed a female, and now he felt the loss inexplicably. He did not know what to do about these strange feelings that raged in him. Perhaps the bump on his head was making him think and act in this bizarre manner.

Or mayhap Florian was right, and some illness was plaguing him that would only be exacerbated by this new injury. The idea was alarming enough to send him out of the hut and into the woods. If he really was ailing, he ought to see a healer. Even the steward's inane advice appealed to Simon in his current state—

when he could not explain the hurt that filled him, a hurt that had nothing to do with his head.

Baddersly suddenly seemed like a haven where he could recoup his strength before returning to check the progress of the undermining. Ignoring the abrupt vision of a dog trailing home with his tail between his legs, Simon straightened and began walking toward the village to retrieve his waiting mount. From there he could ride on to Baddersly, he decided, never suspecting the disquiet his absence from the castle had caused.

"But it's been more than a week!" Florian protested as he faced the three knights who had agreed to meet with him in the empty solar.

"Lord de Burgh has not been gone that long, surely, a few days at most," Quentin said in his most irritating elder knight voice.

Florian pursed his lips. "Before it was a few days. This time he has been missing for a week. I cannot help being concerned—especially considering his poor health."

"And with outlaws about. I, for one, fear that he may have been waylaid again," Thorkill said. Bristling with youthful energy, he obviously was eager to do battle on behalf of the missing Simon de Burgh.

"But we can hardly go out searching for him," Leofwin argued before biting into a small round of cheese he had brought with him.

The rotund knight was always leaving scraps behind, causing a couple of dogs to trail after him wherever he went, and in order to hold the meeting, Florian had been forced to close the door against the mongrels. He threw up his hands in disgust at both the man's habits and his words. "Nor can we turn a blind eye to his disappearance. What will the Wolf say? I shudder to think of his displeasure should we lose his brother!''

Although Florian had never met Dunstan de Burgh, he knew that the three knights had, and he hoped the threat of the Wolf would force them to action. But beyond exchanging wary glances, they did not rouse themselves as Florian had anticipated. ''Perhaps you should send a message to the Wolf, awaiting his command,'' Leofwin mumbled.

Quentin cleared his throat, as if in disagreement, just as they were finally getting somewhere, and Florian muffled an impatient sigh. Leave it to the old man to find a reason to do absolutely nothing! While Florian shifted in annoyance, the knight fixed him with an apologetic frown.

''Actually, I did hear something of Lord Simon's whereabouts after he left the first time,'' Quentin said.

''And why have you said nothing?'' Florian demanded, outraged to be left in the dark.

Quentin cleared his throat awkwardly. ''I did not feel it was my place to say,'' he muttered. ''But he was seen at the alehouse in the village, being quite, uh, friendly with an older man.''

Florian, whose proclivities were known, gasped at the suggestion in Quentin's tone. ''Simon de Burgh is *not* of that persuasion, I can assure you,'' he said with a sniff. Pausing to contemplate a vision of that magnificent knight, he sighed.

Thorkill frowned in disapproval. ''Just who was this older man? And why were they meeting at the alehouse?''

''No one knows, or at least they would not tell me,'' Quentin said.

''Most mysterious,'' Leofwin mumbled.

"Stop spitting cheese!" Florian scolded, although he was more irritated by Thorkill's attitude than Leofwin's manners.

"What of his illness? Perhaps he has been stricken with something and was seeking a healer," Thorkill suggested.

"In an alehouse?" Florian asked, with enough acerbity to make Quentin laugh.

Thorkill flushed. "Perhaps he was searching out information or directions to some local wisewoman."

"Or mayhap he was simply getting a drink!" Leofwin suggested between bites.

"No," Florian said. He was certain that Simon de Burgh was not the type of man to frequent such a place without good reason. He paused to put a finger to his chin. "I wish we could find out what happened when he was waylaid in the woods. I have a feeling it is somehow related to these odd trips of his."

"None of his men are talking about the night they spent in the chase," Quentin said, shaking his head, and Florian frowned. He, too, had been unable to discover the details of that mishap, and it was most annoying. And now this business at the alehouse…

At least Florian was sure that Quentin was mistaken, for he knew full well that Simon's interest lay in women. In fact, he would wager that a certain dead woman who might not be dead was the cause of all these mysterious comings and goings. But where did her former betrothed, Brice Scirvayne, fit in? And the chase outlaws? Like chess pieces upon a board, Florian could see all of them, but he could not guess their placement or their exact relationship to the lord of Baddersly. Something was missing.

"We'll just have to ferret out the story, won't we?"

Florian said with renewed determination. "If only we could talk to one of the outlaws."

Quentin snorted at that, and Florian bristled. And they called themselves knights! They should be out protecting their lord instead of dithering like a bunch of old women! "If not, then perhaps you should venture into the village. Someone there must know more than he's telling."

"Very well," Quentin muttered. "But do not send for the Wolf as yet. Dunstan de Burgh would not take kindly to a goose chase."

Would a search for Simon be foolish? Florian was not sure. He did not like the idea of the visiting lord slipping off without a word, and he worried. It was part of his job of keeping Baddersly running smoothly. And something about Simon de Burgh fairly cried out for someone's concern. The man was simply not happy, and yet he deserved to be. Florian smiled slowly. If there were any way he could arrange it, he would see the great knight content.

And Florian had a suspicion that such a state could be arranged—by whoever was causing his loss of sleep and appetite.

Bethia stayed away all day, spelling the guards at their posts, hunting small game and trying to keep her mind from Simon de Burgh's hard body and playful remarks. If only both did not appeal to her so! His words might have offended another woman, but they had ignited something inside her that was hard to extinguish.

Since leaving her father's home for that of her great-aunt, Bethia had lived a near sexless existence as little better than a servant. Although a few visitors would have liked Bethia to serve them in other ways, Gunilda had kept her well away from the men, unwilling to lose her attendant.

Upon Bethia's return home, she had been thrust at Brice, whose handsome appearance was all too easily eclipsed by his loathsome nature. But even before she discovered his true character, Bethia had felt nothing. Nor had any of the freemen and villeins who joined her band affected her in any way. It was only when she first looked upon Simon de Burgh that fires long banked stirred to life once more.

Why? Why should one person have such an ability to alter her perceptions, her desires, her very self? And why did that one man have to be someone she needed to reach her goal, someone she had to see daily and work with and thank for his help? Someone who had gotten a shovel to the head for his trouble?

With a low sound of exasperation, Bethia finally gave in to the concern she had carried with her all day. It was almost time for supper, but she made certain to be early so that she could speak privately with Meriel, the widow who cooked for the small band of outlaws.

This morning she had sent the older woman to tend to Simon—the head wound, not the lump in his braies—and though loath to admit it, Bethia was anxious to learn of his well-being. "Hmm. It smells delicious," she said when she reached the cooking pot where Meriel stood, stirring some thick stew.

A woman of few words, Meriel only nodded, and Bethia, suddenly impatient for news of her knight, wasted no more precious minutes in idle speech. "So, tell me, is he all right?" she asked, trying for a careless tone but not quite succeeding.

Meriel did not lift her eyes from the pot. ''There was no one there, mistress.''

''No one there?'' Bethia felt the clench of unreasoning panic. ''But where did he go?'' The man had been knocked unconscious, and though it did not appear too serious, he should hardly have been up and about as yet.

''I do not know, mistress.''

Without bothering to respond, Bethia headed for the hut, certain that Meriel had been mistaken. Perhaps the widow had gone to the wrong place or Simon had been out relieving himself when the older woman arrived. Knowing the knight, she was certain he would avoid any fussing over him, even if it was for his own good.

But when Bethia reached the tiny building where she had left him, it was empty. There were no signs that Simon had been there at all except the impression of his body in the straw and a small spot of blood where his head had lain. Bethia stepped back outside, assailed by worry and guilt. She should have tended him instead of running away. He had acted in a most unusual fashion. What if he was out of his head? He could be wandering the woods aimlessly or he might fall prey to one of Brice's men, who would not wait to discuss his identity.

Or he might have taken it upon himself to investigate his own accident with his sword arm. Bethia drew in a harsh breath at the thought, but quickly dismissed it. If there had been a fight, she would have heard of it, and all around her the forest was silent.

Bethia surveyed the surrounding area and noted that none of the growth was disturbed beyond the path. Maybe Simon had been well enough to leave on his own. She frowned, knowing an unreasoning anger that he would depart without telling her. And yet, what was she to him? He was not one of her band and was free to come and go without informing her of his movements.

Still, the thought put her in an ill mood, and she returned to camp, watching warily for Simon's appearance. Firmin and a few others seemed subdued during the meal, and finally she asked the surly archer what exactly had happened to the knight. Red faced, he muttered something about fools who stood too close to working men, but his words trailed off beneath the force of Bethia's stare.

"And just where is he now?" she asked softly.

If possible, the archer's face became more florid. "I thought he was in your hut!"

"He is not," Bethia answered calmly. "And though he might well have returned to Baddersly, I would like to make certain of his whereabouts. Jeremy, head to the village, and see what you can find out there. Will, go over toward Ansquith and question the shepherds who are friendly to our cause. And Firmin, since you are the one responsible for this accident, you can keep watch for two shifts tonight."

While Firmin sputtered, Bethia stood in order to gain everyone's attention. "Need I remind you all that Simon de Burgh is the one who thought of a plan to free Ansquith from Brice's hold?" she asked as her gaze swept the clearing.

"We were doing just fine without him," Firmin muttered.

"Doing what?" Bethia asked, her tone level. "Yes, we were harrying Brice's supplies and stealing from his pockets, but it has become evident to all of us that he is never coming out to face direct attack. What happens when winter comes? How long or well do you think we will survive in these barren woods, running from one hiding place to the next?''

Although Firmin still looked angry, most of the others nodded in agreement. These men needed to get back to their mining, their farming, their shepherding, and only the ouster of Brice would allow them to resume their lives, and in some cases, return to their families. And none were so enamored of this outlaw existence as to want to continue it indefinitely.

''He's probably bringing his army upon us—all because his own bumbling put him in the way of my shovel.''

Bethia knew that Simon was too graceful to make a mistep, but she refused to waste time arguing. ''If Simon de Burgh wanted to bring on his army, he would have long ago,'' she said, sending a quelling look at the archer. Besides, Simon was not the type of man to punish them all for one person's transgression. Was he furious with them? Or with her, for her refusal to tarry with him in the hut? Bethia quickly dismissed the notion, for a knight like Simon de Burgh undoubtedly had his pick of willing women far more beautiful than she.

''Still, it wouldn't hurt to change our camp again, Bethia,'' John said.

Although her heart told her that there was no need, Bethia knew she must consider the others, who did not have as much faith in Simon. ''Very well,'' she said. ''Let's disperse for now. We'll close the mining operation for a day or two, but have someone watch the area.''

It would put them behind, and Bethia knew a bitter impatience to be done with the passage and on her way into Ansquith. She forced it down ruthlessly, for the wait appeared necessary to keep her men at ease. With a curt nod to John, Bethia turned away, telling herself to be satisfied with the day's work. But something twisted in her gut, and it was more than a chafing at the delay.

Worry over a certain great knight assailed her, along with the niggling feeling that she had somehow betrayed him by bowing to the distrust of the others.

Baddersly was no haven.

Only hours after his arrival, Simon was sick to death of Florian fussing over him, of the odd glances sent his way and the gossip he knew was running rampant. He was better off in the woods, he thought glumly, even though the thought of Bethia tightened his throat with a hard knot of something like embarrassment.

He felt like a fool. Ever since he could remember, Simon had known an innate confidence. After all, he was a de Burgh, and along with the name came certain privileges and respect. But Simon had not been content with that alone. Always striving to equal Dunstan's accomplishments, he had easily surpassed his other brothers in strength and battle skills.

Now he felt lost, out of his depth, a *fool*. And his ill mood was acerbated by the company at Baddersly, which seemed intent upon making his life miserable.

They all harped upon his health until he roared out his rage. But the truth was that his poor appetite and sleeplessness had returned full measure. Even though everyone else ate with great relish, to Simon the food tasted bad. And the bed, though elegant and soft, held no comfort for him.

During the day, he felt a restless energy that no amount of riding or exercise with his knights could dissipate. He felt the edge that came with battle, but he had no opponent to fight. The longer this went on the angrier he became. Although Florian spoke ominously of an imbalance of humors, he refused to seek out a doctor when he knew that physically he was fine.

He was not so sure about his mind, for it flitted about in a wholly uncharacteristic manner. One minute, he decided to go back and oversee the undermining, preparing to leave with a boyish eagerness, only to feel a sudden reluctance that made his spirits plummet.

After days of this aimlessness and indecision, Simon felt ready to explode. He could not stand another moment spent inside Baddersly's walls, but neither was he ready to return to the chase. With an angry grunt, he mounted his destrier and headed to the village, seeking a peace of mind that was becoming increasingly elusive.

But the village held no remedy for his ill mood. The early afternoon sun dappled the old roadway, glinting off the occasional traveler or the villein on his way to the fields or a freeman tending to his own croft. Babies played while mothers worked, and the door to the alehouse stood open.

Simon swallowed painfully. Maybe there was something wrong with his gut, for it felt as though his food had lodged halfway down, sticking in his throat. He rubbed at his chest as he left his mount at the smithy and walked through the cluster of buildings and farther on toward the edge of the village.

There his attention was caught by a young woman feeding chickens. A shaft of light caught the thick braid that trailed down her back, and Simon felt a swift ache of loss. What was Bethia doing now? Was she all right? Was she finding shelter and food? Simon grunted in disgust at his own thoughts, for she could probably hunt better than he could. Without volition, his gaze followed the woman, the graceful toss of an arm, the gentle flow of her simple gown around her hips. He saw the flash of a slender ankle and an unwanted heat coursed through him.

As if aware of his scrutiny, she turned slowly, one hand deep in the pocket of her gown in a manner that bespoke caution beyond that of the usual maid. And when she faced him, Simon knew why, for the familiar face of Bethia Burnel tipped upward in wary defiance.

Bethia. Simon tried to speak but could not even form the word, so struck was he by his first sight of her garbed as a female. Gone was the hard warrior, and in her place stood a beautiful woman, still strong, but with the soft curves that had been hidden beneath her man's tunic. Simon's mouth grew dry as he gaped at her, and the air between them seemed to heat and close, heavy and thick with longing.

"Good day, sir knight," she finally said, with a lift of her chin that told him she was still the same fearless fighter.

"What are you doing here?" Simon demanded, rousing himself to speech.

"Oh, I have lots of hiding places, and even you don't know all of them yet." Her words came out in a breathy whisper that teased Simon's senses even as they irritated him, for he would know everything about her, inside and out. He felt like grabbing her and shaking her, making her tell him everything, give him everything....

With a grunt, he inclined his head toward the tiny building behind her. "You are not here alone." It was a statement more than a question. Though Simon knew

Bethia to be skilled with weapons, he did not like the thought of her living close to the woods without any protection. Where was her band now?

"No," she said, and even as she spoke an older woman came to the door of the cottage. Simon recognized her as the cook for the outlaws and of little help in the event of an attack. "I'm here with Meriel. 'Tis her home."

Simon bit back an oath, blood pounding in his veins, loud and fierce, at the idea of her living with one old woman. "That's not what I meant, and you know it," he said through gritted teeth.

"I can take care of myself, and you know it," she answered back. Her braid had fallen forward over one slender shoulder, drawing Simon's attention and making it difficult for him to concentrate. It looked so thick and smooth that he ached to touch it, and when she tossed her head, sending it back behind her, he nearly growled in frustration.

"If you've come here simply to argue, you can go back to your castle," she said with an annoying air of dismissal. As Simon sought an appropriate response, she crossed her arms over her chest, distracting him yet again. It was a familiar pose, but for the first time, Simon saw the pale skin at the bottom of her throat and the rich expanse that traveled down to the edge of her gown, where the gentle curves of her breasts nestled. Simon sucked in a harsh breath.

Suddenly her female clothing seemed indecent, and he struggled for a righteous scold, but his mouth was so dry he could only sputter like a fool. Even as he decried the lush view of her flesh, Simon wanted to put his hand there or his mouth. He wanted to lift her skirts and take her on the grassy ground, without thought to the feeding chickens or the watching widow. He wanted to gather her up and impale her on his throbbing body. Hot, slick and tight.

The urge was so overwhelming that Simon felt dizzy. The cottage, Meriel and the nearby road faded from his awareness until nothing existed except Bethia and his need to have her, thundering through him in a nearly uncontrollable swell.

She must have felt it, for she made a soft sound of distress—or denial. ''I have work to do,'' she said in a low, raw voice that made Simon want to seize her no matter what her words. As she turned, his gaze settled on her braid, and the way it swayed, along with her skirts. The narrowness of her waist, often hidden in bulky tunics, was all too evident, and the pain in his groin grew until he began to sweat. He could throw her over his shoulder and...but she was already heading into the cottage, while Meriel gave him a wary look.

Simon felt like howling his rage and frustration to the skies. Ahead of him the road loomed, with a long walk back to his horse, and he knew he could not make it. Nor could he wait here, unable to endure another moment in the vicinity of Bethia, especially when she was dressed as a woman. He was so stiff he could barely walk, and so he crossed the road with an awkward gait and ducked into the chase.

Once inside the woods, Simon ran forward a few feet, just far enough to insure privacy before leaning heavily against the trunk of a tree. His lungs burned despite the small effort, and his head swam dangerously. Surely this was some malady, he thought with the portion of his brain that still functioned, and he drew in deep drafts of forest air, trying to oust whatever ailed him.

But visions of Bethia swam before him, especially the expanse of throat and chest revealed by her gown. She was a woman, and he wanted her. *Bethia.* Not any of the doxies he'd had in the past. Not any court lady or peasant wench. *Bethia.* And she had turned from him without a backward glance.

Bending over in an effort to ease his distress, Simon reached for himself, and finally giving in to the ache that was crippling him, he yanked down his braies and took himself in a tight grip. With each long stroke, Simon imagined Bethia's hands upon him. Her fingers. Her mouth. Her thighs tightening over him. Then, closing his eyes, he grunted as his body quaked in fierce release.

Simon groaned in the aftermath, his muscles still shuddering violently, before he hastily rearranged his clothes. Sagging against the rough bark of the oak behind him, he tried to catch his breath even as he flushed over his actions. It had been release and nothing more, he knew, yet the swift physical response that had always served in the past no longer satisfied him.

Release simply was not enough anymore, and the knowledge made Simon groan again, for he was not certain what else he needed, let alone how he was going to get it.

Chapter Eleven

Bethia shrank back into the bushes that had hidden her from Simon and shuddered violently in reaction to what she had just seen. The trembling in her limbs made her lean against a tall oak for support, but she moved as silently as possible, fear of discovery making her hold her breath. If Simon found her now, he would despise her, not only because of the privacy she had unknowingly invaded, but for another, far more damning reason.

Bethia knew with a certainty that chilled her that the proud knight would hate her for witnessing what he would call a weakness. Some men might laugh or joke about their bodies' needs and a certain manner used to assuage them. Bethia had overheard snatches of such conversations before and marked them not. But other men were not Simon de Burgh, who held himself so proudly that he bowed to nothing, not even his own urges.

Loosing a low hiss of relief at the fading sound of his footsteps, Bethia sank down to the ground, her legs giving way. Truly she had not meant to watch. She had only followed him because he had acted so strangely in front of Meriel's cottage. When he saw her, he had blanched as if guilty of something, and his usually terse conversation had become even more so, punctuated by long, stifling silences.

Bethia's innate suspicions had been roused, and his abrupt exit into the woods had heightened her anxiety. Not that she had thought he would betray them exactly; she trusted him too well to believe that any longer. But Simon de Burgh could be up to other mischief like some reckless venture that would not gain her approval if she knew of it.

Bethia had never imagined that it was lust that drove him into the woods, especially lust for *her*. She had known but a few men until recently, and although she had received her share of admiring glances even when dressed as a male, she had never dreamed of anything like the sight of the mighty knight straining in the throes of his own passions.

Quaking anew at the memory, Bethia was assailed by the same fierce yearning that had begun the moment she watched Simon touch himself. Although she probably ought to be ashamed, Bethia had felt no embarrassment, only an instinctive response that made her heart race, her breasts swell and her lower body ache. It had taken all her strength of will not to go to him, to ease him and herself.

Kiss me there, Bethia.

His words came back to haunt her, and Bethia had wanted nothing more than to sink to her knees before him and do just that. To learn everything about his hard form, to take everything he would give her. Even now her body throbbed with unfulfilled desire, and for the first time in years, Bethia felt like weeping for all that she had denied herself.

Because of him. With a low sound of distress, Bethia rued the day that she had laid eyes upon Simon de Burgh, for better that she had never known these feelings than have to fight them in addition to everything else. Of all her battles, this one suddenly seemed the most difficult, and she placed her palms upon her thighs, drawing in a slow breath as she marshaled her strength.

Her only solace was that Simon had not called out any earlier than he had, for if he had, she might not have been able to stop herself at the sound of the low growl that had accompanied his satisfaction. For it was no mindless grunt of pleasure she had heard, but her name, torn from his throat as in anguish.

Everything was back to normal. At least that's what Bethia told herself when Simon returned to the chase. He professed an uncertain memory of his accident, and so the threat of retribution was lifted. Their minds eased, her men returned to their posts, the miners began to dig again and Bethia went back to her abandoned hut. All was as it should be—except for the heat of awareness that seized her whenever Simon was near.

He did not try to kiss her again, nor did she witness any displays of his passion. Nevertheless, Bethia felt the heat of his gaze on her like a smoldering blaze waiting to be ignited. Although she had done nothing to inflame him, Bethia felt a vague sort of guilt over it, as though she ought to return his passion with equal ardor.

As well she could. Despite her rough male clothing, for the first time in her life, Bethia felt like a woman. A woman who *wanted*. It scared her, this sudden surge of desire, for it made her vulnerable—something she had never been in living memory.

She had always felt a certain confidence in herself even when just a child, adored by her mother and indulged by a proud father. The skills he taught her, along with her position in the prosperous household, had given her an assurance that continued even after she was wrenched from her happy existence into a world of toil and obeisance to indifferent relatives. Throughout all the frustrating years that followed, they had never managed to break her spirit, and neither had that bastard Brice, for Bethia would not be swayed from her purpose—to one day regain the freedom she had once known.

Her burgeoning feelings for Simon de Burgh threatened that goal of independence, and so she kept a wary eye on both the knight and her own dismaying reaction to him. It would be so easy to give in to these unfamiliar urges, to go to him and learn the mysteries of her own womanhood. And to end up carrying his child, Bethia thought glumly. How then would she battle Brice or rescue her father or lead the outlaw band that had come to depend upon her?

Disgusted, Bethia told herself to ignore his appeal. Instead, she tried to focus on his flaws. He was too often grim and unsmiling, even harsh and rude at times, yet she admired his bluntness. Sighing, Bethia rejected that assessment while searching her traitorous mind for something worse. Her lips curved slowly as she seized upon his terrible temper, a truly deplorable trait! And he was so rigid in his beliefs that he could not accept her own competence until she struck him over the head with it. Or bound him, hand and foot.

As if aware of her preoccupation with him, the sub-

ject of her thoughts strode into camp, and Bethia
sucked in a hard breath at the sight of him in the bright
light of midmorning, glinting with moisture. She had
never seen anything like it, for Simon de Burgh was
the cleanest man she had ever known. It seemed as if
he were always coming or going from the stream that
she knew ran cold even at this time of year. And there
was something about the way he looked afterward,
flinging back his dark hair, dripping wet, his tunic
clinging to his hard body, that made Bethia struggle
even more fiercely against her unwanted attraction.

Although she was no coward, Bethia told herself that
a wise woman avoided temptation whenever possible.
And Simon de Burgh with his tall, muscular body, and
harsh visage that belied his passionate nature, would
have tested the piety of a saint. Ignoring the questioning
glances of her men, Bethia rose and headed for her hut,
feeling craven indeed.

Simon watched Bethia leave and bit back an oath of
frustration. Ever since his return to the chase, she had
been avoiding him so assiduously that even her men
had begun to notice. They gave him black, threatening
looks that he had done nothing to deserve. Well, little
enough to deserve. His eyes narrowed, his mouth thin-
ning into a grim line. So what if he had teased her?

A few randy words were nothing compared to what
she had done to him over their brief acquaintance—
capturing his men, tying him up, torturing him with her
smiles! The litany of the wench's misdeeds would fill
one of Geoffrey's precious books. And yet, Simon had
treated her with courtesy, had bent over backward to
help her and had even gone so far as to believe her far-
fetched tale of rising from the dead.

And what thanks did he get? None! Bethia remained

distant and wary, as if she could hardly bear his presence, and as for the rest of them...Simon's eyes narrowed as he surveyed his companions, who were eating their dinners with relish. Not one of them seemed grateful for his assistance. Indeed, he now wondered if some stood against him in his efforts. Although Simon could remember little of the accident that had stolen his wits recently, he remained suspicious of the surly archer who had caused it.

Simon scowled as he got his meal portion and sat down on a log. As a de Burgh, he was accustomed to loyalty, but now he was surrounded by men whose trust was uncertain, and a few, like Firmin, who eyed him with animosity. Simon could not be sure of the source of the archer's hostility, but he had seen the man watching Bethia, and he did not like it. If not for his promise to the wench, he would bring in some of his own men—and not simply for his own protection. He could handle a few ragged tree dwellers, especially now that he was on his guard against them, but what if they turned on Bethia, too?

Any one of them could be in league with Brice, disrupting their attack plans even now. And if the undermine was discovered, how would they reclaim Ansquith without endangering her father? Simon had never been one to worry; he always made a decision and acted swiftly upon it. This situation was unusual, however. Not only must he be concerned about the mine, but about Bethia, too.

Although she claimed to lead this band, Simon remained skeptical. Deep in his gut he felt uneasy about a woman in charge of men. He knew from personal experience how Bethia could tempt and arouse, and he knew that strong passions often erupted into violence.

Fie, he had to struggle to control himself! What if one or more of these motley characters took it into his mind to have her? Bethia was skilled with weapons, but she had not the strength to hold off a big man—or two.

The vision that formed in his mind was so unsettling, Simon grunted and rubbed his chest. If the wretched woman weren't so blasted stubborn, he would be with her right now, protecting her! But she avoided him, as if he, a knight and a de Burgh, were somehow more of a danger to her than any of these ragtag followers.

That can never be between us. The memory of her words made Simon scowl anew, for he was unaccustomed to being denied. He could not remember the last time someone had told him nay, and he grunted with frustration. *Only Bethia.* The obstinate wench had dared to contradict him from their first meeting when he told her to lay down her weapons and she had not. She had continued the annoying habit until Simon felt as though he would explode.

He wanted to shake her until she bid him yea to everything, especially to that which lay betwixt them unresolved, flooding him with raging, hot sensation at the very sight of her. But she continued to avoid him. Did she not feel this thing between them that made his blood roar? Simon still did not understand her rejection. His name alone was enough to draw the interest of women, yet Bethia seemed to think little enough of it.

The knowledge made him grimace, but at the pull of his facial muscles, Simon lifted a hand to his hard jaw. Perhaps it was his demeanor that put Bethia off. He tried to smile only to grunt in dismay. Although not accounted handsome among his brothers, he didn't consider himself ill-favored. And there was no other man with whom to compete, of that Simon was almost certain. Why, then, was Bethia so adamant in her refusal?

A stray comment of Stephen's echoed in his head, and Simon tensed. Just as there were men who preferred others of their own sex, his worldly brother claimed some women were drawn to...females. Starting at the thought, Simon drew the attention of the others who were still eating, but he ignored their curious glances and rose to his feet. He tossed the remains of his own meal into the fire, his gut churning sickeningly.

Now that the idea had taken root, Simon could not dislodge it. He had never really considered such a possibility, but as he did, it filled him with new frustration. How could a man fight against that? He didn't seem able to draw in enough air. Only after taking a deep breath was he able to bring his body under control, and the errant thunder of his pulse angered him.

He was a fool, shying away from shadows! He had never been one to skulk like a coward, afraid of the truth! Better that he face his enemy—or his answers. With a grim set to his jaw, Simon turned toward Bethia's hut. She would not welcome his visit, of that he was certain, but he did not care. He had to know. Now.

As he strode impatiently through the woods, Simon remembered the kiss they had once shared. Surely he had not imagined her response! Nor had it been an accident, an aberration. A man would be able to tell, wouldn't he? Simon's blood thundered as something like fear licked at his heels. Bethia, the one woman who affected him as no other, had to be within his reach because the alternative did not bear thinking about.

By the time he reached the small hovel where she had taken up residence, Simon's whole body was taut, as if prepared for battle. His hand drifted to his sword hilt before he lifted his fist to the thin wood that served as a door, knocking loudly. Although Simon was prepared to beat it down, his knuckles had barely grazed the surface when it swung open.

"What is it?"

She stood there before him in her man's clothes as she had so often before, but this time Simon felt as if someone had slammed him in the chest. It really didn't matter what she wore, rough tunics or fine gowns, she would always be the most beautiful woman he had ever seen. As she continued to stare up at him, her gaze shuttered and wary, Simon sought the words that would not come.

His tongue felt thick and slow, his mouth dry from the simple sight of her, his lungs heavy with her scent. She filled his senses far more than any bloody battle or forest idyll. Somehow Bethia alone managed to get inside of him, as if she had entered through his very pores. And he wanted to be inside of her, as well.

It was not so much the lust that drove him forward; it was a yearning to make her feel what he was feeling, to share this unfamiliar sensation with the woman who engendered it. He reached for her, and for once, she did not shy away. Pulling her tight against him, he slammed the door behind him and took her mouth with a violence that he had never dared unleash on one of his paid harlots.

And instead of denying him, Bethia met his hunger with her own. Her tongue twisted around his, her arms curved around his waist and her body pushed into his. His earlier worries vanished under the force of her passion, for no woman could feign such raw desire. He curved one hand around her slender neck to hold her to his kiss, while his other palm curved around her hip, tugging her to him. When he yanked her upward against his throbbing hardness, he felt her fingers close over his buttocks, digging into his flesh as if to urge him on.

Lifting his mouth from hers, Simon gulped in air as he paused to study her face. Her eyes were open and flaring with an unholy light that set his loins afire. He wanted to tear her clothes from her, to strip her naked and master this strong, amazing woman with his body, but even as his blood raged, he knew that whatever it was that drove him to her would not be appeased by a swift, feral mating.

Simon pressed his mouth to her throat and ran his hands along the supple form hidden beneath male clothing. When he touched her breast, he groaned aloud, so great was the pleasure. With a low growl, he tugged at her tunic, pulling it downward, so that he could kiss the pale curve gleaming in the dim interior of the hut.

His fingers trembled as he touched the smooth softness of her breast, and he shuddered, his breath labored and ragged. When her thigh slid against his groin, he grunted in agony. He had never felt this way in his life, as if he were burning up from the inside out, as if he were engaged in the most important contest of his life.

He leaned over her, tasting the skin he had exposed, and she arched backward as his cheek brushed against her hard nipple. Vaguely he was aware of her fingers digging into the muscles of his buttocks, but the sharp sensation of teeth biting into his shoulder made him jerk upward to stare at her. She was panting as much as he was, her eyes wild, and he groaned as his hard tarse leaped in response.

Bethia had bitten him, and Simon thought he would explode into his braies at the knowledge. She wanted

him, and the dizzying satisfaction that ran through him
was something akin to exaltation. "Bethia." He whispered her name, his normally focused thoughts scattered wildly. All he could think of now was to get her
on her back on the pallet and thrust into her until this
pounding need was finally assuaged.

"Bethia."

For one dazed moment, Simon thought he had spoken aloud again, but then he heard her name once more.
It was coming from outside the hut, and even as he
lifted his head to listen, he felt Bethia stiffen. She
pulled from his arms and straightened her tunic, a shuttered expression replacing her unveiled passion.

Simon couldn't speak, nor could he move. His body
shuddered in delayed reaction to her withdrawal while
she went to the door and stepped outside. And his
thwarted ardor turned to fury when he heard Firmin's
voice, followed by Bethia's soft reply. Firmin sounded
insistent, and Simon turned and threw the door open
loudly in his eagerness to vent his frustration on the
surly archer.

Bethia looked over her shoulder with a frown, as if
he were meddling, and Simon hesitated, though he was
tempted to intervene in a manner that no one would
mistake. Gritting his teeth, he waited while struggling
against an urge to roar his rage at the skies. He wanted
to throw Bethia over his shoulder, to put his mark on
her, to proclaim to all and sundry that she was his, but
something told him that she might not care for such a
display.

"I'll be along in a minute," she said to Firmin, and
Simon grunted in outraged disbelief. She was leaving
him here—in this state, while she ran off to meet with
the archer? Simon glared at the man, who wisely chose

not to meet his gaze, until he finally, reluctantly, disappeared into the trees. At his exit, Bethia turned and walked back toward the hut, stopping before the doorway as if to keep a good distance. The face that only recently had been taut with passion, was hard and implacable, making Simon even more furious.

"I told you that this cannot be between us," she said, her tone cool. "Please do not approach me again."

Was this the same woman who had taken a bite out of his shoulder? Simon felt like shaking her, but when he took a step forward, she backed away. He slammed one fist into his palm in frustration. "You feel it, too!" he said. "Do not deny that you feel this thing between us!"

"Of course, I feel it," she snapped.

After all the time that Simon had thought himself alone in his ardor, her admission took him by surprise. Why had she hidden her desire from him? Why had she denied him? He felt betrayed, as if he had caught her in a lie or deceit against him, for all the while he had thought himself rejected, when he was not. Was he? Simon's elation at her response was short-lived, and his eyes narrowed as he studied her. "Why?" he demanded.

"Why won't I fall to the ground for a quick tumble, you mean?" she asked.

Simon flinched at the words, for they hit far too close to home. Yes, that was what he had known before, but it was not what he wanted now. Yet how could he tell her the difference when he didn't even know himself? He only knew that he needed something more, something only she could give him. But before he could form a response, she continued in the same cold tone that infuriated him.

"As enjoyable as I'm sure it would be, I have no intention of letting you fill my belly with a bastard babe, when I have no means of taking care of a child. Or had you not even considered that possibility?" she taunted.

Simon reeled as if she had struck him, for he truly had not thought of his seed taking root. It had never been an issue in any of his paid encounters, for he assumed such women knew what they were doing. As the hated flush rose on his neck, he felt the fool yet again, but his pride was used to Bethia's battering, and his desperation was growing stronger. If Bethia's reluctance sprang from caution, then he must respect it, yet his body still throbbed with unspent passion.

He had heard Stephen bragging often enough about his so-called skills with women, of techniques involving hands and mouth that Simon had dismissed as a waste of time. He had always wanted to bury himself deep and take his satisfaction as quickly as possible, but now…with Bethia the hows and whys didn't seem to matter, he only knew that he must have her in any manner possible.

"There are ways to avoid that, other methods I have heard of to find pleasure," he muttered.

She looked at him askance, as if she could hardly believe what she was hearing. And could he blame her? In civilized society, men and women did not speak so boldly, but Simon no longer felt civilized. He felt like a barbarian, ready to take this outlaw for his own at any cost.

For a long moment she simply stared at him, and Simon felt his blood rush, hot and fluid, through his veins once more. But the flicker of desire in her eyes was quickly shuttered as she turned away. Her shoulders were straight, her head held high, but the hint of resignation in her tone made Simon want to howl in protest.

"How can I trust you to control your passions, when I cannot trust myself?" she asked.

She was only a few feet away, but it might as well have been miles, for she had put the distance back between them, shutting him out, denying him yet again.

Although he wanted to drag her back into the hut, to force her submission, Simon knew he could not. On a gut level, he suspected that overpowering Bethia would destroy what lay between them, not unleash it. And, besides, he wanted her to come to him, willing and passionate!

With an angry grunt, Simon let her go. He had what was left of his pride after all, and no mere woman was going to disturb him. He refused to allow it! Slamming a fist into his palm, he vowed to ignore the outlaw wench until she saw the error of her ways, until she approached him and then he might deign to touch her again.

Fie, he swore harshly, she would have to *beg* him for it!

In the days ahead, Simon kept firmly to his resolve. Unfortunately, just the knowledge that Bethia felt this attraction between them, too, and had admitted it, strained his determination. Worse yet was the hot memory of her fingers clinging to his flesh, her mouth on his and the small red spot that lingered on his shoulder.

She had marked him, and in more ways than one.

Simon felt as if his world had upended, and he walked on the broad expanse of sky, a stranger to his own existence. In his experience, women were the weaker of the sexes, to be protected and hidden away. Yet Bethia swaggered about the chase in men's clothes, giving commands and fighting as well as many of those who followed her.

All of his life, he had thought women useless, yet now he felt ineffective and idle in his role as supervisor of the undermine. Bethia ignored him, as if he were some ornament, and only his own fierce determination kept him from returning to Baddersly.

Females were supposed to be the ones who pined away for their knights, who relished romantic prose and song, but Simon caught himself more than once in morbid contemplation of the object of his desire. Worse yet, he was constantly afflicted by a hardening in his braies, and it was beginning to alarm him.

What if Florian was right and he suffered some malady? Although Simon had never heard of a man dying of a stiff tarse, he considered seeking advice from a healer. But the thought of trying to explain his predicament made him hesitate—along with a certain wariness of whatever remedy the doctor or wisewoman would recommend.

So far, a good dowsing in the stream provided his only respite, but though it chilled his body, the water did little to cool his mind—or the fire that seemed to burn in his chest. He wondered if Firmin's shovel had struck him there unknowingly, too, for his insides ached and festered as if fiercely bruised. Throwing his tunic onto the overgrown bank, Simon rubbed a spot just over his heart.

He was getting too old for this, he decided, only to have the thought bring him up short. Age was something he never considered. Dunstan was his elder and always would be because of their birth order, but the years were going by rapidly. With a sudden shudder, Simon realized that Dunstan had already married by Simon's age.

The dismaying discovery made him wonder if his sexual frustration was a symptom of his maturity. Perhaps there was something in a man that drove him to wed at a certain stage of life, to procreate and provide new blood for the next generation. The notion was startling in its simplicity, yet held an answer to so many of his questions that Simon grunted aloud.

Never had he expected to wed, for he had no use for women and cared nothing about reproduction. He had always suspected that with six brothers, one of them was bound to perform that duty of carrying on the de Burgh name. Indeed, Dunstan and Geoffrey had already done so, releasing Simon from the onerous task. He had no need of an heir, no desire to be saddled with a female all his days.

But that was before Bethia, before he had met the only woman he had ever admired, who shared his interests, who matched his strength of will, who fired his senses until he was walking around with a perpetual tent in his braies. And marriage would take care of that. Simon drew in a harsh breath as the possibilities loomed before him. Bethia unafraid of pregnancy. Bethia in his bed. In the woods. In the river. Beneath him. On top of him. In every way possible. His heart thundered while his body strained even further for release.

Bethia, marked as his, forever.

The idea was definitely worth thinking about, he decided, releasing a shaky breath. Why waste another minute? he wondered as he reached for his tunic, a smile tilting his lips. Like the decisive battle that won the war, this was the answer he had been seeking, and the sooner it was done, the better.

Chapter Twelve

It was dusk when Bethia heard the footsteps outside her hut. Someone was approaching, and whoever it was, he certainly wasn't being very quiet about it. In fact, the steps sounded unnaturally loud, as if an angry giant were stomping toward her tiny building at an alarming pace. Having just lain down on her pallet, Bethia rolled off it with speed and stealth as she unsheathed her sword.

Despite her haste, she was barely ready when the door burst open without any warning knock. She had no time to question her visitor, for a huge, threatening figure was already stepping over the threshold. With a skill long honed, Bethia did not hesitate and thrust her sword into the great black shape before it could attack her. But instead of engaging her in battle, her opponent cursed loudly in a familiar voice that sent her weapon thudding to the ground from nerveless fingers.

"Oh, no! Simon!" Bethia cried out in helpless panic. Frantically she reached for him, feeling along his torso in the dimness of the hut.

"What were you doing, trying to kill me?" he muttered as her fingers found a tear in his tunic.

His accusation turned her dismay to anger. "Why aren't you wearing your mail?" she snapped.

"Because I wasn't anticipating an attack," he answered in a harsh tone.

"You should always expect attack!" Bethia argued as she probed the hole only to feel the wetness of his blood. "Faith, I've cut you!" Her panic returned and, turning the big knight around, she unfastened his girdle with shaking hands, letting it drop to the dirt floor in her haste to check his wound. His tunic got in the way, so she lifted it, pushing it upward until he raised his arms to let her remove it entirely. She tossed it carelessly upon the pallet, so intent was she upon her task.

"Here, move into the light," Bethia said, nudging his massive form toward the doorway, but the day was fading, offering feeble illumination, so she knelt to fire the tinder ready in the tiny hearth. Simon stood silently behind her, and Bethia wondered at his acquiescence. He had been unusually docile, for which she blamed his injury. Else why would he let her turn him this way and that, probing at him in the near darkness?

It was only when the wood flared and she turned around that another possibility occurred to Bethia. Crouched low before the small blaze, she looked up and caught her breath on a low, strangled gasp.

Simon stood before her easily, looking huge and formidable and not the slightest bit injured. His upper body was bare, and the firelight gleamed upon his muscular shoulders, the hard expanse of his chest and the dark hair that grew there before arrowing down across his flat stomach into his braies. For a moment, Bethia froze, unable to move or speak at his sheer beauty. She stared at the dark indentation of his navel, feeling his gaze upon her, hearing the rush of her own blood in her ears.

Swallowing hard, Bethia forced her attention to his side, where a fresh stain shone dark against his skin. Forcing herself to focus only upon his wound, she pushed herself to her feet, stepping forward to lean over and examine it. Swiping at the blood with her fingers, she saw that the cut was not deep and loosed a low sigh of relief.

"A scratch," Simon said, as if reading her thoughts. "Was it your intent to mark me with your blade as you did with your teeth?"

The words, whispered in his deep voice, made Bethia still, and she stifled a shudder at the reminder of her recent loss of control. Closing her eyes, she fought against the images that swamped her, memories of Simon and herself here in her hut, his mouth upon her breast, her hands clutching his hard buttocks. Yet she did not move, for she was afraid of straightening, of looking at him, of what he might do. If he touched her now, how would she have the strength to deny him?

"Because," he said, his breath warm on her hair, "if so, I prefer the feel of your mouth to that cold metal."

The arrogance in his tone saved her, for Bethia felt a jarring annoyance at his presumption. Why could he not leave her be? How often must she tell him nay? How many times would he test her? Drawing herself up to her full height, she lifted her chin to look at the man who toyed with her so unfairly.

"You're lucky I didn't run you through, you knave!" she said, crossing her arms over her chest. "How dare you barge in here without knocking? You have no right to—"

He cut off her words with a fierce glare that stopped

them in her throat. "You've driven me mad long
enough," he muttered, a nearly feral light in his eyes.

It startled Bethia, as did the hands that descended on
her shoulders. She knew better than to let him touch
her, especially when her gaze kept dropping to the bare
chest on that amazing body of his. Shaking off his grip,
she stepped back and grabbed up his tunic, thrusting it
toward him, as if to ward off his appeal.

But he didn't take it, and in the ensuing silence, Bethia could hear the sound of their breathing, hurried and
loud even over the crackling of the fire. And though
she refused to look at him, she felt the force of his gaze
with an intensity that seemed to burn through her. Desperation made her brusque.

"Put this on, and leave me be, Simon! I've already
told you that I won't dally with you!" Bethia cried.
She punched his hard stomach with her fist wrapped in
his tunic, but he made no move to do what she bid,
and she felt a sharp flare of panic. Here was the only
enemy she didn't know how to fight, for he would not
be deterred by coldness or harsh words or even the
threat of her sword. She could not ignore him or outwit
him or best him in a fight, and his stubborn will
matched her own.

What if he touched her again? Bethia could feel her
tenuous resolve slipping. They were still too close. Her
fingers buried in his still-warm clothing could easily
unfold to press against the flat muscles of his abdomen.
The fire warmed her back, but it was nothing compared
to the heat that radiated from him, and she took a deep
breath only to draw in the very scent of him, so mas-
culine yet so unique it made her dizzy with longing.

"Then marry me," he said in a gruff voice.

Bethia stilled in shock, clutching the material in her

hand in a fevered grip. Surely she had misheard him. "What?" she asked. At last she dared look at him, at the harsh, shadowed features that had become so dear to her that she was tempted to risk all for his pleasure. But she found no answering affection there.

"Marry me," he repeated, and Bethia felt the heart that she had guarded so zealously splinter despite all her efforts. For this was no passionate offer of alliance, but a command Simon uttered through gritted teeth, his jaw tight, his eyes glittering as if pained.

"Then you will have no fears of pregnancy. Should there be a child, I will give it my name," he said, though he did not appear thrilled by the prospect. Bethia, who had never entertained thoughts of a family, found herself outraged by his attitude toward a blameless babe. But she had no chance to argue, for he continued on in rigid determination.

"I'll oust Brice and wrest back Ansquith, make no mistake," he promised her. "For if necessary, I can march upon it with the might of the de Burgh armies behind me."

Bethia stared up at him in stunned disbelief. It wasn't so much the lack of love in his proposal that hurt her, for she had never trusted to such ethereal emotions. Nor did she flinch at the mention of battles instead of ardor. It was the way he looked at her, as if she were nothing more than a weakness of his body he held in contempt, that made her reel, and the way he spoke, with a total disregard for her thoughts, her feelings, her wishes. Even more alarming were his plans for Ansquith, which he would "reclaim" by himself, without any mention of her.

"And you and your brothers will save my father and

my home while I kick my heels at Baddersly?'' Bethia asked, her voice deceptively soft.

Although Simon appeared surprised by her question, he nodded curtly. "That would be safest."

Taking a step back, Bethia pushed the heels of both palms against him with all her might. The unexpected move made him stumble, and she took advantage of his imbalance, shoving him through the doorway. "Get out!" she shouted, barely able to control her breaking voice. "Get out!"

Ignoring the bewildered expression on his face, Bethia took her dilapidated door and slammed it so hard that the thing slipped from his moorings and hung crookedly. A reminder, she told herself, of men and their crooked tongues, their habits of twisting everything toward their own wants, with careless disregard for anyone else's.

Sagging against the broken door, Bethia vowed not to give a man power over her or her lands. Never again would she live under the thumb of another, unable to enjoy the smallest share of her own freedom. A lifetime of servitude was not worth a few moments of pleasure, of that she was certain, and although she felt a treacherous admiration and kinship along with her longing for Simon de Burgh, she would not let it influence her.

This would make things difficult, she knew, but even if he withheld his aid, she would not bend to Simon's will or to any man's. When the sound of low curses and stomping feet told her he was moving away, Bethia threw herself back down onto her pallet, determined to mend the heart that he had so ruthlessly ruptured.

During the long night, Bethia armored herself well. She had spent years cut off from human closeness, and she had that long habit to draw upon in the solitary darkness of her hut. She also had memories of those lost years, of drudgery and oppression, to remind herself of the cost of volunteering her independence.

Although she did not think Simon would work her to death as Gunilda had nearly done, Bethia chose to focus on that loss of freedom, envisioning a life behind castle walls, where contact was limited to attendants, where Simon would leave her to go where he pleased, doing what he liked while she waited behind, relegated to the tasks he assigned her.

And if sometimes her mind wandered to the more pleasurable aspects of an alliance with the hard knight, Bethia inexorably brought it back to what she would give up, instead of what she would gain. For, indeed, there was precious little for her in his bloodless proposal.

Of course, there would be cold evenings spent in the warmth of his bed, worshiping his fine body and discovering all the mysteries that beckoned her. And once Bethia might have enjoyed the companionship between them, but of late the easy sharing of interests had given way to harsh words and battles of wills. And in the end, he had proved that he had no respect for her skills, seeing her only as a body to be enjoyed and put aside.

If he wanted some useless ornament, why didn't he marry one of the many to be found at court? Why did he torment her, making her think they were so alike when he was no different than any other man? Bethia blamed herself for her own terrible attraction to the first true knight she had known in years. And even as she vowed to retain her freedom, she had wondered what the light of day would hold. Men were temperamental, prideful beings, and if Simon was the same, what would he do in response to her refusal? Would he betray her in his rage?

Uncertain what to expect, Bethia was relieved when he appeared at the mine late in the afternoon. Despite all her armoring, she felt a slice of pain when he regarded her with the cold expression of an enemy, not an ally. But had they ever been friends? Drawing a shaky breath she remembered a night spent talking over shared rabbit and tried to dismiss it, along with all the times they had discussed strategy, command, weapons, the daily demands of this outlaw existence.

Instead she forced herself to recall his face, defiant and hateful when she had first bested him, and all the times they had clashed since then. It was not friendship, but war for supremacy that raged between them, and now the final battle lines had been drawn.

"It's nearly completed," he said stiffly, inclining his head toward the entrance.

"Good," Bethia said. In the awkward silence that followed, she sought the strength necessary to broach the subject that lay between them. Although some cowardly part of her was tempted to ignore it, she could not, for she had to be certain of his position.

"We could not have done it without you. And for that I am grateful," she said, lifting her gaze to his harsh features. Did his gray eyes flicker with pain? Bethia told herself no, for his mouth swiftly set into a hard line. "We can proceed from here."

His harsh burst of laughter annoyed her. "A bunch of ragtag archers against knights? I think not," he muttered with his usual arrogance.

Bethia ignored his insult. "Regardless, I do not mean to hold you to your promise."

It was the wrong thing to say, Bethia knew that immediately, from the taut angle with which he held himself. She could almost see the outrage emanating from him, like heat from a forge. "I am a de Burgh," he said stiffly. "I honor my commitments."

The word he chose made her think of his proposal. Would he be as committed to marriage as to all else? She would never know. Nodding, Bethia turned to go, feeling oddly sick in the pit of her stomach, as if she had somehow betrayed him, when all she had done was look out for herself.

And as she had learned long ago, if she did not, no one else would.

Ignoring Bethia's retreat, Simon moved back to the mine, where he began to dump with unnecessary force the cartload of earth that came out of the tunnel. She was still trying to get rid of him! It was not enough that she refused him, aye, even rejected his suit, but now the wretched woman wanted him away completely! But he would not give her the satisfaction. No matter how insulting she was, he would not shirk his duty to Ansquith. Nor did he intend to hide himself away because she could not bear the sight of him.

Besides, he had tried that last night—returning to Baddersly, where even Florian's fussing had seemed welcome. After Bethia rejected his proposal, Simon felt battered and bruised and in need of familiar surroundings, but the castle gave him no comfort. Fie, he had even sunk so low as to miss his brothers for the first time in recent memory.

Worse yet, he began to suffer a foreboding about the undermine and the approaching battle, going so far as to question his abilities. Bethia's refusal had turned him inside out, making him doubt everything, including himself. And if something did go wrong, who would aid her? Despite her dismissal of him, somehow her safety weighed uppermost in his mind, and he wrestled with the problem late into the night. Finally he decided to send a messenger home, explaining the situation to his father, just in case Dunstan, busy with his own demesne, turned a blind eye to such a small concern near his wife's holdings.

After a nearly sleepless night, Simon dispatched the messenger at dawn and rode alone over the countryside to make certain he knew the land well enough to fight upon it, should the need arise. So far there had been no sign of the so-called mercenaries, and Ansquith had been quiet, but he wanted to be prepared for anything. This one small battle had somehow become more important than any other in his warrior's existence, and he was determined to prevail.

And once it was over, he would be free of any further obligation, Simon told himself with grim determination. When Bethia was installed at Ansquith again with her father, he would leave Baddersly for good. He had told no one, not even his father in the message he had sent, but that was his intention.

He had always wanted to fight for Edward as Dunstan had done, but Campion had disapproved, refusing to allow all of his sons to join the King. Now, however, Simon was determined to go his own way, even if it was in defiance of his father's wishes. They meant little to him, as did everything that had once held meaning. Even the thought of finally joining Edward's knights left him cold. Battles, victory and the ensuing rewards no longer excited him. At last, he had decided to pursue his dream, only to find that it was empty.

But he had no intention of returning home to the

dubious solace of his family. He was not the type to unburden himself to his brothers, and even if he were, they would laugh in derision at his current complaint. And he certainly could not stay here when everywhere he looked held memories of Bethia, when she would be living so close that he would surely see her out riding sometimes, where he might well witness her marriage someday.

That notion had sliced through him like a sharp blade, surprising him with its intensity. In his more lucid moments, Simon was dumbfounded by his own reactions to her rejection. Not only was his pride wounded yet again by this woman, but there was a deep emptiness inside, as if she had sent the surgeon Florian recommended to remove something vital from his gut.

At least the ache in his groin was gone. And for good, probably, because Simon could not imagine ever wanting a woman again. In truth, he could not envision caring about anything. Only the thought of taking out his frustrations on Brice Scirvayne kept him going, and to that end Simon had made his way around to the chase, where he checked on the progress of the digging.

So impatient was he for the passage's completion that he was tempted to help the miners himself, but the thought of going into that dark, dank passage made his breath catch, so he stayed above ground, helping a couple of archers with the removal of earth. And he continued on, eager for the heavy labor, long past Bethia's departure. And after supper Simon returned, as if by very force of will he could command the tunnel's completion.

"My lord!" A faint cry from the direction of the mine made Simon hurry to look into the hole below.

"My lord, we've run into a problem. Could you come down here and take a look?"

Simon swore softly. Had the enemy detected their mine? Or had the miners simply run into a rocky spot? Although he knew numerous problems could develop, he did not relish going below to see for himself. That was not the venue of a knight, but the job of the miners, of…whoever was in charge. With a grimace, Simon envisioned a tunic-clad Bethia descending under the ground and cursed again. Gritting his teeth, he forced his feet down the narrow ladder.

As the darkness settled over him, Simon fought against the feeling of closeness that threatened to choke him. He tried not to think about the damp walls of dirt, of the timber beams that precariously held off the weight of the world above. Drawing in a sharp breath, he focused his mind on Bethia and moved forward.

Almost immediately he saw a glimmer of light that grew into the glow of a lantern held low by one of Bethia's men. "I'm going to get Will. Would you take my place and lend a hand in the meantime?" the man asked, hurriedly passing over the lantern. Before Simon could answer, he was gone, a shadowy blur whose face and clothes were blackened with soil.

Simon paused in the still passage. He would have much preferred to hunt for Will himself rather than assist whoever was ahead, but he would surely look the coward if he raced off after the disappearing man. With another soft oath, Simon steeled himself to go onward rather than back and, crouching uneasily, he stepped forward.

He noted with approval that the tunnel sloped gradually upward, in accordance with his instructions. There was little danger of the defender flooding the passage, but Simon believed in preparing for any eventuality. Unfortunately, nothing could ready him for this slow trek through the dank, stifling blackness. The smell of rotting earth and foul air assailed him, as did the sensation of being trapped.

Refusing to succumb to his own pounding heart, Simon forced himself to think of Bethia. The sooner this undermine was completed, the sooner she would have what she wanted, and even if her desires did not include him, he would fight to the death for them. He was a de Burgh, and his word was good.

With a grimace, Simon realized that he must soon reach the end of the passage, even as he dreaded coming up against a black wall of earth that marked the last of the digging. He would have eagerly rushed through to Ansquith, weapon drawn, but this slow crawl into the bowels of the world made him sweat. It was the heat and not his weakness, Simon told himself, as he stumbled on rough ground.

From the looks of it, he had reached the end, but where was the other man who was supposed to be digging? Even as the thought crossed his mind, Simon heard a sound behind him. He whirled only to see a cart come barreling toward him. He stepped aside as well as he could in the narrow passage, but the edge caught his leg and took him down. In an instant, his world went pitch-black as he lost the lantern and was showered by damp earth from the cart.

For a moment, he panicked, flailing at the soil that covered him until finally he sat up, drawing great gasps of air into his starved lungs. The darkness was complete, and Simon felt a dizzy disorientation. Which direction was he facing? Sucking in an unsteady breath, he forced himself to concentrate and swung to his feet. But it was already too late.

By the time he rose into a crouch, hand on the hilt of his sword, prepared to meet an unknown enemy without sight to guide him, Simon heard the creak of straining wood, the crack of timbers and the thud of earth gaining its release. Throwing himself toward the sound, Simon rolled to the ground even as the ceiling gave way. He covered his head, but clods of heavy soil landed on his back with wrenching force and soon his mouth was filled with it, until nothing existed but blackness and dirt, weighing him in place.

It was only after the thundering sound of the cave-in dwindled to a trickle of falling soil that Simon heard the voice. He groaned in answer, but the only response was the faint ringing of laughter. Firmin. Simon silently cursed when he recognized the voice of the hostile archer. Had the man deliberately destroyed the undermine? To what purpose?

"Now how do you fare, sir knight?" the archer shouted, his tone a savage mockery. "You were warned to stay away from her, but you couldn't keep your filthy hands off her, could you? And because of your fancy name and your fat purse and your so-called army, she let you touch her, didn't she?"

Although Simon could not reply, Firmin raged like a madman, cursing violently. "I saw you yesterday in her hut, half-naked, with the door open as if you would flaunt your use of her, and I knew it was only because of this hole in the ground. Well, now, it's over!" he screamed.

"After this, no one will ever want to dig here again, and she'll be mine! Do you hear me, you bastard? Listen well, for I will tell you just what I'm going to do to her, all the ways I'm going to have her, over and over again. While you lie here breathing your last, I'll have her bending over, like a bitch, spreading herself only for me.''

Blood roaring in his ears, Simon struggled violently against the earth that held him prisoner until finally he could barely draw a breath. And if Firmin was still ranting about Bethia, Simon could no longer hear him. *Bethia.* His chest ached anew at the thought of her. *Kill him, Bethia,* Simon urged silently before he lost all thought.

Although no coward, Bethia had done her best to avoid Simon after their brief meeting, and now she sat on the edge of her pallet alone rather than face him at supper. She was weary and had thought to find solace away from the prying eyes of her men, but the gathering twilight reminded her of the night before when the peace had been broken by Simon barging in to demand that she marry him.

In fact, she could almost hear his footsteps outside. Panic, anger and an odd sort of joy all mingled together as she rose to her feet, swinging wide the door. ''I told you to leave me alone!'' she cried, only to step back in surprise. It was not Simon who stood on her threshold, but Firmin, looking strangely feral in the fading light.

''What is it? Is there a problem?'' she asked, trying to direct her wayward thoughts from Simon de Burgh to whatever difficulty had developed among her men.

''There is no problem,'' Firmin said, shutting the door behind him.

No doubt, the archer was imagining betrayals again that demanded utter secrecy. Unfortunately, Bethia was in no mood to soothe him. Crossing her arms over her chest, she regarded him with impatience. "What, then?"

"I've been with you from the beginning," Firmin said, moving forward. "If it weren't for me, you'd be rotting in that dungeon or married to Brice. And I've never asked for any payment, just followed along, taking your orders like the rest of them when we both know I'm different. And I've waited long enough."

Confused and wary, Bethia stepped back and wondered if the man had been drinking. Firmin's face was red and he seemed unusually agitated, as if he had been up to something. Before she could decide what, he threw himself at her, pressing her back against the side of the hut, the hardness between his legs unmistakable as it dug into her belly. And her gasp of shocked protest only gave him the opportunity to put his mouth on her.

Bethia nearly gagged as he thrust his tongue down her throat, and with an angry grunt, she tried to bite him. He only groaned and put his hand between her legs. The awkward position made it hard for her to move, for he had trapped her arms between them, gripping her wrists. She could not break loose to reach the hilt of her sword, and his weight made it difficult to kick him.

For a moment, Bethia thought him drunk or delirious and no serious threat, but when he stuck his hand inside her braies, she realized he was in deadly earnest. "Now I'm going to have you, like I've always wanted, and you'll forget all about that bastard de Burgh," he said. To Bethia's horror, she felt him fumble with his braies as he pushed his red face against her neck. "I've taken care of him, for good," he muttered.

His words, even more than his movements, startled

Bethia into action. With a force born of desperation, she lifted her leg to stamp down hard upon his foot, and when he recoiled, she smashed her elbow into his face even as she unsheathed her sword. Now it was Firmin who backed across the tiny space to the wall, the point of her blade against his belly.

"What did you do to him?" Bethia asked, her voice hard and even, her hand steady.

Firmin swore loudly. "He doesn't matter, he and his stupid mine. It's gone, all of it, and him with it! Now you belong to me!" He lurched forward with a snarl, reaching for her again, and Bethia reacted instinctively, protecting herself from his wild attack with the weapon she had long mastered. The ensuing look on Firmin's face was nearly comical. Even as he stared helplessly down at the sword Bethia had plunged into his stomach, he seemed disbelieving.

"What?" he asked while the blood gurgled. And although for Simon's sake, she would grant him no mercy, Bethia would not let a dog die from a hole in his belly. With one more swift stroke, she made sure he was dead.

Then she called for her men.

Chapter Thirteen

When Bethia reached the clearing, the men who were finishing supper rose to their feet with sharp cries of horror. Only then did she realize that blood covered the front of her tunic, startling evidence of the life she had taken.

"Firmin's dead," she said. "He attacked me, and I had to kill him." A rumble of murmurs and gasps greeted her announcement and Meriel stepped forward as if to help her, but Bethia waved her back. She had no time to waste on herself or the fallen archer.

"He said he destroyed the tunnel, and I think…" For the first time, Bethia's voice broke, and she paused to clear her throat and square her shoulders. "I believe Simon is down there."

In an instant, John was organizing the men in a way that Bethia could not manage in her current state of agitation, sending most of them past her to the digging site at a run, while others were dispatched to fetch the miners and stand guard. When just she and John were left, he moved to her side. "Are you hurt?"

"No," Bethia said. And it was true. Physically she was unharmed, but the pain that filled her seemed far worse than any wound. Indeed, she felt as if she were bleeding from the inside out, from her very heart, with each drop accountable to the knight who might already be dead. "Do not worry about me. 'Tis Simon who must concern us," she said.

John studied her for a moment, as though to make sure she was truly well, then he nodded slowly. "Let us go and see about this knight of yours," he said, turning to follow the others. Without bothering to contradict his claim that Simon belonged to her, Bethia made haste to join him.

By the time they reached the mine, some of the men were already below. "It's a cave-in all right! It looks like the bracing timbers were cut," someone shouted. Bethia fought against the urge to push aside everyone in order to see for herself, for she knew little of the digging operation. She needed to stay out of the way, she knew, yet it was hard to relinquish even that small bit of control.

Just as it had been for Simon. Was he so different from herself? He did what he thought was right, certain that he was the only one who knew what was best. For everyone.

Choking back a sob, Bethia crossed her arms as if to ward off the ill news that would surely follow. Men had been killed mining the iron ore of the chase, she knew that well enough. Sometimes the earth gave way, burying them, and if they were not fatally injured by the falling debris, they soon smothered to death, deprived of life-giving air.

A sound escaped Bethia's throat as she imagined Simon dying by that slow torture, and she reacted in the only way she knew how, with anger at the great knight. He ought to have known better than to go below! Why was he poking around in the mine anyway? Bethia knew of his hatred for enclosed spaces, especially those beneath the earth.

And yet, the undermine had been his idea. Without giving thought to his personal misgivings, Simon had tendered his professional advice and made sure that it was carried out correctly. All for her. The knowledge made Bethia's eyes burn and her throat close, and her sharply indrawn breath sounded suspiciously weepy.

Blinking rapidly, Bethia told herself that Simon had only done what he should, as any true knight would do, but the explanation was no comfort. Nor did it stop the myriad feelings that rushed through her. For when she was fighting for her very life, an outlaw allied against authority, no one else had stepped forward to do what was right.

Oh, others had helped her escape from the dungeon and in her strikes against Brice, but Simon alone had pledged himself with no motive except his own finely honed sense of justice. He had swept into her life like a force of nature, unstoppable and untamable, intent only upon doing good. For her.

A tear ran down Bethia's cheek as she realized that, despite his arrogance and stubbornness and his tendency to command anyone and everyone, Simon meant more to her than she had dared acknowledge. Even though he tried to order her life, more often than not against her own wishes, she craved his presence, his body and his gruff voice like some kind of tonic. It made no sense to an ordered mind, but Bethia had the suspicion that logic had little to do with such things as love.

Love. Bethia had thought herself strong and immune to emotions she had long held in contempt. But as she waited in the growing darkness, fetching lanterns and tools and emptying buckets of soil, she admitted what she had refused to concede over these past weeks. All her efforts to guard and mend her heart were in vain, for it no longer belonged to her.

Simon de Burgh had stolen it from her.

"Firmin must have cut the supports, but I don't know why Simon would have gone down there." John's low tone made Bethia turn. He stood beside her, breathing heavily and dusting off his hands.

"It was his mine, from the beginning," she answered.

John gave a sidelong glance that told her he guessed at Simon's hatred of being underground, but did not care to comment. He simply shook his head. "But why now? And how did Firmin catch him unawares? That knight was more than a match for any of us."

Bethia tried to shrug and failed. "Perhaps he was...distracted," she muttered, remembering their recent argument and cursing it. All too well, she recalled the cold look in his eye, the hurt she thought she had glimpsed there. Lord knows she wasn't as strong as she thought. Maybe Simon wasn't, either. Maybe, just maybe, he felt something for her besides lust, and if so, he might have been affected by their falling-out, his sharp instincts dulled.

Guilt gnawed at Bethia, slowly transforming into anger. The man had always been careless and reckless! Hadn't she told him to wear his mail? Hadn't she warned him to always anticipate attack? He should have known better! A harsh sound bubbled up from Bethia's throat only to die away as she heard a shout from the direction of the tunnel.

"They've found a foot!" One of the archers called

out the news with excitement, but the announcement made Bethia feel sick. Although she had never swooned in her life, her knees swayed, forcing her to lean against a tree for support. A *foot*. The word conjured up images that were too horrible to contemplate. Was Simon's magnificent body maimed beyond recognition?

Bethia sagged against the bark of the ash, pressing her palms to her thighs in a vain effort to regain her composure. She had suffered the loss of her home, her freedom, her heritage and her father's love, and yet, looking upon Simon de Burgh's prone form seemed to be more than she could bear.

"We've got him, Bethia!" Her fingers jerked at the shout, and she knew a cowardly urge to turn her back, burying her face against the sturdy wood behind her. Instead, she forced her attention toward the mine, for no matter what condition Simon was in, she would see to him. She owed him that at least.

"He's alive!"

An odd strangled sound rang in her ears, and Bethia realized it came from her own throat, as she trembled uncontrollably. Relief rushed through her only to be swiftly replaced by her natural wariness. Against all odds, Simon had survived, but for how long? With what kind of injuries?

Forcing herself to stay where she was, Bethia waited until they had brought him up from below, but when she saw the two men carrying his still figure, she ran to his side. Without conscious volition, she placed her hand on his chest, reassured by the beat of his heart. Yet he remained silent, his eyes closed, his breath shallow. His body, always so clean from his frequent baths in the stream, was covered with soil. That small fact suddenly made Bethia's eyes burn, and she swiped at them impatiently.

"Will he be all right?" Bethia heard herself ask in a voice that sounded wholly unlike her own. When no one answered her, her heart hammered in trepidation, but she looked up at the sea of dirty faces that surrounded her. All glowed with concern in the lantern light, but no one spoke until one of the miners cleared his throat.

"He wasn't down there long, mistress, and it's a queer place under the ground. Sometimes a foul wind will get you and sometimes pockets of air will save you. That looks to be what happened to him. He's a lucky one. It seems we got to him in time. If he had been down there all night…" The man lowered his gaze and shook his head.

"That's what Firmin intended," Bethia whispered. The black-hearted archer had planned to spend the night cavorting with her, while Simon lay below, dying a long, slow death. Sucking in a sharp breath, Bethia knew she should be thankful that the Judas had hurried to her hut to brag about his misdeeds. For if he had not, Simon would surely be gone. The knowledge made her shudder as she stared down at his dirty, drawn features. "Take him to—"

"My cottage."

Bethia looked up in surprise to see Meriel among the crowd. "I'll stay with my sister and her brood while you tend him," the widow said softly. The offer was generous, but Bethia hesitated. Meriel's cottage was farther away and across the village road. It was full night now, but if anyone found them with the prone body of Baddersly's lord, explanations might be difficult, especially for a known band of outlaws.

Bethia weighed the risk, then thought of the other places available. An abandoned mine? A cave? A tiny hut? Although small and spartan, Meriel's home would be far more comfortable than any makeshift camp. And there was a well for water and a wide hearth for heating it.

"Very well," Bethia said, sending Meriel a grateful glance. Her men remained quiet, patiently awaiting her decision, and she realized, belatedly, how much trouble Firmin had fermented among the ranks. Now she would have peace, but at what cost? "Put him in the farm cart. I'll take him," she added, unwilling to involve the others.

"I'll help you," John said. His somber gaze brooked no resistance, and Bethia was not inclined to offer any. Once the cart had been dragged from its hiding place and a horse borrowed from the smith, she and John made their trip under the cover of darkness in the guise of a late-returning farmer.

On her perch beside John, Bethia forced herself to stare straight ahead although every nerve in her body screamed to turn back to where Simon lay. As they proceeded slowly through the blackness of the chase, she cursed each moment of delay, certain that her knight was breathing his last while jolted on his hard wooden bed. Although his heart was beating steadily when last she checked, Bethia had no opportunity to look for wounds and he showed no signs of awareness.

Pushing aside the panic that threatened, Bethia remained still and silent as they traveled through the woods and across the road to Meriel's cottage. She and John managed to get Simon out of the cart and onto a pallet inside, though the knight was huge and heavy.

Once he was lowered, John turned to her, a bit breathless from his exertions. "Shall I stay?"

"No, you had better return the cart. It would look odd sitting here at the widow's cottage," she said. He met her gaze for a long moment as if determined to assist her, but what could he do? He was no healer. Nor was there anyone with any great knowledge of such things in the small village.

Finally John nodded, but he gave her an odd look. "Are you sure you're all right?"

For a moment, Bethia did not know what he was talking about until she glanced down at her stained tunic. She stifled a wild urge to laugh then, for in the wake of Simon's accident, she had completely forgotten about Firmin's attack. "Yes, I am fine, for 'tis all his blood," she explained. "Bury him."

John's expression grew cold. "'Tis more than Firmin deserves."

"Yes," Bethia agreed, although she knew that John would take care of the body, despite his personal feelings. Grateful for his help, she walked with him to the doorway, waiting there until he disappeared from sight before shutting herself in with Simon. She moved to the hearth to light the wood laid there, in case she should need the fire.

Once it flared brightly, she turned and stepped toward where Simon lay, kneeling beside him easily. With a trembling hand, she felt for the beat of his heart, breathing a sigh of relief at the steady thump beneath her palm. Her fingers brushed against the soil that clung to his tunic, and she pushed to her feet. First, she needed to wash him. Then she would be better able to determine his injuries and help him heal.

As gently as possible, Bethia stripped him of his

clothing. Although the night was warm, she put a bucket of water over the hearth. When it had warmed slightly, Bethia moistened a cloth and started wiping away the grime. She began with his face, her ordinary task becoming much more as she tenderly swept the harsh features that meant so much to her. Here was an opportunity to touch him, and she relished it, hesitating only a moment when she reached his mouth before running her fingers over his soft lips.

With a rush of feeling, Bethia remembered the hot pleasure of kissing him, and instead of denying her own response, she wanted desperately to do it again, to breathe life into his still form, to see the flare of passion in his eyes and know the rough touch of his hands, as frenzied as her own while they struggled to get closer.

Her breath catching, Bethia tried to push away the images. Simon might never recover, might never be able to…choking back a strangled sound, she continued to bathe him, moving her cloth down his throat and across the wide expanse of his chest, her fingers catching in the crisp hair and gliding over the flat nipples.

Although she had never lingered over her own toilet or washed any of the guests at Ansquith during her days there, Bethia took her time, performing her task lovingly, each swipe of the linen a tender stroke of wonder and discovery. She neglected no part of him, even lifting his feet to attend to the arched toes and passing her cloth up the inside of his thighs with trembling hands. But his body did not react.

"Wake up, Simon," Bethia urged softly. "And I will let you tease me all you wish. Aye, I will do whatever you bid me," she promised in a broken whisper, but there was no response.

Setting aside the water, she tended to his cuts and

bruises as best she could, cleansing the worst with
wine. Although she found no signs of broken bones,
she knew he could be hurt inside or suffering from a
blow to the head. She had heard tell of those who bore
such wounds and never awoke, existing in a netherworld until they wasted unto death. But that would not
happen to Simon, Bethia told herself. She would not
allow it.

"You're going to recover, Simon de Burgh, or I'll
kill you myself!" she threatened shakily. When even
that harsh warning garnered no answer, Bethia turned
away, tossing off her bloody clothes and washing herself with the remaining water. Then, dressing herself in
one of the gowns she kept at the cottage, she returned
to the pallet, covering her patient with a thin blanket.

Although weary enough to seek her own rest, Bethia
knelt beside him once more, sliding her palm across his
chest to feel the reassuring beat of his heart. She
watched him for a long time, fearful that his condition
would change, but it did not, and finally exhaustion
claimed her. Dropping her head onto an arm, she slept.

Bethia blinked and lifted her head, wincing when her
neck protested. She was seated among the rushes in
Meriel's small cottage, her arms crossed upon the pallet
where Simon...a small sound escaped her throat when
she realized that he was gone. Lurching to her feet, she
took a step toward the door only to halt as a tall figure
filled the entrance.

Simon. He stood on the threshold, and in the light of
day his body was sorely bruised and battered and startling in its nakedness. For a long moment, Bethia could
not draw a breath as her shaky relief was replaced by

a host of emotions, including a raw hunger for that glorious body. She lashed out sharply in reaction.

"What are you doing outside?" she demanded. He moved into the small cottage without the least bit of chagrin or modesty, and Bethia forced her attention to his face. His features were set in a tight expression, his face pale, and she hurried toward him. "You should be lying down, you fool!"

When he shrugged off her assistance, it seemed as if everything she had been holding inside her for hours, days, even weeks, exploded in a uncontrollable burst of passion. "You stupid oaf! You're lucky to be alive! Why did you go down there? Why?" Bethia swore and pummeled his wide chest with her fists until he grabbed her wrists.

He held them fast, glaring down at her with a black expression, and something pulsed in the air around them. Suddenly Bethia realized how close she was to his great, naked body. Without volition, her gaze dropped to his groin, where his member stood stiff and erect. She was already panting; now her breath caught and her heart launched into a new, furious beat. Slowly she lifted her head, and her eyes met his only to find her own powerful desires reflected there.

His jaw tensed. "I'll not beg," he said.

The reminder of all the times she had refused him did not make her flinch, for Bethia was beyond such trivial annoyances. She had played at being a man for too long. Now she wanted to be a woman, no matter what the price.

"Then I will," Bethia said, lifting her mouth to his. For a moment, she thought he would spurn her despite the desires of his body, for he still grasped her wrists, but she had no intention of letting him thrust her away.

Every hidden yearning and stifled craving had burst into life inside her and would not be denied.

Then, just as his lips parted against her onslaught, his fingers slid down her arms to her back, and Bethia was pressed against the tall, hard, naked length of him. But it wasn't enough. She wanted to feel every muscle, every bit of skin on his magnificent form. Impatient, she ran her hands over his shoulders and down his chest, along his sides and over the taut curves of his buttocks.

Tearing her mouth away with a gasp, Bethia kissed his hard jaw, the thickness of his throat, the rough hair on his chest. Reaching his nipples, she grazed one with her teeth and heard his harsh exhalation in response. She moved downward, dipping her tongue into his navel, thrilling at every inch of flesh, every grunt and jerk that told her he was alive and strong.

She began to sink lower, prepared to kneel before him, but he tugged at her skirts. "Bethia, Bethia," he muttered in a hoarse whisper that made her feel inflamed, as if the streak of sunlight that caught them in its path was too hot, her clothes too confining. She wanted to be as free as he and so she let him lift her gown and pull it over her head. Beneath, she wore only a shift, and with an impatient grunt, Simon removed it, too, tossing it aside.

"Bethia." Grounding her name out like a curse, he pulled her to him, rubbing her breasts into his chest with a rough sound of pleasure. Then he lifted her so that his hardness nestled between her thighs. His callused hands ran over her skin, lifting her higher as he moved against her throbbing core. Clinging to him tightly, Bethia nipped at his ear, then harder on his throat.

He stumbled, muttering a string of oaths before he lowered her hurriedly to the pallet. Spreading her legs wide, her knees high, he settled between them, his weight heavy but welcome. His hands were rough, his movements frantic, but no more so than her own. Bethia ran her foot down the thick muscle of his calf, as she met his gaze, smoldering, demanding. His dark hair fell forward onto his forehead, his features taut, his jaw tense, and she loved every grimace.

"I won't stop," he muttered, as if daring her to gainsay him.

But Bethia was not about to argue. Inside her, a frenzied pulsing had begun, urging her on with reckless abandon. This was life. This was love. And she could not deny it. "Don't. Don't stop," she said, and something passed between them, hot and elemental.

Simon groaned and Bethia buried her face against his throat, biting into his shoulder at the first thrust that broke her maidenhead. The pain was gone as quickly as it came, and she wrapped her legs around him, eager for his full penetration. She clutched at his back, digging her fingers into his muscles, relishing each harsh breath, every hard thrust. Faster and deeper he went, but still it wasn't enough. She wiggled impatiently until his hand closed around her hip, lifting her to him.

"Bethia…" The low growl ignited something inside her, and she heard her own answering moan. Her pulse beat to the rhythm of his movements, and each time he plunged forward, sensation spiraled through her until she arched against him, unable to get close enough, unable to…

And then she stiffened as pleasure ripped through her, so intense she could not contain a joyful cry. The sound was swiftly echoed in Simon's shout as he plunged into her one final time before shuddering, his head thrown back, his muscles working with the force of his release. For long moments, his body jerked until finally he fell upon her with a harsh groan.

Bethia welcomed him, her hands smoothing his skin, slick with sweat and taut with the evidence of his strength. At the end, he had called out her name, and she felt an awed wonder at the force of their shared passions. Although she had no experience with these matters, Bethia sensed that something had been forged between them here, a bond that would not be easily broken.

Whether that was good or ill, she refused to consider, especially when Simon was alive and well and holding her. And so, trembling, she lay her head against his shoulder and ignored all else.

Simon drifted in a slumberous state, halfway between waking and sleeping. His body, especially his chest, ached with an intensity that sought to rouse him, while a heavy satiation urged him back to a netherworld. He felt a contentment such as he had never known in his quest to better Dunstan's achievements, an elation far more heady than the greatest triumph in battle, yet cloaked in a peace he had discovered only within the forest. It was a deep, abiding satisfaction, with an edge of excitement to it, hinting of new pleasures to come.

Bethia. Awake in an instant, Simon drew in a ragged breath heavy with the scent of her, mingled with the aroma of their lovemaking. The perfume made his body stiffen, and he realized that he was still buried deep within her. Had merely a moment passed or more since he had spilled his seed into her womb? All Simon knew was that he did not care to leave her. His past encounters had been swiftly concluded and easily forgotten, but now he wanted to stay where he was, surrounded by her, touching her, smelling her, feeling her... forever.

He inhaled again, reveling in the small act, and nuzzled her neck while he ran a hand over her buttocks to draw her tight against him. Her skin was smoother than the finest fabric—a curious mixture of soft curves and lean muscle that made his body lurch in response. He had been so frantic to get inside her before that he had not noticed much beside his driving need. Now he put his lips to her throat, aware of the sudden leap of her pulse, and, remembering the hot pleasure of her bites, he grazed her with his teeth.

The sound of her gasp made him want to please her, and Simon rubbed her bottom, massaging the soft mounds and exploring the crevice between that led to where they were joined. Yet he remained still, and so did she, as though holding her breath. He found that if he listened closely, he could tell where she was most sensitive.

The knowledge excited him in return, and Simon slid his fingers up her back and around to her chest. There he played, discovering the shape and feel of her breasts, while Bethia fell back, panting. Her breasts were not heavy, but firm, and she liked it especially when he rolled the nipples between his fingers. With a low grunt of approval, he sucked at her throat and the smooth skin of her shoulder. He nipped her there, giving her back some of her own, and she uttered a low sound of surrender that made his tarse jerk inside her.

She felt it, for her gaze flew to his, the light in her

eyes soft yet fierce. "Simon..." She whispered a word for what they were doing that inflamed his blood.

Ever before he had been glad to be done with his brief couplings, but now...now he had a mind to have her again. And again. Simon studied her face, her usual cool, competent expression replaced by the impatience of her ardor. "Again?" he asked aloud, purposely withholding his movements.

"Again," she demanded, raising her mouth to his as she wrapped her legs around him. Groaning, Simon kissed her deeply, with a slow heat that had been lacking from their earlier, frantic mating. In answer she clutched at his back with strong fingers and arched toward him.

"Bethia," he whispered as he drew himself out, only to glide slowly back into the slippery heat of her. He took himself nearly from her, grunting when she snatched him back, and he grinned, but she would have no teasing from him. Nipping at his neck, she pulled him to her, and he thrust forward in a series of long, sure strokes that had them both panting.

As he looked down at her, her wheat-colored hair shining in a patch of sunlight, her face softened by passion, Simon wanted to spend the rest of his life here inside her, prolonging the pleasure for which he had once sought a swift end. For a moment, fear clutched at his heart that this was all a dream, and he was still buried in the mine after Bethia had rejected him.

He could not bear such a fate, he thought, thrusting deeper and harder as if to stake his claim to her body, if not her soul. "Bethia!" Muttering her name, Simon gripped her chin with his fingers, forcing her to look at him. Then he took her mouth with his, telling her in no uncertain terms that she belonged to him now. And forever.

The days that followed Simon's rescue passed far too quickly for Bethia, for it was an idyllic time spent mostly on the pallets in Meriel's small cottage, losing herself in their shared pleasures. Supposedly Simon was on the mend—having sent word to Baddersly—and she was tending him, but outside of some scrapes and bruises on his glorious form, he was much as he had been before.

The miners were back at work, and John stopped by daily to report on the progress. Luckily Firmin had destroyed only the very end of the passage, and the cave-in was cleared away without delay. Indeed, if the weather held, the tunnel would soon be completed, though Bethia was not as overjoyed at the news as she would once have been.

Without conscious agreement, she and Simon had seized on his recovery as an excuse to linger at the cottage—and with each other. If he had not already taken possession of her heart, Bethia would have given it over to him countless times as he stroked her with his rough hands, murmuring hoarse words of encouragement until he shouted her name in completion.

Sometimes they came together in a leisurely fashion that made her moan and cling to him. At other times, he swiftly lifted her skirts, penetrating before she had a chance to catch her breath. No matter what the manner, Bethia was always eager to take him to her, for she was all too aware of the temporary nature of their interlude.

The days had taken on an unreal quality, as if she and Simon existed in a world of their own making, but

Bethia knew it could not continue indefinitely. They had spoken, long, whispered conversations about their pasts and soldiering and likes and dislikes. But, as if by tacit agreement, they had said little of the future.

To Bethia it loomed ahead like the black hole of the mine, but with no opening in sight. Did Simon still want her to marry him, or was he content with their current arrangement? Bethia had no idea. Worse yet, she was even more uncertain of her own feelings. Although she loved him, she could not disregard the reservations that had been honed from years of wariness.

Pressing her palms against her gown, Bethia looked up at the sky. Clouds were darkening it to gray, and she wondered if John would arrive before the rain. As much as she longed for an end to her fight to save her father, Bethia found herself wishing for a storm that would delay the inevitable, that would keep her here in a limbo between duty and desire.

As if to remind her of the latter, Simon appeared in the doorway of the cottage, and Bethia drew in a sharp breath at the sight of him. He wore only a simple tunic, but the clothes did little to hide the arrogance and power that emanated from him. Her heart lurched painfully, but she hid her sudden fear for tomorrow behind a composed expression.

"John is late," she said, lifting a hand to shield her eyes as she looked toward the woods. A stray breeze caught at her skirts when she turned.

"Perhaps he avoids the coming storm," Simon answered, stepping forward to join her. He had stayed close to the cottage to avoid recognition, but the road was deserted this afternoon, the clouds presumably keeping travelers and farmers alike at home.

''He thought they would finish today, unless a heavy rain damages the passage,'' Simon said.

Then let it rain, Bethia thought rebelliously. After all these months of frustration, of fighting vainly against Brice, of impatient preparation, she wanted to put off the final moment. ''Are you sure you are well enough to lead the attack?'' she asked, earning a frown of contempt from Simon.

''Think you that I have not the strength to do battle?'' he asked, his brows lifting slightly.

Despite her misgivings, Bethia smiled, for she suspected that a demonstration of his endurance was in order. Sure enough, he advanced on her, dark promise in his eyes, until he had backed her up against the outside of the cottage. But even as she felt an answering passion surge within her, Bethia knew the weight of concerns that would not be swept aside by Simon's kisses.

When the time came, Simon, and, indeed, all of them, would be risking their lives in the attack upon Ansquith. Simon planned to send word to a few of his select knights and soldiers to join him, but no battle was assured. And now, when the moment was at hand, suddenly the manor and all that it stood for did not seem so important. Somehow, during the past idyllic week, Simon had gained precedence in her life.

And no matter what happened on the morrow, Bethia sensed that these precious days would not be repeated. Even should they recapture Ansquith, they could no longer sleep together each night, waking to mate in a slow, sensual rhythm until they fell back again, exhausted, their slick bodies entwined. Things would change, and Bethia, ever the realist, looked forward with a leery eye.

Forget the mine! Let's not do it! The words screamed in Bethia's head even as Simon took her mouth with his own. If only they could continue on indefinitely as they were... But she could not forget about her father. Even though he had abandoned her, she could not do the same, especially when he might be ill and weak. And if she did not go to Ansquith, where would she go? What would she do? There lay her only hope for independence....

As Simon leaned over her, his hands braced on either side of her head, Bethia felt a faint drop of moisture on her hair. The rain had begun, and she was glad. Lifting her arms, she wrapped them around his neck. "I'm getting wet," she whispered when his lips broke from hers to blaze a hot trail down her throat.

He raised his head at her words to meet her gaze, and his held a fierce, demanding light. "Good," he muttered, and she knew he did not refer to the rain. He pressed his body against hers just as the light shower descended, and the combination of heat and coolness made Bethia shiver. She laid her head back against the cottage blissfully while Simon reached for the hem of her gown.

With a hunger that incited her own, he pushed up her skirts and parted her thighs. Bethia gasped when she felt the brush of his knuckles against her while he yanked at his braies. His sex sprang free, and she moaned as the thick head nudged her opening. With one hand he lifted her higher, while the other took hold of her chin, forcing him to look at her in that way of his. It was unsettling, as if he were branding her, but she could not deny his possession. She was already panting, her body ripe with expectation of what was to come, and she welcomed the first hot rush of pleasure as he entered her.

His mouth came down on hers even as he plunged higher inside her, and the gentle rain dripped from his dark hair onto her breasts. Her back thumped against the side of the cottage with each heavy thrust, but Bethia writhed and moaned and clutched at him with frantic fingers.

Dimly she realized that they were making love out of doors in full view of anyone, but no one was about, and what would they see? Only she knew that he was buried deep inside her, so deep that she...with a cry, Bethia hid her face against his shoulder, biting down hard as the spasms took her. She heard Simon's urgent, muffled groan and felt the violent shuddering of his body that signaled his own release.

It was only after Simon had slipped from her that they heard the shout. With shaking fingers, Bethia righted her soggy clothes and stepped away from the wall even as Simon was already moving around the side of the cottage. Neither of them had a weapon, and Bethia cursed her own distraction, but it was only John, hurrying across the road in the rain. Sparing a moment to be grateful that he had arrived no earlier, Bethia eyed his wide grin with wariness.

"They have finished!" he said as soon as he reached them. "All that is left is a few feet of earth to break through, and we can enter the bailey. If the rain doesn't soak the passageway, we can attack on the morrow!"

Simon, no doubt eager for battle, joined in John's hearty enthusiasm, and who could blame him? Bethia knew that she, too, should be celebrating, but her smile was forced. The goal for which she had worked so hard now seemed an empty triumph, the independence she had once coveted a cold replacement for the knight who stood at her side. Instead of a new beginning, Bethia saw an ending.

Her idyll was over.

Chapter Fourteen

"We're going to be attacked!"

The cry echoed throughout the great hall until Florian lifted his head to see what the shouting was about. "Attack? What's this about an attack?" he demanded of the youngster who was spreading the word. When the boy ignored him, Florian grabbed the miscreant by the back of his tunic, effectively halting his headlong race across the tiles.

"Ow! Let go, Master Florian. Please!" the boy cried, his feet dangling.

"Only if you tell me why you're scaring the women and children with such a tale." He lowered the boy to the rushes but received no apology.

"We *are* under attack," he insisted. "My brother saw it! A whole host of armed men, on horse and on foot approach, coming from the north!"

Florian frowned. "Tedric, isn't it?" he asked, and the boy nodded. "If a party is headed toward Baddersly, it does not mean that they plan to lay siege. You must be certain of your information before shouting it to all and sundry. Now run down to the gate and find out what's really happening and report back to me.

At once!'' Grinning happily at such an official chore, the boy took off at top speed.

Florian shook his head and wondered what, exactly, Tedric's brother had seen. If visitors were coming, he was unprepared, and supper was still being cleared away! He turned on his heel, ready to shout for one of the guards when Quentin strode into the hall with a purposeful gait.

"Ah, there you are, steward!'' he said.

"Who is coming?'' Florian asked him, without preamble. "I've had no message from travelers, but who would attack us? Tell me it's not that upstart Brice! Didn't someone claim he was hiring mercenaries to destroy the forest outlaws? Surely, he would not dare send them against us?''

Before Quentin could answer, Leofwin ambled in behind him. "'Tis not mercenaries, nor invaders, either, but Baron Wessex who approaches, with a huge party,'' the knight said. "I hope you have plenty of stores, for it will take a fortune to feed them all.''

"The Wolf,'' Florian whispered. "What is he doing here?''

"I told you no good would come of his brother's disappearances,'' Quentin said sagely.

Florian bristled. "I believe 'twas *I* who told *you,* and Lord de Burgh has not really disappeared. He is simply absent again.''

"How long has it been this time?'' Quentin asked.

"Just a few days, I think,'' Florian answered glumly. They had not heard a word from him recently as Quentin well knew. Florian wrung his hands. "Oh, dear, what shall we tell the Wolf?'' He stared at the door, as if expecting deliverance, but he soon discovered that one did not tell Dunstan de Burgh, the Wolf of Wessex, anything.

They entered the hall in a group, the Wolf and his men, their footsteps heavy, their mail creaking and their voices raised. Towering over his entourage, the Baron of Wessex prowled among the assembled household like his namesake, demanding that his brother attend him. But, of course, Simon was nowhere to be found.

Florian swallowed hard and stepped forward. "Welcome, my lord. We had no word of your coming, so I fear that you find us unprepared, but we will have rooms readied at once and a late supper laid out."

"You! You are the steward here, by name of Florian?" the Wolf asked with a growl of impatience. He was even bigger than Simon and more imposing in his manner, for where his brother seemed cold, Dunstan seemed fierce and far more dangerous.

"Aye," Florian answered, wishing, for once, that he had never been placed in charge of Baddersly.

"Where is my brother?" the Wolf demanded.

"Well, my lord, that is a matter of some question," Florian said, smiling in a placating manner.

Unfortunately, the Wolf looked as though he were not easily placated. Sweeping the room with a green gaze so different from Simon's, he practically roared his displeasure. "What goes on here?"

"Your brother is gone, my lord," Thorkill said with an earnest expression. Florian had to admire his spirit if not his intelligence, but the knight had come from Campion, so perhaps he had become used to these frightening de Burghs.

"Aye, he comes and goes," Leofwin said.

"Gone more than he comes, really," Quentin said with a dry cough.

The Wolf stopped his prowling. Like a giant beast, he stood in the center of the gathered onlookers, surveying them all with a jaundiced eye. "I can see that he is not here. *Where* is he?"

Leofwin scratched his head. "Well, that's a matter of some debate."

"We don't know exactly," Florian interjected before the knight could get himself in deeper. "But we think he's in the chase. You might try looking for him there upon the morrow."

"Or leaving a message for him in the village," Quentin added.

"He's gone off alone?" Another man, obviously also a de Burgh stepped forward. "Without even his squire?"

"Ah, yes," Florian admitted. "But 'tis not so unusual. In fact, he seems to be in the habit of it."

"In the habit of it?" The fellow, his dark thatch of hair falling forward over an intelligent face, turned to the Wolf with a look of bewilderment.

"Aye, my lord Geoffrey," Thorkill spoke up. "He has come and gone several times since his arrival here."

"Yes, that is quite so," Florian confirmed. "He's here for a day, then gone for a week. Absent most of the time, really." Florian nodded at the Wolf, whose expression grew more thunderous.

"What is going on here?" he shouted. He turned to the one called Geoffrey, who only shook his head.

"That doesn't sound like Simon at all," Geoffrey admitted.

"We feared he was ailing," Leofwin said. "For his behavior ever since his arrival has been markedly odd. Hasn't been eating at all."

"Aye," Quentin echoed, and Florian felt like strangling them both for bringing up this topic. He stepped forward, cutting in delicately.

"Actually, I think I know the affliction from which he is suffering," Florian said, his ready smile faltering under the intense regard of all these fierce-looking knights. He drew a deep breath and clasped his hands together. "Lovesickness."

Six dark heads swung toward him, eyes wide as they regarded him in silent astonishment, then every one of those infernal de Burghs burst into laughter. Florian frowned. He had never met the Wolf of Wessex before, but so far he was not favorably impressed by him or his rabble of brothers, who all guffawed and slapped their thighs as if they had heard the most amazing jest.

Florian raised his voice to be heard over the hooting. "I would think that your brother would prefer your support, rather than your amusement," he said tersely. "He has been quite despondent of late, so I would guess that all is not going well in his, uh, affair of the heart." Florian leaned forward, his voice lowered to a conspiratorial tone. "I believe he has been concerned about his chances of success."

One of the brothers, a breathtakingly handsome man, scoffed loudly. "Simon? Simon has never had a doubtful day in his life. He was born thinking he was invincible and proceeded to prove it."

"Aye," muttered one of the smaller ones. "He's never been like you, Stephen. Never cared a bit about women or his looks, that's for sure."

Florian pursed his lips in disapproval. As Simon's siblings, these six should be sympathetic, not derisive. No wonder the poor man was so stiff and unyielding, if this was an example of the devotion of his family.

"Nevertheless, I can almost certainly assure you that your brother is taken with Bethia Burnel, late of Ansquith, and most recently of Burnel Chase."

At his words, the Wolf shot a glance toward Geoffrey, and the amusement left their faces, replaced by a kind of dawning horror. "She's the one he talked about in his message!" the smallest one piped up.

"Poor Simon," the Wolf muttered.

Geoffrey shook his head. "How the mighty have fallen."

"Pah! I don't believe it for a moment," Stephen said. "You there, pretty maid, fetch me some wine, if you would be so kind," he said, flashing a blinding smile at one of the serving girls.

Florian lifted a brow. This was one to be wary of, he noted, even as he nodded toward the girl. Taking a deep breath, he bowed low. "Yes, sit, my lords. Supper is over, but we can serve you well." He clapped his hands, and the servants scattered. "Tomorrow you can search for your brother in the chase."

Five of the brothers moved toward the benches, led by Stephen, but Dunstan stalked up and down the hall, studying the knights who had assembled for his presence. Pausing in front of Leofwin, who sucked in his breath until he was red faced, the Wolf swung round.

"Where is Arthur? And Hal?" he asked. "Have not all the men-at-arms turned out?" At Florian's confused look, he turned back toward Leofwin. "Where are those who arrived with Lord Simon?"

The portly knight only shook his head, and a shout went up to summon the missing men. Florian hurried toward the kitchens, but he did not need to see Dunstan's expression to know the Wolf was not pleased.

Glancing out at the darkening sky that signaled the close of the day, the big knight cursed loudly.

"Something's afoot," Geoffrey said.

"Aye," muttered the Wolf. "And on the morrow, I intend to find out what."

The rain had come and gone, barely soaking the ground with a summer shower and denying Bethia her hoped-for delay. Instead, she had risen with the dawn as plans for the attack went forward. She could not even claim one last, hurried mating, because the floor of the cottage was littered with Simon's men. Despite her misgivings, he had sent for them after talking with John, and they had arrived before nightfall, so as to be ready come morning.

Escaping behind a blanket, Bethia had dressed in her men's clothes, her sword at the ready. Although she expected a rebuke from Simon, it did not come. He simply held her gaze with his own for a long moment before warning her curtly, "Stay back and out of trouble." In no mood to argue, Bethia said nothing. Let him think what he liked, she had no intention of tagging behind like a stray cur.

The knights' horses had been left with the smith, so they all went into the chase on foot, the dozen men whom she had once ordered bound hand and foot and returned to Baddersly in a cart. Although they dared not reveal any animosity toward her in front of Simon, Bethia had every intention of keeping her wits about her in the hours ahead. Her natural wariness had only been reinforced by Firmin's betrayal, and she planned to keep an eye out for both herself and Simon.

By the time they reached the tunnel, the miners were nearly through the last bit of earth, and Simon ordered all to follow him, two by two. When he relegated Bethia to the rear, she swallowed her protest, but when he ordered one of his men to protect her, she swore softly. Only the importance of the battle ahead kept her from having her own altercation with one hardheaded knight in front of everyone.

Oblivious to her anger, Simon descended the ladder. If he had any reservations about going back down into the mine that had trapped him before, he showed no signs of it, and Bethia spared a moment to admire him. His eyes were alight with excitement, his jaw tight in concentration, his personal power nearly tangible in the early morning light. With a kind of awed wonder, she realized that these men, herself included, would follow him without question into the depths of hell.

Tearing her gaze away, Bethia turned to her own small group of archers, selecting a handful to join her, but when she turned to lead them forward, she ran into the man Simon had assigned to protect her. ''Stay out of my way,'' she warned in a fierce whisper. And pushing him aside, she stepped onto the ladder.

In the darkness below, even Bethia felt a tremor of uneasiness, as far ahead the last earthen barrier to Ansquith was breached. All too easily, she remembered Simon buried here, and it took a goodly amount of strength not to call out or even whisper ahead to him, especially when she felt the press of bodies ahead and behind.

Then, at last, they were moving, and those in front of her rushed upward into the daylight at the other side, drawing their weapons. Bethia followed, brandishing her sword, but found no enemy with whom to do battle. Simon and his men were arrayed about the bailey, looking huge and threatening, while a small group of servants and household members cowered before them. Indeed, they appeared so terrified that Simon, in exasperation, called for someone to fetch Brice.

Bethia tensed, for surely the cowardly bastard would take the opportunity to try to best them. He would never fight himself, but he had a handful of miscreants who had arrived with him and had gathered more. Backing against the wall, Bethia waited, alert for his tricks. Indeed, she wondered if he would even appear, and she watched for any escape routes he might take.

However, to Bethia's surprise, Brice soon arrived, attired in the finest clothes, no doubt bought with her father's money. Far from appearing concerned about this attack, he moved with the languid ease of a nobleman whose morning toilet had been disturbed. But Bethia was not fooled. Behind him came four of his henchmen, with more perhaps hanging back in the shadows, and she softly ordered the archers to slip behind the small buildings that crowded the bailey.

"What is this?" Brice asked, waving a perfumed kerchief in front of his nose, just as if those who had erupted from the bowels of the earth carried a foul stench. His manner made Bethia long to rush forward and slit his throat, but she held her place, deferring to Simon with difficulty.

"Lay down your arms for the brother and emissary of your liege lord, Simon de Burgh," one of the knights proclaimed, and all eyes turned to see Brice's reaction.

"My lord!" He stepped forward with a smile that fairly gleamed, and Bethia choked back a cry. She wanted to shout out his duplicity, to run him through without preamble, so that he had no chance to sway the assemblage with his honeyed lies. Only extreme force of will kept her where she was, but again she eyed the likeliest escape route, should the coward turn tail and flee.

"My lord, I am so pleased to meet you," Brice claimed, bowing low to Simon. "I have been trying to get messages to you for weeks, but the cursed outlaws have intercepted my every effort. I wanted to let you know that Edward is dispatching an armed force to eliminate the brigands," he said, staring pointedly at John and the other archers.

"Edward?" one of Simon's knights echoed.

"Yes, I taught his children, you know, when I served at court. Traveled around with them for years," Brice claimed with a false modesty that made Bethia want to vomit.

"Was that before or after you were an advisor to the archbishop?" John called out, his voice heavy with derision.

"Probably thinks he birthed Pope Nicholas himself," one of the other archers muttered, turning to spit loudly in a show of contempt.

Brice's smooth expression hardened. "I certainly do not expect you to comprehend the wealth of experience beyond your sorry little lives, outlaws," he said. Dismissing them with a wave of his hand, he inclined his head toward Simon. "But Lord de Burgh, certainly you've heard of Edward's plans. You're in his confidence, aren't you?"

Bethia recognized the ploy immediately but choked back her comment, for Simon would not be so easily gulled. Perhaps a lesser man would have lied to save face, but Simon was not the type to be influenced by flattery. By the set of his jaw, she knew that he had not been taken in by Brice's spurious charm or false claims.

"The King is sending no force here," Simon said.

"But I will gladly send a messenger informing him of your nefarious deeds."

Brice brushed aside the threat with a smile and a sweep of his arm. "Really, my lord. I'm afraid you've been a victim of malicious gossip. I have done nothing here but visit with an old and dear friend."

"Whose daughter you tried to kill?" Simon asked.

A hush fell over the crowd that had gathered, and all eyes turned to Brice, who shrugged off the accusation with another one of his ingratiating grins. "Rumor spread by my enemies. The poor girl died from the illness that has laid her father low." He made a great show of bowing his head as if in grief. "And I still weep for her."

Bethia kept her own outrage in check as Simon grunted angrily, his fierce temper barely restrained. "Then you'll be overjoyed to find that she's been resurrected just like Lazarus," he said through gritted teeth.

Seizing her opportunity, Bethia stepped forward, throwing back the hood that shielded her distinctive hair, and her appearance was met by a round of gasps from the onlookers. Brice's eyes grew wide, and he glanced about him like a rat searching out its escape hole. His smile fled and he dropped his conciliatory manner with a sudden leap backward.

"Attack!" Brice shouted, and the men who had waited behind him surged forward, joined by several others hidden in the shadowy doorways. They rushed Simon, and Bethia was tempted to fight by his side, but his men were there, and she had no intention of letting Brice get away.

Ducking and running along the edge of a small hut, she emerged from the rear of it to catch a glimpse of

Brice's fancy tunic as he raced toward the great hall. She gave chase, blinking when she reached the dim interior before she saw him heading for the stairs. Whether he intended to hold her father hostage, destroy evidence of his misdeeds or try to sneak away, Bethia was not certain. She only knew that she had to stop him.

"Hold, coward!" she shouted, and he looked over his shoulder, his brows lifting mockingly. But he finally stopped, turning to face her when she had nearly reached him.

"Ah, Bethia! Or is it? Difficult to tell in those rags, I must say," he taunted. "As amusing as I find your costume, I fear I don't have time to dally with you."

"It won't take long for me to kill you," Bethia said, and he threw back his head in a burst of laughter.

"Bethia. Bethia. Do you really think you can?" he said. Finally drawing his sword with a flourish, he began to circle her, his white smile taunting. "You play at being a man, but you cannot best one."

Ignoring his words, Bethia reined in her feelings and concentrated on his movements, for she knew that Brice would strike quickly before others could arrive. When he did, lunging forward as if to knock her weapon from her hold, she repelled his attempt easily, and he drew in a sharp breath of surprise.

"So, your forest criminals have taught you to hold a blade. I'm sure that's not all you learned in the woods. Was it worth it, Bethia?" he asked. When she did not answer, he circled again. "You could have shared a bed with me, but you would rather lie in the dirt with a host of villein rabble. I never thought you were such a nasty thing." He clicked his tongue and lunged, but Bethia parried. "Naughty girl, you surely do not think to best a real swordsman?'' he asked, launching himself forward.

Bethia did not respond to his words, but centered her attention on fighting well. In a battle against Simon she could not triumph, but Brice was no knight. His skills were limited, and though he soon abandoned all pretense of technique in the hope of winning through brute force, neither was he very strong. Bethia was quicker and more deadly, and she showed no mercy.

Soon Brice was breathing hard, a wild light in his eyes that indicated his flagging energy. "Well, well. You are good. I will give you that, Bethia, but come now," he said, backing away. "I have no quarrel with you. Let us part on friendly terms. Lay down your arms and I will give you a share of my wealth."

Bethia made a sound that mimicked one of Simon's grunts, and slipped her blade beneath his, slicing open his arm. Howling like a babe, Brice stepped back to clutch at it. "Mercy!" he wailed. "Mercy, Bethia, for you need me! Put down your sword, and I will give you your father's life!"

Uncertain, Bethia faltered, and Brice seized upon her show of weakness. "Let me live, and I will provide you the antidote to the poison I've been feeding your father." The knowledge that Brice had caused her father's illness, just as she suspected, made Bethia hesitate. She knew little of healing. What if Brice did possess some secret to her father's recovery that would die with him?

"That's a girl," he said. "Just let me stop bleeding all over the floor. Oh, I…" He swayed on his feet, as if faint, and Bethia moved forward automatically only to jump back as Brice lunged forward, thrusting his sword at her belly. The tip of it scraped her flesh but did not find its mark, and he had lost his chance. With grim intent, Bethia swung around and sent her blade into his heart.

He fell backward, stumbling until he lay in the rushes, his tricks spent, his deceits done. Once certain that he would rise no more, Bethia leaned over, palms on her thighs, and sucked in great drafts of air. Not only was she spent emotionally, but her whole body shook from the force of the battle that had strained every muscle and pushed her to the limits of her endurance. She had just begun to catch her breath when an ungodly roar filled the hall.

"Bethia!"

Simon. He was alive and well and here, and she was glad. But when she lifted her head to look at him, Bethia saw his face was contorted with rage. He thundered toward her, stopping suddenly at the sight of Brice's prone body. Then, with a ferociousness she had never seen, he swung upon her.

"Fie on you, you foolish, stubborn wench! What did you think you were doing? I told you to stay at the back! I told my man to protect you, but you deliberately evaded him!" His anger fueled her own, and she straightened slowly.

"You have no hold over me, Simon de Burgh. Nor can you dictate to me," she said.

He reached for her then, his big hands closing over her upper arms. "Can I not? You're mine, do you hear me? Mine! And I won't have you recklessly endangering your life for the likes of him!" He was shouting in her face, his grip digging into her so forcefully that she thought he might shake her.

Staring up at him in horror, Bethia felt her eyes burn. She had thought Simon different, but he was like all men. He could not see a woman as a warrior, but only as a drudge to sit back and do his bidding. Well, no matter what had gone between them, she would not submit herself to his will.

"Let go of me, you great lout!" she cried. Jerking free, she pulled out her knife, brandishing it in front of her. "Don't ever touch me again, you bastard!"

For a moment, they faced off, as they had countless times before, the very air pulsing with the force of the passions that erupted between them. Hurt, humiliation and rage at his defection warred in Bethia as she stood there, chest heaving, ready to take on another enemy. She would never have attacked him, but she was determined to stand her ground until a shout rang out from across the hall, diverting her attention.

"Bethia, come quickly! Over the hillside!" Bethia rushed to the doorway, Simon close behind, only to gasp in horror at the sight that met her eyes. Arrayed over the country outside Ansquith's walls was a huge army.

"The mercenaries!" she cried. She swung toward Simon in dismay, but he seemed little affected by the news. Unmoving, he stood eyeing the force, his lips curving slightly.

"Don't let them hear you call them that," he said dryly.

"Why? Oh, what are we to do now?" Bethia cried.

"Open the gates!" Simon shouted.

"What?" Bethia wondered if he had lost his senses as she surveyed the approaching knights and soldiers whose numbers far outstripped their pitiful force. "Why?"

"Because those men are no ill-bred mercenary rabble," Simon said with a tight smile. "Those are my brothers."

Chapter Fifteen

At the sight of his siblings, the driving heat of Simon's anger began to ease. Although they knew well his temper, he suspected that even his brothers would have been shocked by his recent display of rage. Yet Simon could claim no control over his wrath ever since he had glimpsed Bethia taking off alone after Brice.

Frustration had filled him, for he could not call her back, nor could he follow, because of the men who rushed toward him. He had cut down the two who came at him immediately, such was his fury, but there were others, and for once in his life, he cursed each moment of battle, eager only to have it done. If anything happened to Bethia…Simon had felt such pain in his chest that he had glanced down expecting to see an ax thrust through it, but he sported no visible wound—only the agonizing knowledge that Bethia had gone after her enemy.

And might be hurt. Or dead. Consumed by fear such as he had never known, Simon had fought on furiously, swiftly putting an end to the brief skirmish. None beyond Brice's own hirelings had the heart to strike against their master's liege lord and his daughter, too.

And so they had laid down their arms as soon as Brice's men were vanquished.

Simon did not wait to treat with them, but ran after Bethia, his usually inactive imagination conjuring all manner of ends for her. When he had heard about that business with Firmin, he had wanted to lock her away in Campion's tallest tower, and after this, he vowed that he would…if only it wasn't too late already.

When Simon saw her still standing, his relief could not moderate the rage that boiled in his veins. Had she no thought to what she had put him through? Had she no sense at all to pursue that bastard by herself? Brice would be desperate, and such men were twice as dangerous.

Even the sight of Brice's dead body was no comfort to him, for Simon was too overcome to rein in his tumultuous emotions. They burst from him in a thunderous shout. He wanted to shake her, to warn her never to do that to him, to never risk her self for *anything.* She meant so much to him that it frightened him— almost as much as did the thought of losing her. And he was not a man accustomed to fear. But caught in the grip of his own overwrought passions, Simon had been unable to express any of that in his speech with her. Everything had come out wrong, and Bethia had been outraged.

Simon slanted a glance at her beside him, silently watching the arrival of his family, and he loosed a harsh breath. He had not sought an argument; he just wanted her to see that she could not be so careless. He would not allow it, Simon swore silently, even as he felt a growing unease.

She claimed he had no hold over her, but she was wrong, and he would prove it to her soon enough. Just not yet, he thought, shying from the cold cast of her features. Now that his temper was spent, he realized that he could have handled the situation better.

"Bethia," he began awkwardly, but when he turned to face her, she was already slipping away, hurrying toward the stairs. She was probably going to find her father, Simon concluded, reaching up to rub his mailed chest. For a moment, he hesitated, unsure whether he should go after her or not, but he knew she would want a private reunion with her sire, while he should meet his brothers. With an impatient grunt, Simon strode forward.

He stepped outside to stand naturally before the entrance to the great hall as they rode into the bailey: Dunstan, Geoff and the younger ones, too, from Campion. And as he lifted a hand in greeting, Simon realized that for once, he was glad to see them all.

After his stormy conversation with Bethia, the rough affection of his siblings was welcome, and when Dunstan clasped his arms loosely around him, for the first time Simon felt no trace of competition between them. He even lingered a moment, patting his elder brother's back, causing Dunstan to draw away with an odd, questioning glance.

"Perhaps that fool steward was right," the Wolf muttered. Before Simon could ask Dunstan what he meant, Geoffrey was grabbing him, and soon he was engulfed in the often annoying but sometimes comforting presence of his family. They were all there, except their father, Campion, and Simon drew back in surprise when he saw how much the youngest, Nicholas, had grown.

"What are you all doing here?" he asked, looking his fill at each of them.

"I was concerned about your last message and thought I'd take a look for myself at this troublesome demesne Marion brought to the family," Dunstan answered gruffly. "Geoff was at Wessex with Elene, showing off his daughter, so he insisted on coming along."

"You left Elene there with Marion?" Simon asked, earning himself a frown of assent from Dunstan and a warning growl from Geoffrey, who was unaccountably sensitive about his bizarre wife. Turning away from him, Simon held out his hands to encompass the rest of them. "And you—Stephen, Reynold, Robin, Nicholas?"

Stephen wore a disgusted expression that said he had been coerced into coming, but the other three appeared more enthusiastic. "Father said you might need us!" Robin explained. And instead of taking his usual umbrage at such a claim, Simon felt oddly affected by his father's concern.

"But where's the fight?" Nicholas asked. He was turned out in brand-new, shining mail, obviously eager for a battle. At the sight, Simon felt something catch in his throat, and for once, he was glad that there had been little to the clash of arms here. Nicholas suddenly seemed too young to embrace a warrior's existence. While he, Simon admitted ruefully, might be getting too old.

"It looks like the fighting's over," Geoffrey said, surveying the bailey.

"No battle at all? That's not fair!" Nicholas protested. "And you don't even look sick," he accused, stepping forward to inspect Simon closely.

Sick? He was going to throttle that inane steward! "I am not ill!" Simon muttered.

"Oh, I don't know," Stephen said. Sprawling into one of the few chairs, he called for a cup of wine just as if this were his own hall. "Simon looks a little pale around the gills to me. But, tell us, where is this female who's turning you inside out?"

Simon clenched his fists, consumed by the old urge to knock some sense into his sibling, but he had no time for it now. Other, more important matters, required his attention. Brice and his men needed to be buried and the last of his minions must be ferreted out of the household. Was Sir Burnel alive, and if so, what was his condition? And as for Bethia…turning his back on Stephen, Simon called for his men, and so he missed the startled glances his brothers exchanged on his behalf.

"Maybe he really is sick," Nicholas whispered in wonder, and Stephen gazed dolefully after his brother. Simon had always been fun to taunt, for even the mildest comment would send him sprawling across the table after one of his siblings. From the beginning, he had been a born fighter, his temper renowned, so when he stalked away instead of brawling, Stephen knew something was different.

Either Simon had developed some dreadful new maturity or Florian was right. The infamous warrior was in love. Reaching for the cup a servant handed him, Stephen took a long, fortifying drink before setting it down with a thump. Truth to tell, he had been reluctant to join the others in this little road trip, but suddenly the visit had taken an interesting turn.

Propping his feet up on a nearby bench, he grinned and leaned back to watch the entertainment.

Bethia was avoiding him. Although Simon had been busy all day, he sensed it always on the edge of his awareness. He had directed the household after the battle, sent word to the miners to fill in the tunnel and explained the situation in full to Dunstan. The Wolf immediately pardoned the archers, who cheered and headed back at last to their homes, outlaws no more, as Simon wished them well. He had even spoken with John, a strained, curt conversation that left Simon feeling as though Bethia's man was accusing him of some perfidy even though Ansquith was returned to its rightful owners.

Simon had heard through a servant that Bethia was still closeted with her father, who had been moved back to his old chamber and was being plied with broth and wine. The rumor running throughout the manor house was that Brice had been poisoning the old man since his arrival, which explained not only Sir Burnel's decline, but his poor decisions. Presumably Brice had kept him alive to maintain the pretense that Burnel still ruled. Although Simon understood how herbs could work on a man's mind, he still found it hard to forgive Bethia's father for welcoming Brice in the first place, let alone urging his daughter to marry the bastard.

It was only when supper had come and gone and the servants were finding quarters for his brothers, that Simon began to wonder about his own bed. All evening his brothers had sent him sidelong glances that urged him to demand Bethia make an appearance, but he knew that it was never wise to demand that Bethia do anything. And he still harbored a vague sense of guilt for his outburst this morning that made him reluctant to face her.

Finally, as his brothers drifted off to find their own rest, Simon could wait no longer, and, ignoring Stephen's amused look, he took a deep breath and headed up to the great chamber, where Bethia supposedly lingered. His steps faltered as they had not since he was a child called before Campion for some minor infraction.

Grunting in disgust, Simon marched to the door only to find it guarded by a man-at-arms. Although the man probably had been placed there by Bethia to protect her father, Simon knew a rush of annoyance. Now that he had taken Ansquith, there should be no need for soldiers in the hallways—especially ones he did not command.

"I would speak with Mistress Burnel," Simon said, gritting his teeth at this supplication.

The guard looked as if he wanted to quake in his boots, which only made Simon angrier. "Well? Let me pass, you idiot!" he demanded.

The man shook his head. "I was told not to let you in, my lord," he explained, his expression apologetic. "She, uh, she said that she does not wish to see you."

"What?" Simon roared. He had no intention of believing this scrawny soldier's sputtering nonsense. Nor would he let the fellow keep him away from Bethia. Pushing the man roughly aside, Simon wrenched open the door, and the soldier, in his first show of intelligence, did not try to stop him.

With an outraged bellow, Simon burst inside, only to stop when he saw Bethia seated beside the bed, where a white-haired man reclined against the pillows. A brace of candles illuminated the area, adding a lustrous golden glow to Bethia's wheaten locks. She was wearing some kind of soft robe that revealed the curve of her breasts, and Simon swallowed, his mouth suddenly dry.

"Get out!" she said, without moving. "Can't you see my father needs his rest?"

"What? Who is it, Bethia?" the old man whispered.

"'Tis Simon de Burgh, Father, the knight whose brother is lord of Baddersly," she answered. "He helped me regain my place here." The last was admitted with a grudging glare, and Simon felt as if she had slammed her fist into his chest. He had known she was displeased with his earlier behavior, but to treat him thusly? He reeled from the blow even as he struggled with his temper.

"Aye, I am Simon de Burgh," he said, his gaze flicking to her father, and decided the time had come to assert his claim. "I am also the man who is going to marry your daughter."

Although Sir Burnel made no comment, Simon heard Bethia's low gasp. She rose to her feet, and her loose, flowing attire could not hide her fighter's stance. Simon felt as if a battle had been fought of which he knew nothing. *And he was the loser.* "I fear you are mistaken," Bethia said, her voice cold. "He did propose to me once, Father, but I refused him."

Simon grunted in dismay at her denial. Fisting his hands, he struggled against the urge to grab her and shake her until she took back her words, or to stop her cruel mouth with his own, to show her with his body just how much store he put into her denial. But when he looked into her set face, Simon felt all the fight leave him in one long, shuddering breath. The memories of her past rejections returned in a rush, along with the pain that only she had the power to inflict.

He had sworn never to beg her again, and he was a de Burgh, a man of his word. Perhaps it was time to retreat, aye, even surrender the war that did nothing but tear him apart. With a low growl, Simon held himself tall and gathered the tattered remnants of his pride around him. Then, without a backward glance, he turned and left the room.

He found Stephen still seated in the hall, and though they had never been close, when his brother offered him wine, Simon welcomed it. Anything to dull the pain, to take away the vision of Bethia's features, expressionless, as she shunned him yet again. He ought to be used to it by now, Simon thought dismally, but after the past week they had spent together, he would never have expected this.

Had she used him only to regain her home? Simon refused to consider that the fearless outlaw he had admired would do such a thing. With a groan he downed his drink and let Stephen pour him more. But what did he really know of her? Although he had been drawn to her from the beginning, Simon admitted that he had never understood Bethia, especially her behavior toward him, which had run the gamut from violence to indifference to passion and back. He could be sure of only one thing: she might as well have run him through, for the way he felt was worse than any wound.

"I never thought I'd see you fall," Stephen mumbled.

Simon ignored his brother, except to reach out to take the drink that would dull his senses, deadening his very soul until he was like Stephen, a shadow of a man unworthy of his name. For once, the truth about his brother failed to induce the usual contempt in Simon, and he smiled grimly. Maybe he should give up his knighthood and become a useless drunk, too.

"God's wounds, Simon, I've told you all time and again to spread yourself among the ladies, but you wouldn't listen. Not you nor Dunstan nor Geoffrey, and now look at you all!'' Stephen shuddered.

Simon merely grunted, holding out his cup for more, and Stephen poured unsteadily. ''When your steward told us that you were in love, we all laughed, but when he explained that—''

Simon cut him off with a low growl. *''What?''*

Stephen leaned back in surprise. ''The steward at Baddersly, by the name of—''

''Florian,'' Simon muttered as he envisioned just how to kill the meddlesome steward. With his bare hands, perhaps. It would be his final act in his brief tenure as lord of the castle and more satisfying than anything during his stay in this wretched part of the country.

Except for that time he took Bethia up against the cottage wall. In the rain. Simon groaned, closing his eyes against the images that assailed him. Or that first time, when she had begged him. Or that second time, so slow and languorous. Or the morning after when he had woken with his face buried in her wheaten hair spread across the pallet. An agonized sound escaped his throat, and he recalled the hot pleasure of her body, the heady joy of her company, the low, husky sound of her voice, the wonder that was Bethia, maiden and warrior, lover and friend.

''Well, it's obviously too late now. All I can do is give you my sympathy, and I do,'' Stephen muttered. ''I wouldn't wish love on anyone—even you, Simon.''

Simon jerked upright at his brother's words. Was it true? Was he *in love* with Bethia? His immediate reaction was denial, but even as a refusal rushed to his lips, Simon felt that same dizzying sense of upheaval that he had known ever since Bethia had waylaid him in the woods, upending his very existence. Indeed, how else to explain what she had done to him? And Stephen had a point. Had he not seen Dunstan brought low by the same thing? And he had watched Geoffrey weep like a babe when that termagant he married had disappeared.

With a snort of disgust, Simon vowed never to cry over Bethia, although his chest hurt so that each breath burned. He was stronger than his brothers, even the Wolf. He had been through battles and won, and he would not let one outlaw wench break him. After they were finished at Ansquith and Baddersly, he would pursue his plan to join Edward's forces. And he would never look back.

But in the meantime, he would have more wine.

Simon awoke to a dull throbbing in his head and a roaring noise that sounded suspiciously like one of Dunstan's growls. He blinked blearily and lifted his head only to find himself slumped upon the table in Ansquith's hall. And Dunstan was growling. Loudly.

"What is the meaning of this?" the Wolf roared.

"Well, I think that's obvious."

Stephen's purring tones made Simon jerk up only to bang his knee on a sideways bench. He groaned and reached for his aching head, which somehow felt worse than the leg.

"Our dear brother cannot hold his wine," Stephen explained in an annoying, conspiratorial voice.

"What did you do to him?" At Dunstan's hushed demand, Simon swung around, trying to see who was talking, only to find all of his brothers arrayed behind him. Dunstan was glaring at Stephen, who looked his usual charming self and not the slightest bit weary after drinking until all hours. Simon groaned again.

"See?" Stephen said with a cluck of his tongue. "Sad, isn't it? But I guess we all can't share the same talents—"

"You left him to spend the night here?" Dunstan demanded angrily.

Stephen shrugged with his innate grace. "I found more…appealing accommodations myself, and he seemed comfortable enough, sunk over the table with his face in a puddle of wine, just like a—"

With an angry grunt, Simon lurched to his feet, intent upon slamming one of his fists into Stephen's perfectly groomed features, for he recognized his brother's tactics well enough. Stephen was enjoying making him look bad, for it wasn't very often he had the chance of appearing more virtuous than one of his siblings.

It was only when Simon swayed slightly, his head pounding, that he began to remember the previous night more clearly, including his own vow to become a worthless drunk just like Stephen. Blinking unsteadily, he studied the rogue de Burgh, who did not look so useless this morning.

"Day of God, get yourself a bath," Dunstan advised, eyeing Simon askance. "You reek! And I would advise you not to let your lady see you thusly."

For a long moment Simon could not speak, his tongue thick in his mouth, but he straightened to his full height and turned slowly to glare at each of them in turn. "I have no lady," he finally managed with some degree of ferocity.

"Ho! What's this?" Robin asked, looking puzzled.

"Uh-oh," Geoffrey whispered.

Dunstan swore under his breath. "So that's why you've suddenly taken to drink."

"But the steward said—" Nicholas began, only to stop at the sight of Simon's furious face. Simon could see them all exchanging glances, but he had no wish to elaborate. "I'll bathe so as not to offend your delicate sensibilities, Dunstan, but then I have every intention of leaving, so don't ride off without me."

"Leave? Why, we wouldn't think of it," Geoffrey said. Something in the tone made Simon suspicious, but his head hurt too much to reason well. "Isn't that right, Dunstan?" Geoff said, nudging Dunstan.

"What? Oh, right," Dunstan said with a grim nod. "We can't leave until Sir Burnel is sufficiently recovered. A few days at least, maybe more."

Simon's eyes narrowed, and he felt as though he had just been tricked into buying Saint Hubert's shinbone from Stephen. But Dunstan wore an expression that brooked no argument, and Simon did not feel up to taking on his elder. How did Stephen drink so much and never look the worse for it? Simon felt like they ought to just kill him and be done with it. Instead, he scowled and trudged for the stairs.

Several days? He had no intention of remaining here that long. With a grimace, he called for hot water and realized he did not even have a room, but a nod and a word from Dunstan sent a servant hurrying ahead to direct him. Apparently he was reduced to sharing a chamber with his brother, when he had just fought a battle to regain this blessed place! Grumbling to himself, Simon did not hear the conversation that continued in the hall below.

"All right, I give in. Why are we staying here in this reasonably comfortable but small manor house when

you have a perfectly good castle at your disposal?''
Stephen asked, arching a brow at Dunstan.

''Yes, why is that?'' Robin asked.

''Don't look at me! It was Geoff's idea,'' Dunstan
growled.

''Didn't you see him? He's miserable!'' Geoff said.
''We are obligated to do something to help him.''

''Help Simon?'' Stephen snorted. ''Isn't that a con-
tradiction in terms?''

''Perhaps, but why then did you pour wine down his
throat last night?'' Geoffrey countered.

''Not out of some misguided attempt at matchmak-
ing,'' Stephen said in disgust.

''Is that what you want us to do? Make a match for
our own brother?'' Robin asked, his tone incredulous.
''Why, it's tantamount to betrayal!''

''You wouldn't think that if you were in love,''
Geoffrey said.

''A lot of nonsense,'' Reynold said with a grunt.

''Poor Simon. I almost feel sorry for him,'' Robin
said, shaking his head.

''Me, too,'' Nicholas said, eyeing the others with
bewilderment.

''You might as well just stick a knife in his back,''
Stephen said mildly as he reached for a cup. ''But I
must admit to being a little bored lately, and this certainly ought to liven things up a bit. By the way,
where's the girl? I've a notion to view the female who
could bring down our warrior brother.''

At that, everyone glanced at each other and
shrugged, and Stephen laughed in amusement. ''Dunstan, as the mighty liege lord, I'd say you are just the
one to summon her!'' he taunted. When Dunstan
growled angrily, Stephen only laughed harder. ''Well,

then, bring on the entertainment,'' he said. Although
he thumped his cup loudly, his smiled faded as he saw
the puddle of spilled wine where his brother's head had
lain.

"But for the record, don't ever do me any like favors."

Simon lifted his head, relieved to feel no ill effects
from the motion, and glanced toward the narrow window of the tiny room. After his bath, he had fallen
asleep, and by the looks of the light, he had missed
dinner. Just as well, for he did not care to face either
his brothers or any other residents of Ansquith.

At the thought, the pain rushed back, as if he were
freshly wounded, and Simon swore, long and fluently.
Drawing a harsh breath, he willed himself to ignore it,
just as he would any injury, even though this one was
deeper than all others and probably permanent. Shrugging aside the knowledge, Simon swung to his feet,
grateful that the world did not spin under his feet, even
though he suspected it would never be righted again.

A knock made him rise to stand, and he cursed the
anticipation that coursed through him, though not of his
own volition. It would not be Bethia, he told himself
as he opened the door, and indeed, it was naught but a
servant, who quailed beneath his hard stare.

"Sir Burnel sends you his gratitude and requests that
you attend him since he is too ill to come to you," the
man said.

Simon frowned, dreading a conversation that might
include Bethia, but he was not a coward and, nodding
curtly, he strode toward the great chamber. Scowling
at the man-at-arms who still guarded the entrance, he
hesitated, certain that he would rather crawl into a mine

than proceed. Indeed, it took more courage than he had ever mustered just to step inside.

But it was all for naught. The room was dim and silent, empty except for the old man who reclined upon the pillows. Simon moved forward, his breath shuddering from his body in a low hiss of relief. Or was it disappointment?

"Ah, Lord de Burgh! Thank you so much for attending me, but here, please come closer and sit by me. My voice is not what it used to be," Sir Burnel said in a hoarse, rasping tone barely above a whisper. With a nod, Simon walked toward the old man, although he despised sickbeds and had no wish to further his acquaintance with Bethia's father.

"I owe you my life," Sir Burnel said as Simon sank onto a low stool, trying not to imagine Bethia sitting here, where he had last seen her. "And, more important, my gratitude for your part in my daughter's triumphant return."

Simon struggled not to grimace. "You need not thank me, for I was honor-bound to do what I could for my brother's vassal."

The old man coughed and wheezed, but his hazel eyes, so much like Bethia's, bored into Simon, as if assessing him. "Ah, yes, honor. The de Burghs possess it in abundance, as I recall. Nonetheless, you did more than most would have, and I thank you. But, tell me, what of this betrothal? When will you wed my daughter?"

Simon choked back an oath and surged to his feet. "'Twas a mistake. You heard her. She has refused me." And more than once, Simon thought, as he felt the familiar flush rise on his throat.

"Surely, a de Burgh would not give up so easily?"

the old man asked, and Simon flinched, eyes narrowing upon the lined face of Bethia's sire. "Especially when the prize is so rare."

Hands fisted at his sides, Simon had to rein in the temper that threatened to burst forth. "Strange words coming from a man who abandoned his own daughter and then would wed her to a man such as Brice Scirvayne," he said. But he took no pleasure in the shadow that passed across the old man's face at his taunt.

"You are right, of course," Sir Burnel said, his expression bleak. "But having made mistakes, a man can hope to right them, can he not?" he asked, turning to look at Simon. But Simon had had enough, and he gritted his teeth as he shook his head.

"Not this time."

Chapter Sixteen

Bethia went down to supper with misgivings. She had kept busy during the day, tending her father and inspecting the household, determined to right Brice's wrongs, but by evening, she was plagued by an uneasy feeling, as if all her work were prompted not by devotion to duty, but by weakness. And when her father urged her to see to her guests, the de Burghs, rather than take her meal with him, she was forced to admit it.

She was being a coward.

She did not want to see Simon, for her emotions were still raw from the events of yesterday. Oh, she had known that her idyllic trysting with the great knight would end, but she had not been prepared for such a terrible conclusion. During their days at the cottage, he had treated her as an equal, lulling her into thinking that such was his opinion of her.

But yesterday he had proved his true colors well enough, raging like a madman, as if she were nothing but his chattel, a mindless thing that he would command according to his will. And after months of freedom, Bethia would not enslave herself again. Sinking

onto a stool in her small chamber, she wiped angrily at
her burning eyes. Willingly she had given Simon de
Burgh her heart and her body, but her spirit she could
not surrender.

Having made her decision, Bethia knew she must
live with it, but seeing him again was almost too painful to bear. Why could he not leave? Surely it would
be easier to forget him once he was gone! But all the
de Burghs lingered, eating up the manor's stores, and
Bethia knew she had hidden behind her father's illness
long enough. It was time to make an appearance. Bracing herself, Bethia lifted her chin, straightened her
shoulders and headed toward the great hall.

She had nearly reached the bottom of the stairs when
she halted, stunned by the sight that met her eyes. Although she had seen them at a distance, now they
crowded around the high table, making it look small,
making the entire hall seem too little to contain them
all, seven men so alike that she caught her breath.

Never before had Bethia seen such great, strapping
knights together. They were different, she could tell,
but all had the same dark hair, and all were handsome,
most more so than Simon. In fact, he shared the harsh-
est features of the group with one other, yet it was his
face that drew her, his form that made her eyes sting
perilously.

Watching him among his siblings, Bethia realized
that Simon came by his arrogance naturally. How could
anyone growing up among these powerful men fear that
anything could touch him? Even to her eyes, they appeared invincible, and Bethia could not stop staring,
although it soon became apparent that her presence had
been noted. While she gawked, they rose to their feet
as one, wide shoulders jostling each other, but straight-

ening their tall bodies with an inborn grace that Bethia
recognized.

"Mistress Burnel! Come take your place at the head
of the table." The largest, most formidable one spoke,
and Bethia knew him as the Wolf who held Baddersly,
for he had spoken briefly with her father. His welcome
was courteous, yet Bethia hesitated. Although she had
commanded men and captured them, these seven would
daunt even the most fearless, and she was not feeling
especially brave this evening.

But she was no coward, and drawing in a sharp
breath, Bethia forced herself to move forward. It was
only when she stepped closer to the table that she realized Simon was still seated, and as she neared, he
pushed aside his trencher to surge upright. With a fierce
glance in her direction, he stalked away, causing six
dark heads to turn toward him. Worse yet, once he
strode off, those six gazes swiveled back to her, and
Bethia nearly flinched.

For a moment, she wished that the tiled floor could
swallow her up. But it did not, and there was nowhere
to go but forward. Although it took all of her courage
not to turn and flee from Simon's contempt and his
siblings' curiosity, Bethia moved to take her place at
the high table in utter silence.

And then everyone started talking at once. If not for
her heartache, Bethia would have laughed as each of
them began speaking to her, for she did not even know
their names. Finally, the Wolf growled for quiet and
introduced each de Burgh in turn: Geoffrey, Stephen,
Robin, Reynold and Nicholas. Although Bethia greeted
them cautiously, none censured her. She had not been
sure what to expect, but certainly not this kind treatment. Yet, how else would a de Burgh behave? They

all wore their honor like mail, bright and gleaming and pure.

Bethia suspected they would not be so welcoming if they knew how she had once mocked Simon, scoffing at his name and the esteem in which he claimed it was held. Now, of course, it was well evident. Anyone with eyes could see that these were good men who used their strength and power for right.

The knowledge was disconcerting, and though the de Burghs continued eating and speaking, Bethia merely toyed with her food. She was not hungry, and the presence of Simon's family made her feel her loss more keenly. This is what she had given up, she knew, even as she told herself that her freedom was more precious than kinship to these men.

Finally Bethia pushed aside her trencher, and the de Burgh to her right, quieter than most, took the opportunity to lean close. "Is there aught I can do for you, mistress?" he asked, his brown eyes filled with concern. "I know that Simon is a hard man, with a fierce temper, but he is also fierce in his devotion to those he cares about."

Bethia swallowed hard against the temptation to confide in this gentle man. "I fear I do not know what you mean, Geoffrey," she said as evenly as she could manage.

The look he gave her told her he was not fooled, but he did not argue the point. "Affairs of the heart are never easy. Perhaps you two simply need some time," he said gently. "We can stay as long as you like."

Was this why they lingered, prolonging her suffering? Bethia wondered. Outrage warred with distress and, placing her palms upon her thighs in an effort to maintain her composure, she pushed to her feet. Holding herself straight, she shook her head and spoke as plainly as she could. "Go then, for there is no reason for you to stay."

Bethia stood behind the shutters, back from the window so that she could not be seen as she watched the de Burghs mount their horses. She had spoken briefly to Dunstan after the midmorning meal, making her formal farewells on behalf of Ansquith. Of Simon, she had seen nothing, and although she judged that to be to the good, Bethia still strained to catch a glimpse of his distinctive form among his brothers.

"Are they all leaving?"

Her father's hoarse tones brought Bethia across the room, for she knew it was still difficult for him to speak loudly, and she took a seat upon the stool near the bed. "Aye, they will soon be well away," she said, her own voice cracking.

"I am sorry, daughter," her father said softly.

Bethia laid her hands upon her lap, covered now in a fine yellow gown that appeared strange to her eyes. "You have apologized aplenty, Father, and are forgiven. 'Twas the herbs working on you, as was Brice's intention."

"Ah," her father mumbled, but he turned his head toward her. "Yet your knight took me to task for sending you away in the first place."

"Simon? You spoke to Simon?" Bethia asked, startled.

"Aye," her father said, his gaze gentle. "And he is right. I should never have agreed to let you go with Gunilda. I was so stricken with grief at your mother's passing that I could not think clearly, and when Gunilda said I was raising you improperly, I thought to right a wrong. I soon regretted my hasty actions, for I missed you most dreadfully.''

Bethia jerked her gaze to his. ''Missed me? But why didn't you send for me or answer any of my letters?''

A shadow fell over her father's features, and he grimaced, as if in pain. ''I received no messages from you, Bethia, and so thought you happier in your new life.''

Gunilda. Bethia was too spent and weary to summon the appropriate outrage, but she knew well what had occurred. ''She never sent them on.''

''Nor let you see mine, did she?'' her father asked. Bethia shook her head. ''What cruelty you have suffered, my child, and because I was too foolish to see the truth!''

''Nay,'' Bethia murmured. ''I, too, should have suspected something amiss, so 'tis my fault as well. And I was all right, Father, well fed and clothed and warm,'' Bethia added in an effort to ease his mind. None had abused her, and she knew her life of drudgery could have been far worse.

''Well, despite all the ill for which Brice is responsible, I guess something good came of his stay, for you have returned at last,'' her father said, reaching out to squeeze her hand. And Bethia realized that Simon must have left her a small piece of her heart because it swelled and pulsed with an unfamiliar sweetness.

''Now that I am in my right mind, I would never force you to marry,'' her father said, and Bethia breathed a sigh of relief. That was what she wanted to hear, wasn't it, that she would always have her freedom?

''But what of your knight?'' her father asked. ''I wish you would reconsider his proposal. He seems to be a man of strong passions, but a good man, clever and brave and honorable and quite taken with you.''

Bethia drew in a sharp breath. Actually Simon glowered at her whenever she was around, but to others that might look like something else, she supposed, such as hunger. Or desire. Pushing aside such thoughts, she recalled instead the expression on his face when she had denied their betrothal and shuddered painfully.

''No. I am…grateful for Simon's aid, but I cannot marry him.'' Or any other man. Bethia had come to the difficult realization that she was a freak of nature, a woman with a character ill suited for her sex, an anomaly with no place in the world but her own. How could she explain that to her father, who was responsible for her skills and would surely take more blame upon himself?

Bethia drew a deep breath. ''He won't allow me to be who I am. Although he pretended to admire me, he cannot stomach a woman such as I for a wife. And I cannot change.''

Her father made a small noise of disagreement. ''Simon seems to crave you just as you are.''

''No. He made himself quite clear after I killed Brice.''

''My dear, did you ever think that his temper was brought on not by any disapproval of your skills, but of fear for you?'' her father asked. ''A man has his pride, and there is nothing worse for it than to stand by helplessly and see things you cannot control, especially loved ones in danger.''

When Bethia simply stared at him, her father closed his eyes, as if tiring, and she rose to her feet unsteadily, considering his words. She had taken Simon's outburst at face value, but perhaps her father had a point. Heart thundering, Bethia hurried toward her room, even as she wondered if it could be true.

She remembered her own frantic rage at Simon's recklessness, her confused feelings when she had found him up and around after his brush with death. She had been so angry with him for getting hurt, and yet she still loved him—enough to show him in that most physical of displays. She and Simon were alike in many ways, could this be one of them? Did they both react with anger when worried for another?

By the time Bethia reached her chamber, she was seized by a desperate need to find out if her father was right. With increasing horror, she realized that she and Simon, both reticent, had never discussed their emotions, let alone the future. She had dismissed it out of hand, but perhaps there was a way to compromise, to come to some kind of accord without losing herself in the process. Driven by a rising excitement and hope she had thought long dead, Bethia raced to the window only to discover that she was too late.

The de Burghs were already out of sight.

Simon searched for the peace that he had once found in the forest, but it eluded him. His thoughts were still upon Ansquith, where, after two nights of torment, he had finally managed to take his leave. Weary of his brothers' clumsy efforts to throw him together with Bethia, he had drawn Dunstan aside and told him the truth—that she had refused his proposal and that he would quit the place with what little pride he had left. Dunstan, head lowered as if in sympathy, had grunted his agreement.

Bethia had not even come to see him off, and although Simon knew he ought to be grateful to be spared one last sight of her, some betraying part of him longed for it. But it was too late now, for he moved farther away from Ansquith with each step of his great destrier. Yet even his departure could not banish Bethia from his thoughts, and he cursed the woods that were haunted by the presence of the woman he had left behind.

Dunstan had insisted on taking the forest road, though Simon would have preferred another. Bowing to the Wolf's wishes, he let his brothers and their trains go on ahead, so that no one would witness his suffering as the memories assailed him. He could see her everywhere, of course, and even the knowledge that the outlaws were long gone could not rid him of her presence. She was there in the leaves, laughing at him, fighting with him and simply being Bethia, the likes of which he would never know again.

Although he had traveled this way often enough, Simon paused before a thicket that seemed to have been thrown across the road and gazed at it stupidly, wondering why Dunstan and the others had not removed it. Or had it fallen but recently, after the passage of the trains? When a sound drew his gaze upward, Simon blinked in astonishment as a brown-garbed form appeared on a low branch in front of him.

"Halt and state your purpose here," a familiar voice called out, and Simon lifted a hand to rub his aching chest. He studied the figure eagerly, recognizing the lithe limbs clothed in male costume and the strength evident in the arms that held a bow, its arrow directed disconcertingly toward his torso. And he knew her aim was true.

"Get off the horse, slowly, and lay down your weapons," she ordered, and Simon didn't know whether to be enraged or exasperated. But he couldn't help the thrill of excitement that surged through him, along with a rush of hope. Ever she had affected him thusly, like the joy of a battle joined, and yet....

Sliding from the saddle, Simon carefully laid his sword on a nearby rock. ''The dagger, too,'' she said. What now, wench? he wondered as he turned around. To Simon's utter astonishment, she had disappeared, and he started when she dropped behind him, wrapping a length of rope around his wrists. Although he could have easily escaped, he offered no resistance, so curious was he as to her intent.

''Just what are you doing?'' he asked.

''Sit,'' she commanded, pushing him onto a stump. ''We're going to talk, Simon de Burgh, and I'm not letting you go until I get some answers.'' Simon sat, feeling an eerie sense of familiarity. Was this all happening again or was he still on his mount, dreaming of it?

''You claim to want to marry me, but I would know if you want a docile and dutiful wife, for I cannot be one. I am a warrior, like you, and I would not be aught else.''

Simon grunted in annoyance. Of course, he didn't want some silly, useless maid, for he had seen his fill of those. Only one woman had ever captured his admiration and interest, and she stood before him, sword drawn. Her stance was familiar yet exciting, and Simon felt himself harden at the sight. ''Foolish wench! I want you and no other,'' he muttered.

''You don't want to change me?'' she demanded.

''No!'' he growled. He wanted to reach for her, and the bonds that loosely held his hands chafed at him. He struggled against them gingerly.

"You'll let me train with your men?"

Simon frowned. He had never thought she would make such a wild request, but as long as he made certain she did not get hurt, he supposed it could do no harm. Indeed, the activity might keep those muscles of hers well formed, he thought, eyeing her up and down until his groin tightened painfully. "Very well," he said, impatience making his voice harsh.

"I warn you, Simon, do not think you can order me about!" she said, pointing her blade at his heart for emphasis.

He nodded mutely.

"I will not be relegated to my chamber while you are out and about!"

Simon shook his head.

Bethia smiled, and he felt as if he would come apart right then and there. "Very well, then. I'll marry you," she said. "If you still want me."

"I still want you," Simon said through gritted teeth. "Now get these infernal ropes off me."

Crossing her arms over her chest, his betrothed gazed at him with an expression that bordered on the wicked. "I don't know about that. The idea of having you at my mercy holds a certain appeal." And before Simon could react, she pushed him down into the leaves and straddled him.

"Didn't I warn you always to wear your mail?" she asked, clicking her tongue as she pushed up his tunic to run her hands across his chest. Simon shuddered at the sensation, even as he grew more anxious to be free.

"And while you're bound, I have a confession to make," she said, situating herself directly over his throbbing groin. "That day in the woods, I watched you…touch yourself."

Simon's breath left him, and he jerked at the rope angrily, the familiar flush climbing his throat as never before. Shame, resentment and rage all warred within him until she leaned over, her fat braid sliding across his chest.

"It excited me," she whispered, and his temper fled as he felt her nip his throat. Lifting his head, he tried to kiss her, but she only laughed and dropped her mouth lower, her teeth grazing one nipple and then the other until Simon felt as if he were on fire. Chest heaving, he yanked at the bonds behind his back.

"Untie me, Bethia," he commanded, but she only moved down his body, her mouth brushing across his hip as she pulled at his braies. "Bethia..." he warned.

"Poor Simon! Look how swollen you are," she said when his tarse sprung free, and he growled at her angrily, until he felt her tongue touch him. Then he drew in a harsh breath, his heart pounding wildly. "And I think I know just how to ease it," she promised in a husky tone that made his body jerk eagerly.

Then she took him in her mouth, and Simon groaned at the moist slide of her tongue, the hard scrape of her teeth. He reared upward, calling her name, frantic until she tugged at her own braies and stepped over him, straddling him once more.

"Release me, Bethia," he demanded, but then he was inside her and nothing mattered except the hot feel of her taking him deep. Thrusting upward violently, Simon heard the soft cry that signaled her release, felt her body milking his own, and he shouted in hoarse pleasure, shuddering uncontrollably until Bethia fell, panting, against his chest.

For a long moment, Simon could do nothing except gasp for air, but finally when he could breathe again, he growled low in her ear in a voice that brooked no resistance. "Release me, Bethia."

Lifting her head slowly, his betrothed eyed him with a look of a woman well loved—sated and slumberous. "I don't know, Simon," she whispered, her lips curving slyly. "I think I like you better like this. You're a lot less imperious and definitely more manageable."

They were married at Ansquith as the last golden glow of summer gilded the countryside in natural glory, soon enough after the retaking of Ansquith that all of Simon's brothers, having been persuaded to linger at Baddersly, could be in attendance.

Although Bethia wore an elaborate, elegant gown that Simon could not help admiring, he suspected that she itched to get back into the tunic and braies she had worn off and on for the two weeks of their betrothal. Personally he preferred she wear nothing at all, which was the costume he had planned for tonight.

Simon wondered just how soon they could escape from the guests who wandered outside and through the great hall, where trestle tables groaned under the weight of the feast. Already he was impatient for their first night in a real bed, legally wed, and he glanced eagerly toward his wife.

Unfortunately, he would have to wait a while longer, for Dunstan approached, and Simon suffered the congratulations of his siblings with an awkward smile. He was more accustomed to their teasing than their good wishes, but all seemed heartily given. In fact, Dunstan was grinning from ear to ear, as if well pleased by the alliance.

"Why are you looking like the cat that swallowed

the cream?'' Stephen asked, alert despite the wine he had been drinking ever since the ceremony.

''I never thought to hold Simon to Baddersly,'' Dunstan said. He turned to give Simon a hearty thump on the back. ''But now you will not be marching off to Campion and can watch over my property indefinitely.''

With a frown, Simon shook his head. ''Nay. My place is here at Ansquith.''

''But—''

The look on the Wolf's face was enough to make Simon grin. ''No, Baddersly's too big,'' he said, enjoying his brother's bewilderment. ''Too many people. And Florian would drive me mad within a month.''

''But—'' While Dunstan struggled with his surprise, Simon held firm. Baddersly was not what he wanted. He no longer felt a need to compete with his brother, for he had his own dreams and desires, and they were well fulfilled by Ansquith and Bethia. Indeed, he could ask for nothing more than a lifetime of challenges from his warrior wife. *Let the battle begin,* he thought, smiling in anticipation.

''But who will hold Baddersly for me?'' Dunstan asked, turning to the surrounding de Burghs. As was to be expected, Stephen stared into his cup, pointedly ignoring the question, while Reynold stepped away, rubbing his bad leg. Simon's eyes narrowed in annoyance, for he remembered a day when Dunstan would never have asked his family for aid. Would they repay his respect by refusing him?

''I'll do it, Dunstan, if you think me capable,'' Robin piped up, and Simon gazed at him in surprise. Although seven years younger than he, Robin was past twenty now and well into manhood. And he seemed to handle a weapon as easily as any of the younger de Burghs. Still, he was so inclined to jest that Simon found it hard to imagine him taking his duties seriously. He sent Dunstan a questioning glance, but the Wolf seemed to have no reservations.

"Thank you, Robin. I am grateful for your offer. Of course, you are more than able, and Simon will be close by should you have need of advice," Dunstan noted. He gave Simon a fierce look that was soon tempered by a smug smile. "Will it not be a comfort to you, to have some of your family nearby?"

"Pah! I don't need to be close to any of you to suffer your presence, for you all haunt me like the effects of a bad meal," Simon said, and he realized it was true. Somehow, despite all his efforts to make his own way, his family had become so ingrained in him that he carried them with him always. Whether he willed it or not, he could sense his father's concern, Geoffrey's admonitions, Dunstan's advice and Stephen's…Simon felt a betraying flush at the knowledge that he had used that one's suggestions more than once.

Indeed, they were all a part of him, and with that acknowledgment came an acceptance and affection for them he had never felt before. "Fie, I can practically hear Geoff urging me to caution at the most annoying moments," Simon admitted.

Six dark heads jerked up in astonishment, most particularly Geoffrey's. "But you never listened to me when I was right there arguing with you!" he sputtered.

They all hooted with laughter, while Simon turned to his brother. "When I don't have to look at your face I do," he said, sending them off again.

"So when will we see your scowling visage again?"

Stephen asked, making Simon pause, uncertain of his answer.

"You must go home and show Campion your new bride," Dunstan noted. "And you know he'll want us all home for Christmas, although he would never ask it of us."

"And he'll be wanting another grandchild, so you might get busy with that," Stephen suggested, his admiring gaze drifting to where Bethia stood not far away.

"More likely, he'll be anticipating the next wedding," Geoffrey added with a sly grin, and the four remaining de Burgh bachelors backed away as if he brandished a flaming sword in their midst. Indeed, Geoff had touched upon the family weakness, and those who still feared marriage made no effort to hide their wariness.

"Aye," Dunstan said, clearly enjoying their discomfort. "Which one of you will be next?"

* * * * *